The
Werewolf's
Daughter

The
Werewolf's
Daughter

M.R. Street

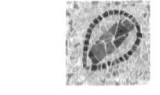

turtle cove press

Published by Turtle Cove Press
www.turtlecovepress.com

Turtle Cove Press and the sea turtle mosaic design are
trademarks of Turtle Cove Press.

Library of Congress Control Number: 2012951951

ISBN: 0985943807
ISBN-13: 978-0-9859438-0-6

To my grandparents and Phil's grandparents;
and to our kids' grandparents,
Tom, Gay, Mary Anne, Emory, and Mary,
with love.

Homo homini lupus

CHAPTER 1

"I saw your mother," Dad says, his gravelly voice crunching like fall leaves. "Did you see her, Lani?"

"Mama's dead, Dad." I tuck the three layers of quilts under his chin. Even with the thermostat set at 90, Dad can't get warm. Meanwhile, sweat plasters loose strands of auburn hair to my forehead and cheeks. If I look like I feel, the phrase *drowned rat* comes to mind.

"She's not dead," Dad says, insistent even through his weakness. "She's cursed."

"Go to sleep, Dad. I have to do laundry."

"Do you have on your ring?"

"All the time." I show him the milky-white moonstone ring on my right index finger. I never take it off, even in the shower. I promised Mama before she died.

"Good, good. It'll help protect you from the curse."

I gather the dirty clothes that have piled up this week. "There's no curse," I mumble, more to myself than to him. God, ever since he came down with this flu, all he's talked about is some imaginary family curse!

"There *is* a curse," he insists. "It's why we had to

leave Georgia. And it's why you have to kill your mother."

"But, Dad, she's already dead. And if by some miracle she survived the car crash, which she didn't or she'd be living with us, the last thing I'd want to do is kill her."

Dad presses his lips together, two grey lines, and stifles a cry so nothing escapes but a whine. He shuts his eyes tight, squeezing out a trickle of tears. He burrows deeper under the covers, and just like that, he's asleep.

I yawn with exhaustion as I take the basket of dirty clothes outside.

Kill my mother? What is Dad thinking? I'd do anything if she were still alive. Anything to be with her.

A shiver skitters across my shoulders and arms, but it's not from the cool summer breeze that brushes my skin and whips my hair off my neck and cheeks. It's from the memory of the night my mother died.

I breathe deeply, letting the faint sweet smell of Confederate jasmine and blackout lilies from Dad's flower garden out front sweep away my sad thoughts.

The sky is dark, the moon a sliver away from new, but my night vision is pretty sharp.

I walk down the front deck stairs. The mossy yard, spangled with tiny purple wild violets, feels soft and cool under my toes.

As I cross the yard, Boulder Man stares at me with moonstone eyes the size of racquetballs. Dad and I built the nine-foot-tall stone sculpture when we first moved to Cloud Pass. Dad drove a friend's tow truck up the mountain and hoisted the massive boulders into place, one on top of each other like a snowman. But long after the snowmen I built each winter melted into slush, Boulder Man remained, a constant guardian over the back yard.

The laundry shed is nestled against the ancient hemlock woods in the far corner of the back yard. Beyond that, nothing but mountain wilderness. The shed is pungent with the scent of mouse. The ceiling light is burned out, so I leave the door open to let in the meager starshine and the light from Dad's window.

Through the milky window above the washing machine, a shadow moves through the woods. But there's no noise. Even a lizard sounds as big as a bear on forest leaf litter.

The night is still as a tomb. Not even crickets or cicadas sing.

Then I hear the *wok-wok* of an owl. It must have been the owl's shadow I saw as it swept noiselessly through the night.

With the washing machine loaded and water whooshing in to fill its tub, I decide to rest outside a while. Dad's asleep, I tell myself. He'll be okay by himself for a few minutes. I lean against Boulder Man, letting his coolness infuse me. I just want a few minutes away from the sauna-like cabin. A few minutes to gaze at the stars and the sliver-thin moon as I think of Mama and Dad.

Dad and I left Georgia in the middle of the night, in a thunderstorm, without Mama.

I rub the moonstone in my ring. Has Dad been seeing Mama's ghost? I don't believe in ghosts, but maybe Dad does. Or maybe it's a side effect of whatever flu bug he's caught.

Why did we have to leave like that? So suddenly, and without Mama? Dad would never explain, deflecting my questions with non sequiturs like, "She would have been so proud of you" and "You have her russet hair, and her peridot eyes."

With my body curved against Boulder Man's cool granite side, I look at the stars blinking between shadowy hemlock boughs. If Dad dies, what will happen to me? I have no cousins on either side. No family here in Cloud Pass; no family back in Georgia. No-one to take me in, to keep me out of foster care. Nothing in Georgia except my mother's grave. My mother, who my father wants me to kill, except that she is already dead and buried. My chest fills with heartache when I realize I don't even know where she's buried. There must be a cemetery in Lafayette. Why hasn't Dad ever taken me there, to lay flowers on her grave, to tell her I miss her?

A motion at the edge of the yard attracts my attention.

A pair of lights glows in the woods. The eyes of an animal.

I peer into the darkness, trying to determine what kind of animal it is.

A cold chill runs through me. I heard a hiker was killed by a bear near here, just last week. What if it's that bear?

The animal steps out of the woods and tiptoes across the yard. *A wolf!* It creeps toward the house, toward the square of light from Dad's bedroom window.

I hold my breath as the wolf sniffs the wall. It stands on its hind legs and peers into Dad's window. Its reddish-brown coat shines in the glow from the window.

"Go away," I yell. "Get out of here!"

The wolf turns toward me. It has a jagged black line across one side of its face. It pushes away from the side of the house but doesn't run away as I expect it to. It walks toward me, its head low and its eyes glowing like coals. The ruff of fur across its neck bristles.

The wolf snarls as it pads toward me, fangs flashing.

Wild animals don't come up to you unless they're sick.

I stand with my back against Boulder Man. I know not to run or the wolf will be on me in a heartbeat. Besides, where would I run? The wolf is between me and the house.

"Go on," I yell, my voice trembling. "Get out of here!"

An owl hoots, two quick barks like before. But this time it sounds like a warning.

The wolf stops. As quick as a ghost, it lopes across the yard and disappears into the woods behind the shed.

I stumble to the front of the house, scramble up the stairs to the deck. I rush inside and slam the door behind me.

Once I catch my breath, I tell myself the wolf probably wasn't rabid after all. It wouldn't have run off when I yelled if it were rabid. Maybe it was just hungry, looking for food.

Now I wish I had stayed where I was, still and

quiet, blending into Boulder Man, so I could have watched the wolf.

I've calmed down enough that my exhaustion has returned. Before I go to bed, I have to check on Dad. I crack open the door to his bedroom.

He's crumpled on the floor by the window, crying, "Melani! Melani, come back!"

"Dad, get back in bed!" I put my arm around his waist and try to lift him but he squirms out of my grasp.

"It was her! Your mother! She'll kill you if you let her!"

"Then why in God's name are you calling her to come back?"

"Because I love her! I've never stopped loving her. You must kill her!"

I squat beside him and drape his arm across my shoulders. This time he doesn't resist. He's lost a lot of weight, and I hardly have to strain at all to help him to his bed. I tuck the quilts across his chest, under his arms.

Dad's snow-white hair hangs lank and stringy below his shoulders. His beard-stubble has grown since I shaved him this morning. His breathing is deep but ragged when he exhales.

"She's gone," he sighs.

"I know, Dad. I know." Tears slide down my cheeks. "I dream about it all the time. The accident."

"Not dead, Lani. Just gone, gone for now. You must find her and kill her. You must save yourself."

"Lay back and rest, Dad. I'm calling the doctor first thing in the morning."

"Haven't you been listening?" He flings the quilts away. "I don't need the damn doctor! I must be close to a hundred now. An old man. There's nothing he can do for me."

I feel the tears well up again. I swipe them away and lean over Dad to kiss his forehead. "I can't take care of you myself anymore. I need help."

"Yes, yes, of course," he mumbles as I re-tuck the quilts and sleep folds over him. "You need help."

Back in my room, I flop down on my bed. I just want to rest my eyes for a few minutes. A few minutes of rest, then I'll check on Dad again.

I know I've fallen asleep because the nightmare is back. I'm so tired, I can't even wake myself up to avoid what I know is coming.

***

Dad drives fast through the rain, leaning over the steering wheel to peer at the road. He slows down as we approach an old covered bridge with a red tin roof.

I'm five years old, and I bounce in my seat with excitement. "Mill Creek House!"

The car tires rumble over the ancient planks as we drive through the long, narrow building. The wipers screech as they pass over the windshield. I watch the headlight beams sweep across the wooden walls with their X-patterned boards that remind me of barn doors.

"Mama says Mill Creek House is safe," I tell Dad.

He cuts his eyes at me, then back to the road ahead. "Yes, that's right," he says, his voice so soft that I can barely hear him. He leans back against the seat. It's as if his anxiety of a moment before has been soothed by the cocoon of the bridge.

"She says my room is safe, school is safe, but most of all, Mill Creek House is safe." I tick off each place on my fingers. "She says this ring will keep me safe, too." I hold up my right hand and wiggle my fingers to show Dad the ring with the milky white stone. It's way too big for me, so Mama wound sticky tape around and around to make it fit my index finger.

"God, I hope so."

"Safe from what, Dad?"

We are off the bridge and Dad guns the engine. The car fishtails on the waterlogged road. Dad slows down and hunches over the steering wheel again.

The road curves and runs alongside the creek. The full moon, peeking out between rain clouds, twinkles on the rushing water.

As I watch the swollen creek, a dark shape climbs up the bank.

"Dad, look! It's Mama. Why is she in the rain?"

Suddenly Mama darts into the road ahead of us.

Dad slams on the brakes. "My god, no!"

I lurch forward. White light like lightning sears my vision as my head slams into the dash. The next moment, my body jerks back against the seat. I put my hands over my face and feel a warm, gooey trickle.

At that second, the windshield shatters as we hit my mother.

Shards of glass rain in my lap and scratch my arms.

"Mama!" I scream.

But the face protruding through the broken windshield isn't Mama's any more. Before my eyes, she turns into a wolf, with rancid breath and yellow fangs. Blood trickles from the wounds on her muzzle where she broke through the glass. She paws frantically, trying to climb in on top of me, her teeth gnashing an inch from my face.

CHAPTER 2

It's almost noon when I wake up again. In a panic, I rush to Dad's room.

He's sitting up in bed, looking weak. He has circles under his eyes, and I don't think he slept much. I feel guilty for falling asleep.

"Do you want to use the bathroom?"

He shakes his head. "Just give me a clean shirt and some privacy."

I lay a fresh shirt on the bed and turn away while he changes.

I listen for the rustling of cotton that means he has taken off the old shirt, the tiny groans that he tries not to let me hear as he puts on the new one. I turn around and shake my head.

His grey-white hands tremble at his neckline, trying to unbutton his shirt.

"Dad, you haven't changed."

"I have changed for the last time," he says, taking deep breaths every couple of words. I have changed more times than you know. Lani, when I die, promise me you will go after your mother and kill her."

I pull his shirt over his head. I feel like a mother

helping a child. "You are not going to die. I'll take you to the doctor and he'll give you some medicine and you'll be – Oh!"

I gasp when I see Dad's naked torso. His chest and arms are covered in thick hair like an animal's, matted with sweat so it glistens like an otter's pelt, only snowy white.

"You are repulsed by my body," he says, not an accusation but a statement filled with sadness.

"No! No, I'm not. I just never realized how much hair –. I mean, I see your arms all the time. But your chest. You never take off your shirt in front of me, even when you're working in the yard."

"I am like Esau, the hairy twin. He was cursed as well."

"You're not cursed." I pull the clean shirt over his head and help him get his arms in the sleeves. "Lean back and put your legs under the covers."

"It is a family curse," Dad says firmly. He obediently slides back against the pillows and tucks his legs under the covers. "Just like the descendants of Esau."

"So now you're saying I'm cursed too?" I try to laugh but the sound strangles in my throat.

"I tried to save you from it. I tried to protect you. I thought taking you away from your mother would be enough, but now I know I was wrong. The curse will claim you when you turn sixteen, just like it got –."

"Dad, can I fix you some tea?" I don't want to talk about the stupid curse. I tuck the quilts under his armpits, a bit more roughly than necessary.

"I've only ever been in one fight," Dad says.

"A fight? What made you think of that?"

"It was a stupid thing to do. I never hurt anyone else, ever. But that one time, it was –." He shakes his head. "The things we do for love. What I did was, I made enemies."

"Are you kidding me? Everyone likes you. Look at Ben. He worships you."

"Ben," he grunts. "Watch out for that Ben."

"Ben's a true friend, to both of us. You think Billie Mae Wrenfield's been up here once to check on me since you got sick? She's *supposed* to be my best friend, but she hasn't even called to see if she could help. Ben, on the other hand, comes to check on us every day."

"Listen to me. You have to protect yourself."

"I'm safe, Dad. We're safe."

"Just do what I tell you. First, get the chisel from my toolbox. It's out in the shed, on the shelf by the door."

"Your chisel? Why?"

"You'll need it to take out Boulder Man's eyes."

I back away from the bed. "I know Boulder Man's just a pile of rocks, but I can't take out his eyes. Dad, that's too freaky. And how is that going to protect us? I can find rocks down by the river to arm myself with."

"Just do what I say," he says again. There's a fierce clarity in his eyes that I haven't seen all week, a firmness in his voice that belies how weak he has become. "Take out the moonstone eyes. Keep them with you until all the werewolves are dead."

"Werewolves! Dad, there's no such thing as werewolves."

"Lani, you are a beautiful, intelligent young

woman. But you don't know everything. Werewolves are real. Your mother is a werewolf, for one."

"What? You must've been dreaming again, Dad. Believe me, I know how real dreams can seem." *Like my werewolf dream about Mama. It's seems to come more and more often lately. How freaky is that? Dad and I are both dreaming about werewolves.*

"You're almost sixteen. I won't be able to protect you after you turn sixteen. Even if I'm still alive."

"You are *not* going to die." A shiver runs up my spine and down my arms until my fingertips tingle.

"I've sent for help. Promise me you will kill your mother before it's too late."

"You've asked someone to help me kill my mother? My mother, who's already dead."

But Dad doesn't answer. He closes his eyes, finally worn out enough to sleep. He sinks into the pillow and begins to snore.

I close Dad's bedroom door, then sit cross-legged on the couch in the living room and punch in the number for the doctor on my cell phone.

The receptionist picks up on the third ring. "Doc Hammond's office. Is this an emergency?"

"My father needs to see the doctor right away." I give her Dad's name and our address.

"Cloud Pass? Isn't that where that hiker was killed the other day? Attacked by a wild animal?"

"That's right. About my father –."

"Guess everyone's totin' a gun up there, keeping their eye out. What was it? A rabid dog?"

"They don't know. When can the doc see my father?"

The woman huffed through the phone, obviously disgruntled that I won't take the time for small talk about something more exciting than scheduling an appointment, which was, oh, only her job.

"How about tomorrow at two?"

"You don't understand. He needs help today." My voice trembles and I clamp my teeth together to keep from crying.

"Can't be today, dear," the receptionist answers.

I wonder if it's payback for not chatting with her. "It's urgent," I plead.

"The doctor has two more patients and then he's leaving for the afternoon. Hold on a minute."

I hear muffled voices through the phone and know the receptionist has cupped her hand over the receiver while she talks to someone in the doctor's office.

She comes back to the phone. "Melani, are you still there?"

"Yes, but I go by Lani. Melani was my mother."

"She passed away, if I remember."

"Ten years ago."

The woman's voice takes on a sweeter tone. "Now listen, dear. Doc Hammond says he'll cancel his last two appointments if you can get your father here by three this afternoon."

I thank her and hang up.

There's a knock on the door. I open it and see a tall, gangly teenager, glossy black bangs hanging across his pale blue eyes.

"Hey, Ben! Come on in." He's wearing the green-and-brown plaid flannel shirt that I gave him for his birthday last month. The sleeves are rolled up to just above the elbows, showing off his muscular arms. A thought flashes through my mind, *I might have to rethink my use of the word "gangly."*

"Why don't you come out here?" Ben backs up and gestures to the bench that's built into two sides of the front deck. "I don't want to disturb your pa. I just came by to see how he's doing."

"See, that's exactly what I was telling Dad."

We sit in the corner of the front porch bench.

"What were you telling him?"

"Mainly that you're so considerate. You're a much better friend than Billie Mae Wrenfield."

Ben grins. "Can't argue with that, but what brought up that conversation?"

I can't tell Ben what Dad said about him, that I should be careful around him, so I pick at a splinter on the railing. "We were just talking, is all."

"Is he doing any better?"

"He had a rough night, but he's finally sleeping."

Ben looks at me sheepishly from under his jet-black bangs. "You could use some sleep yourself. You look plum worn out."

I slap his knee playfully. "Boy, I thought your mama taught you better manners than that."

"Guess I'm a disappointment to you and her, both."

"You can make it up to me. Help me get Dad to town later? He has a doctor's appointment."

"Sure, no problem. Anything else I can do?"

"Stay and keep me company for a little?"

"Again, no problem."

I lean back and gaze at Eagle Ridge rising up from the ravine on the other side of the road. Down in the cut, the Garnet River runs by, and my head fills with the sound of the rushing water.

Ben squeezes my knee, clears his throat, opens his mouth like he's about to say something.

"What?"

"Do me a favor. Don't go wandering around by yourself, okay?"

"Like I do that a lot. You're the one who's always dragging me off to some secret waterfall or tree fort or something."

"Still, we're not far from where that hiker was mauled last week. I don't want you running across the, um, bear what killed him."

"You sure it was a bear?"

Ben rubs the back of his neck. "They think it was a bear sow with cubs. Mama bears are real protective when they have cubs. They get super aggressive."

I think about the wolf I saw last night. "But are you *sure* it was a bear?" I ask again. "Not a wolf?"

Ben tenses. His eyebrows scrunch together and he fixes me with a crystal-blue stare. "You seen any wolves around here?"

If I tell him about the wolf, he'll want to hunt her down.

"Not around here," I say, telling myself the wolf was around back, not around front where we're sitting, so it's not really a lie.

Ben shrugs. "Just promise me you'll be careful. The rangers haven't been able to track it down yet."

"You sound just like my dad."

"I'm not your pa, Lani. Just someone who cares a lot about you." Ben gives me a serious look. "How's your pa doing, Lani? I don't mean just that he's finally sleeping. If you're considering the doctor, and he's not complaining, it must be serious."

I drop my head and rub my eyes, feeling the strain of the last week like a weight on my neck. "Oh, he's complaining, all right.   But I'm really worried. Doc Hammond's canceling his afternoon appointments so he can see him today."

Ben reaches over and clutches my hands in his. His hands are warm, strong, reassuring. He quickly pulls his hand away and sucks the flesh between his thumb and forefinger. "Ouch!"

"What is it?"

"I must've nicked my hand on your ring. Maybe you should get rid of that stupid thing."

"My ring?" I touch the oval moonstone in the ring. "There's nothing sharp on my ring. You probably got a splinter from the deck rail. Besides, I promised my mother I would always wear it."

"But it hurts," he pouts.

I've never noticed how cute he can be when he does that. Like his inner little boy is pleading for a cookie, and you'd have to be real strong to resist.

But I've known him so long, I'm immune. "You'll live." I pat his hand and stand up. "Guess I should go in and check on Dad again. Thanks for sitting with me."

"Cut it out, you big baby."

We agree that Ben will pick Dad and me up around two o'clock. He lopes down the steps and runs to the foot of the driveway. For a gangly sixteen-year-old, he runs with the grace of a deer, quiet and fluid. Yeah, gangly might not be the best adjective for Ben.

He turns back and yells to me. "There's something I want to show you later. Down by the river."

"Not another tree fort, I hope!"

"Better!" He waves as he skips backward a few steps, then turns and dashes away.

CHAPTER 3

Dad's still asleep, so I go to the kitchen to make myself a cup of hot tea and a sandwich.

How long has it been since I've eaten? I've been so focused on taking care of Dad that I haven't thought about feeding myself. As I pile sliced roast beef on whole wheat bread, I feel my mouth flood with saliva. I'm actually drooling. I swipe slobber off my chin and take a huge bite of my sandwich. And another. And another. Before I know it, I have wolfed down the whole thing.

I drop my plate in the sink and decide to take a shower.

I strip to my bra and underwear and suddenly I'm overcome with exhaustion. I lie down on my bed to rest for a few minutes. I don't mean to go to sleep, but wake up to the jangling of the telephone.

I jump to answer it, stubbing my toe on the china hutch. By the time I pick up, there's only a dial tone.

I guess whoever it was will call back. Maybe it was Ben, although he usually calls me on my cell phone.

Maybe it was the doctor. Panicked that I've slept through Dad's doctor appointment, I check my watch, but it's only 1:45.

Yawning drowsily, I grab a clean pair of shorts and pull a tank top over my head. Nursing my big toe, I limp to Dad's room and sit on the edge of his bed.

He's breathing with the slow, deep rhythm of sleep. Wisps of sweaty hair stick to his forehead.

I brush a strand of hair off his face with a fingertip.

His eyes flutter open and he holds my hand to his face, smiling. "Your mother was here again."

"What do you mean? Where?" I look around the room, half-expecting to see my mother's ghost in the corner.

"They try to keep her locked up," Dad says, his eyes twinkling. "But they can't keep her there."

"Keep her where?"

"Hunt House," he says.

I shake my head. "You're confused, Dad. You're the one who had to stay at Hunt House. You had a nervous breakdown or something after Mama died."

Dad sits up and grips my hand tightly in both of his. "You must listen to me!"

His fingernails, long and sharp, dig into my flesh. His sudden burst of energy scares me.

"Dad, you're hurting me."

"It was a lie," Dad rages, spittle flying from his lips. "A made-up story to help a little girl get past the horror of what happened."

I pull back against the rough way he holds my wrist and the insanity of what he's telling me.

"If you weren't in Hunt House, and Mama wasn't dead, why did I have to stay with that old woman?"

"Aurelia? You remember her?"

I haven't heard that name in years, but I remember it. It brings back a memory of a woman with long eyelashes, claw-like fingernails, and a glittery, purple headscarf. Dark, wide eyes set deep in a wrinkled face. Tears glistening on her leathery cheeks. I remember the woman saying, "I did it for my daughter. I had to."

"Is she my grandmother?"

Dad's raspy voice reminds me again of autumn leaves being crushed underfoot. "She will help you. She owes it to you. To our family."

He reaches for the photograph on the nightstand but misjudges and knocks it off kilter. I try to catch it but it tumbles to the floor, the glass shattering. I pick up the photo and look sadly at the scene of our family, now separated by a crack in the glass that runs from top to bottom, right between Mama and Dad.

"She was so pretty," I say softly.

"You look so much like her. She has more red in her hair, but you have her eyes, her cheekbones."

"I'll never be as pretty as she was."

"You are beautiful, Lani. And so is she. Not *was*. She looks the same now as she did in that photograph. Except ..." Dad touches a finger to his cheek.

"Except she's dead and gone." I put the photo back on the nightstand, slamming it a little harder than I intend.

"Neither dead nor gone. I tell you, she was right outside my window last night. I saw her eyes, her beautiful eyes. While I have turned into an old man, defying the curse, she has stayed young. Young and dangerous."

What kind of curse keeps you young, I wonder. *Why*

would you defy it if without it, you grow old, old before your time?

"Dad, I'm taking you to the doctor. Ben's coming over and he's going to help us."

"Ben," Dad scoffs. "He won't come near me. Not in this house. He wouldn't dare."

I've never heard Dad talk about Ben this way. "He just wants to help. I asked him to."

"Make sure you have Boulder Man's eyes," Dad says. His voice rasps like sandpaper on rough-hewn wood. "And promise me you'll be very careful when you go after your mother."

I can't tell him I'll be careful when I track down my mother because I don't intend to track down and kill my own mother. Who's already dead, anyway.

But I don't want to rile him up again by arguing.

"I'll be careful," I answer, vaguely enough that it's not a lie. I'm getting good at this, lying-but-not-lying to Ben and now to Dad. Not that I'm comfortable flirting with the truth, especially to the two people I'm closest to in the world.

"She'll be . . . on her way . . . home . . . by now," Dad says, the air rattling in his chest when he breathes in.

"Home? You mean, Georgia?"

"Georgia." He nods weakly. "Promise me . . . you will find her . . . and remove the curse."

"How am I supposed to get to Georgia?"

"I've sent for help. Promise me, Lani. Say you promise." He tries to raise himself out of the bed again, but his strength is gone.

"Please lie back and rest until Ben gets here."

"Promise me."

"I promise," I say, cold with fear and unable to blink the tears away any longer.

He falls back against the rumpled pillows and damp sheets, exhausted but with a look of relief on his face.

Air clatters in his chest. It comes out of him for a long moment, and then the room is deathly quiet.

I place my trembling hand on Dad's still chest, willing him to inhale, waiting for his next heart beat.

"Dad?" Tears roll down my cheeks and splatter on the front of Dad's shirt. I jostle him gently. "Dad?"

How can death come so quickly, and steal your only family in front of your very eyes? My last words to him were an empty promise. Not *I love you.* Not *Don't leave me.* A promise that I have no idea how to keep.

A rap on the front door jerks me to attention.

I swipe the tears away and stagger to the door.

Ben stands in the doorway, framed by the golden glow of the afternoon sun filtering through the hemlocks.

I throw myself against his chest and wrap my arms tightly around him. "Ben! Oh, Ben, it's too late."

"What happened?" he asks.

"Dad is dead!"

"When?"

"Just now. One minute we were talking," I say through sniffles, "and the next minute he was gone."

Ben smoothes my tangled hair, brushes a stray wisp off my face and tucks it behind my ear. I grasp his hand and lead him inside.

"The old man finally gave up the ghost," Ben says.

I stop dead in my tracks and pull my hand out of his.

He takes in my dumbfounded look. "I'm sorry, Lani. I didn't mean anything by it." He spreads his arms wide, inviting me to forgive him, to accept whatever comfort he can give. "Just that he lived a good, long life."

I wilt into his arms and smell his earthy scent. "He's only forty-nine. *Was* forty-nine."

"Really? That's four years younger'n my pa would be, if he was still around. I always thought he was older."

"I should have done more for him," I choke out between sobs.

"You did everything you could do for him."

"He never got over Mama's death. I guess it made him old before his time." I blink up at Ben. "It's my fault. Taking care of me was too much stress for his heart."

"You know that ain't true," Ben says. "You were everything to him."

I burrow my face into his shirt. My head pounds with grief, guilt, and the realization that now I'm all alone. An orphan. "What am I going to do?"

Ben cups my face in his hands, his fingers under my hair. He tilts my face with the gentlest of pressure, to make me look him in the eyes. "My ma will take care of everything," he says. "Don't you worry."

His closeness is confusing. He's my friend, my best friend, but he's acting different. Like he's decided he's my boyfriend or my bodyguard. I'm not sure I want him in either role, but right now, I can't deal with the confused emotions swirling in my head. Ben's here for me. And I need that, so I take it, selfishly ignoring what he might read into it.

Ben tenderly walks me to Dad's room. I stand beside him at the side of the bed. He holds Dad's wrist, checking for a pulse. He looks at me and shakes his head, but it's an empty gesture. I already know Dad's gone.

"Goodbye, Mr. Morgan," Ben whispers as he pulls the quilts up over Dad's head.

He takes a deep breath and exhales through his mouth, puffing his cheeks. "You don't have any other family, do you?" Ben wraps his arm around my shoulder and leads me back to the living room.

I almost tell him what Dad said about my mother still being alive, but what good would it do? I don't want Ben to know how crazy Dad had gotten at the end.

I shake my head.

"You can stay with us till things get worked out," he says. "I'll take care of you, like I promised I would."

The warmth of his body, the hypnotic way he smoothes my hair, the calm way he takes charge – relieve my fears and allow me to forget, at least for now, how alone I suddenly am in the world.

Over the last few weeks, I became the parent, caring for Dad as if he were my child instead of the other way around. Snuggled against Ben, I pretend I'm the child once more, and let him comfort me the way Dad would have done, or a big brother, if I had one.

On the way out, Ben flips the thermostat setting from heat to cool.

CHAPTER 4

Later, we sit side-by-side on Ben's couch. If I concentrate on the grandfather clock ticking, it drowns out the whooshing in my head that sounds like wind rushing through the Garnet River cut.

Just after the clock chimes nine, Mrs. Stoat breezes in with a bag of groceries filling both arms, her chunky black purse dangling from one elbow. Her silver hair is piled in a neat bun on top of her head, accentuating her soft, round face.

Her smile fades when she sees the look on our faces. "What is it? What's wrong?"

Ben takes the groceries from her arms and talks to her quietly. I know he's telling her what happened, that Dad is dead.

"I'm so sorry, dear," Mrs. Stoat says, throwing her purse and keys on the table by the door.

"Thank you." My voice is as raspy as Dad's was.

"I thought Frank was going downhill fast. I surely did. But I never --." She wraps me in a hug, enveloping me in soft, saggy arms and a cedar scent. "You lie down a while. You can use Jolie's room, and I'll call the coro – I'll call someone to take care of your father."

Mrs. Stoat leads me to the bedroom that belonged to Ben's sister, Jolie. She gave away lots of Jolie's stuff, but a teddy bear and quilted throw pillow are propped on the bed, I guess just the way Jolie left them when she died.

"Try to get some rest, dear," Mrs. Stoat says.

As soon as Mrs. Stoat shuts the door, I move Jolie's teddy bear and throw pillow to the night stand. I tell myself it's out of respect for Ben's sister, but really it's to minimize the creepiness factor of lying in a dead girl's bed.

Minutes pass. Hours. Millennia. I lie on the bed, staring at the ceiling, unable to relax.

Mrs. Stoat knocks on the bedroom door and opens it a crack. I must have fallen asleep because it's light out now. "Do you feel like some breakfast? Then we can go down to your house to pack up some things. I imagine you'll be here a few days, at least."

"But Dad will be . . ."

"You need not worry, child. The ambulance took him away last night."

I sip hot tea at a hand-hewn table while Mrs. Stoat clinks around in the kitchen.

I can't take my eyes off the beautiful inlaid roses that frame the table. I've sat at this table probably thousands of times, but never really looked at it.

"Beautiful work, isn't it?" She sets a plate of toast and scrambled eggs in front of me.

"Did my father do this?"

Mrs. Stoat laughs. "Frank wasn't the only man with talent on this mountain. My George made that. One of the last pieces before he departed." She makes it sound as if he died, rather than left in the wake of his family's tragedy, when Ben's sister died.

Mrs. Stoat points at my plate. "Aren't you going to eat nothing?"

I pick up my fork but my stomach feels like I've swallowed a boulder.

"That's all right. I understand, I surely do. You'll get your appetite back by lunch time."

"I'm sorry I wasted your food."

"It won't go to waste. Ben'll eat it when he wakes up."

We walk down to my house and Mrs. Stoat follows me up the stairs to the deck. "So many steps," she says, panting. "All these years of living in the hills wear on a body, they surely do. Especially the knees."

She waits while I open the front door.

As I pass Dad's bedroom I see his empty bed, a quilt half-fallen on the floor. It's like I'm sleepwalking, moving on autopilot. The whooshing sound fills my ears again. I pull an old gym bag out of the hall closet and stumble to my room.

Mrs. Stoat waits in the living room. "Can I help you collect your things?"

"No, I don't need much. I'll just be a minute."

"Take your time, dear," Mrs. Stoat says. "My goodness, I forgot how lovely your house is."

"I guess you haven't been here for a while."

"A coon's age. Your father and I were friends when we were little, just like you and Ben are now. But that was long ago. A lot of water has passed under the bridge since those days."

"Dad says he and my grandfather laid every stone

by hand when they built the house. That was when Dad was little, but Dad says he did most of the work himself."

"I remember your grandfather," Mrs. Stoat says. "He was a talented stonemason. Your father got his knack for building things from him."

Building things like Boulder Man. The rocks snuggle together so that the whole structure stays in place without mortar. *Take Boulder Man's eyes.* I don't know if I'll be strong enough, even with the chisel.

Under different circumstances, I would have asked Mrs. Stoat to tell me more about my father's childhood. But now, everything seems so surreal that it's hard to hold on to a train of thought, much less carry on a conversation.

I pack some clothes and my Kindle, thinking a good novel might help me get my mind off of things. Last but not least, I pull my favorite hoodie out of the armoire. It's faded and worn, but it used to be my mother's. It used to feature a skull and the word *Genius,* a reference to an album by an old rocker named Warren Zevon, but the lettering is worn off except the top of the "G" and the "us."

"Got everything?" Mrs. Stoat asks. A bead of sweat has trickled down her cheek and clings to her angular jaw line.

"There's just a couple more things." I put on the jacket and zip it up halfway.

I go back to Dad's room.

I shiver and rub my arms, breathing heavily as I look at the empty bed. For the last week, Dad's room has been a furnace. Now it seems cold as a morgue. It's like Dad's dying has taken the life force out of the whole house. Of course it's just because Ben turned on the air conditioning. Probably to keep Dad's body cool until the coroner came to collect him.

I suddenly feel more alone than I've ever felt.

I pick the quilt up and smooth it out on the empty bed.

A slight indentation in the pillow marks where Dad's head rested. A faint, tangy fragrance hovers in the room. The shaving cream I had used when I shaved him every morning for the last week of his life.

I shudder with a wave of sadness.

"Are you all right?" Mrs. Stoat asks from the doorway of Dad's room.

"Fine. I'm fine." I pick up the framed photo of my family – two thirds of us gone now – and snuggle it between the clothes in my bag.

Mrs. Stoat follows me around back to the shed. I slide his dented, duct-taped toolbox off the shelf and set it on top of the washing machine.

"Dad's clothes! They're still in the washer."

"Let me help with those," Mrs. Stoat offers. She squeezes my shoulders and I move the toolbox from the top of the washer to the top of the dryer.

"Is that a toolbox?" Mrs. Stoat asks as she transfers clothes from the washer to the dryer. She doesn't take them out by handfuls like I do; she pulls each piece out one at a time, shakes it, and slings it in the dryer. "What do you need from an old toolbox?"

"Tools," I answer, stating the obvious. Of all the building tools Dad used to keep in here – several hammers, nails of every size, a metal tape measure that

I loved to pull out and watch zip back into its housing – only two are left. A tiny hammer and chisel. They look like toys. They fit easily in the back pocket of my jeans.

"Why on earth do you need tools?"

"Dad wanted me to get the moonstone eyes."

She stares at me, holding one of Dad's shirts by the shoulders. "Moonstones?"

"From Boulder Man. The statue out back? Dad told me to take the moonstones."

"Whatever for?"

"Protection," I answer before I can think about it. "I know how weird that must sound."

Mrs. Stoat smiles sadly. "It surely does, child. You have nothing to fear. Let's just go on home." She tosses the shirt in the dryer, shuts the door, and turns the knob to set the dryer to life.

"No, I promised Dad."

"Well, let's be quick about it, then."

She steps out of the shed and waits for me in the yard, rubbing her arms as if she's caught a chill.

I'm about to close the toolbox when I notice a thick envelope taped to the underside of the lid.

"Melani" is scrawled in Dad's slanted handwriting, in blood-red ink. Is it for me, or did he address this to my mother, after his illness had made him think she was still alive?

Dad knew he was dying. Maybe he hid away some money, to keep me out of foster care.

I pull the envelope free from the box lid and shove it in my jacket pocket.

I trot past Mrs. Stoat with both hands shoved in

my pockets. Standing in front of Boulder Man, I look for the familiar toe holds, niches I used when I would climb up and sit on his shoulders when I was a kid.

Mrs. Stoat watches from a distance, biting her fingernails, as I squeeze my foot into the first toe hold at the base of the huge rock sculpture.

I'm almost at eye level when my foot slips.

"Be careful," Mrs. Stoat calls out.

"I'm okay."

I reposition my foot. When I look up, Boulder Man and I are eye to eye.

It's hard to work the hammer and chisel and keep my balance, but fortunately the baseball-sized moonstones aren't sealed in mortar. Like the rest of the statue, they are held in place by their perfect size and shape. After a few taps, I wiggle them out and put them in my pockets, one on top of the letter from Dad.

That night, I still haven't found my appetite. After scraping my fork through the roast, mashed potatoes and gravy for fifteen minutes, I excuse myself from the table. "I think I'll just go to bed."

I lie down on Jolie's bed without even turning off the light or changing into my pajamas. I put my hands in my jacket pocket and hold the cool moonstones. The envelope crinkles under the weight of the rocks. I take it out and study Dad's writing on the front. "Melani." Possibly the last thing he ever wrote.

A knock on the door startles me.

"Lani?" Ben calls softly. "Can I get you anything?"

"No, thanks. I'll see you in the morning."

I rub the wax seal on the envelope, then slide my fingertip under the flap. Inside is a single sheet of paper, rubber-banded around a stack of cash. This must be what he really wanted me to find when he told me to get his tools and take out Boulder Man's eyes. After all, why are moonstones so important?

I count the money – twenty-five, one-hundred-dollar bills. My first thought is, *This will keep me out of foster care,* although I'm not sure how, exactly. Maybe I'll use it to buy groceries and pay the electric bill so I can stay in our home. I won't even have to tell Child Protective Services I'm an orphan, living on my own.

Maybe the letter explains what Dad wants me to do.

I unfold it and read words that make me as cold inside as Dad must have felt these last few days.

> *My dear Melani,*
>
> *Running away didn't work. The curse has found me. I'm certain now that it will find Lani, too. By sending her to you, I may be sending her into the jaws of death. If it wasn't my only choice, to save her very life, I wouldn't do it. But I know of no other way.*

I stare at the words in disbelief.

> *If you are reading this, it means that I am dead. I believe that God is a loving and forgiving being who cares for all His children, even those who become beasts. Even those who become werewolves like you and me.*
>
> *I hope with all my heart that this is true. When Lani reaches you, I pray she is able to save herself. If she is successful, you and I will meet again soon, be*

it in heaven or hell. Melani, know that I loved you till the end.

> *Love always,*
> *Frank*

I slowly fold the letter and slide it back in the envelope, then put the envelope back in my pocket. I hide the wad of cash in the bottom of my backpack. After I turn off the light, I try to make sense out of what has become a cauldron of confusion – my life.

My father is dead.

My mother is a werewolf.

My family is cursed.

I'm as cold as Dad in his coffin, as cold as the moonstones that I hold inside my pockets as I curl into a ball, shivering under the covers in a dead girl's bed.

It must be midnight when I wake up. That same hoot owl calls, or maybe it's another owl answering the one I heard last night. I lie there half-awake and listen to the lonely sound.

When the door creaks open, I think at first it's Dad checking on me. Then I remember that Dad is dead and I'm not even in my own house.

I pull the sheet up to my chin. "Who's there?"

"I didn't mean to wake you, dear," Mrs. Stoat whispers. "I just wanted to check that you was all right."

"I'm fine," I answer sleepily.

"Sweet dreams, dear," Mrs. Stoat says. She closes the door and I hear her slippered feet shuffle down the hall.

The next morning, I still have no appetite. I fix a

cup of hot tea and take it to the Stoats' front porch where I curl up on the swing.

About mid-morning, Mrs. Stoat peeks her head out the screen door. "I'm making arrangements for your father's service," she says. "Is there anybody you'd like me to call? To come to the funeral or just to let them know your father passed?"

I shake my head. There's no one.

I hear Mrs. Stoat making phone calls. The funeral home, the florist, the preacher.

They'll all have fees, even the preacher. I have no idea how much it'll all cost, but it must be expensive. I retrieve the cash from my backpack and stand in the hallway near where Mrs. Stoat sits at a desk, talking on the phone and scribbling on a note pad.

She hangs up the phone. "What is it, Lani?"

I thrust by arm out, the cash rubber-banded in a thick stack on my palm. "Here. It's twenty-five hundred dollars. It was Dad's. I know the funeral will cost more, but I'll get a job and pay you back."

Mrs. Stoat smiles at me, but her eyes are moist with almost-tears. She slips the money out of my hand and places it on the desk. "I don't think you realize how much more."

"I'll pay it all back. I will."

Ben comes out of the kitchen with a glass of milk and a sandwich on a plate. He's freshly showered, his black hair shiny wet, stray strands poking up on top from where he toweled it. "Everything okay?"

"Fine. Just fine," Mrs. Stoat replies. She sweeps the cash off the desk and stuffs it in her apron pocket. "It surely is, son."

She picks up her pen and notepad and glides down the hall.

Ben is tall and lanky where his mother is round and cushiony, but Mrs. Stoat walks with the same quiet gracefulness as her son.

Ben pokes the air with the sandwich plate. "I was bringing you a sandwich. You hungry?"

"Not really."

"I'll eat it then." He sits in the chair just vacated by his mother and attacks the sandwich. He swallows half the milk in three gulps.

"Glad I wasn't hungry," I say.

"I'm headed to a little place down by the river," he says. "Been wanting to show it to you. You wanna come?"

Any other summer day, I would tag along on whatever adventure he thought up.

"Not today, okay? I'd just be a downer."

Outside, a car door slams. We go out to the front porch, followed by Mrs. Stoat.

A sheriff's cruiser is parked in the drive. A tall, big-built deputy walks toward me.

Mrs. Stoat wipes her hands on her apron. "Can I help you, Officer?"

"Deputy, Ma'am. Deputy Burns. Are you Sally Stoat?"

"I am. This here's my boy, Ben."

The deputy tips his fingers to his hat. "And the girl?"

"That's Lani Morgan."

"Sorry to hear about your father, Miss Morgan." The deputy stands with his feet shoulder-width apart, his hands on his holster belt buckle. "I just came by to let you folks know, the Park Service hasn't located the wild animal that killed that hiker. Keep your eyes open for any animals exhibiting unusual behavior."

"It was a bear, right?" I ask.

"Could have been a bear. Or a mountain lion, or a wolf. Hard to say at this point. Best to be alert around any apex predators."

I'm pretty sure a wolf is considered an apex predator, and a wolf peeking in my father's window would be considered unusual behavior, but I don't mention it. The Park Service might end up hunting it, and I'm sure the wolf I saw wasn't responsible for the hiker's death. If it was a killer, I would be in the funeral home alongside my father.

"Thank you, Deputy," Mrs. Stoat says. "We'll be careful."

"One more thing," the deputy says, reaching into his shirt pocket. He hands Mrs. Stoat a business card. "Could you please call this lady at Child Protective Services?"

A cold rock lands in the pit of my stomach at the mention of the state foster care agency. "Why do we have to call them?"

"Standard procedure. You folks have a nice day."

After the deputy leaves, I ask Mrs. Stoat, "Are you going to call Child Protective Services?"

"I've got too much else to take care of at the moment. I surely do." She tucks the card in her apron pocket, where I can still see the bulge from the cash I gave her. "I'll call her in due time. All in due time."

Later, I ask Ben to take me to town. "I need to pick

up some flowers from the garden store."

"Mama's already taken care of all that," Ben says.

"I want to have some flowers that are especially from me."

He stares at me intently. "You're a flower." His cheeks glow red and he casts his eyes down. "I'll get the car," he says, and runs away as if escaping his embarrassment.

What has gotten into him? He's never talked to me this way before. It must be his reaction to my father's death.

He pulls his faded blue Chevy around from the work shop behind his house and I get in. Ben hooks his arm around my shoulders, pulling me close to him. I lean against him, not completely comfortable with this new development in our friendship, but not wanting to pull away, either.

"You know, Lani, I like having you around the place," Ben says as we drive down the mountain. "Even if you are less company than a hibernating bear." All the windows are open so the breeze tosses our hair around and makes kites out of the collection of old hamburger wrappers in the back seat.

"I'm sorry I've been so quiet." I twist a strand of hair around my finger. "I just have a lot on my mind right now. I have to figure out what I'm going to do."

"What do you mean?"

"I'm fifteen. Child Protective Services isn't going to let me stay in my home by myself. Unless I can think of something, they'll take me off the mountain and put me in a foster home or an orphanage or something."

A cortege of pansies and petunias lines the

entryway to the garden center. I usually like the petunias' cinnamony fragrance, but today, their scent seems heavy and suffocating. Inside, customers buzz around like bees, loading little red wagons with mulch, pruning shears, and trays of annuals.

A large banner announces, "70% off Fourth of July" over a large wooden barrel stuffed with flag-themed yard stakes, red-white-and-blue bird houses, and tangle-free flag poles topped with eagle finials.

"What do you think your Dad would have liked?" Ben asks as we wend our way through aisles of hummingbird feeders, fertilizer, and pet memorial stones.

I think of Dad's garden with its flashy cardinal flowers, firewheel daisies, and smoldering red blackout lilies. "I want to get him something red, but not roses. They die too soon."

Like Dad.

A man with two little girls, each pulling miniature plastic versions of their dad's red wagon, stops me in the aisle by a towering display of wind chimes.

"You're Lani Morgan, aren't you? We're going to miss your father."

"Thank you. I will, too."

"Was it sudden?" the man asks.

The trio has blocked the aisle, trapping me. My heart starts to thump. I turn around and shove past Ben, running in the opposite direction. I take a hard right down the first aisle I come to and spy a shelf of velvety red gloxinias in black plastic pots under a grow lamp. In my mad panic, I have come across the perfect tribute for Dad.

Ben lopes up to me.

"What's wrong?" he asks. "You took off like you was stung by a bee."

"I just don't want to talk about my father with a stranger, in the middle of a store."

"He was only being polite."

"I know. I'm sorry." I pick out a gloxy – Dad's nickname for the plant – with thick, fuzzy leaves and three bright red blossoms. "I'm ready to go."

An older couple in the check-out line ask if I need anything. "Your father was all the kin you had left, wasn't he?" the husband asks.

"I might have some family down in Georgia," I say, trying to make up for the way I acted with the man in the aisle, and at the same time, wondering if it could be true.

"What's going to happen to you?" the man asks.

"Earl! Don't be so insensitive," the wife scolds.

She turns to me. "I'm sure you'll be fine, dear. Come on, Earl, grab those two ferns and help me with the weed-and-feed."

"Sorry to hear about your Dad," the woman at the check-out register says as she rings up my plant. "He did so much for this community. Built the little chapel practically by hisself when he was just a scrawny boy. Why, I remember – "

"We really need to be going," Ben interrupts.

"Oh, of course," the woman says. She hands me my change and puts the gloxy in a brown paper bag. "My condolences, sweetie."

"Thanks for rescuing me back there at the check-out," I tell Ben as we drive home. "I guess I better get used to people giving me sympathy. It's kind of overwhelming, though."

"You told that lady you might have kin down in Georgia?"

"I don't know why I said it. It just slipped out." I pick at the brown paper bag holding the gloxy in my lap. "Something Dad told me, but I'm sure he was remembering a dream. Or maybe he was thinking about before my mama died."

The next day is the toughest. It rains that morning, and I remember the old Indian saying about rain washing away the footprints of the dead. When the rain clears, steam rises off the land like spirits departing. Bluebirds call to each other in the hemlocks.

Ben comes out on the porch and stands beside the swing where I'm sitting. He lightly strokes my hair, then squeezes my shoulder. "Would you like to walk down to the river?"

"Today's the funeral," I remind him.

"But not till this afternoon. We have a couple hours." He's wearing bib overalls and the plaid flannel shirt I gave him, its sleeves rolled up to just below his elbows. He looks like a little boy busting at the seams to share a secret. He holds out his hand to me and wiggles his fingers. "Come on."

I take a deep breath, thinking the calm babble of the river might relax me, maybe even help me face the funeral. I put my hand in his and let him pull me to my feet. We walk around the side yard and into the woods.

"You must've put these rocks in here." Granite rocks, about the size and shape of footballs and shot through with pea-size garnets, line a path carpeted with the tiny needles of the hemlocks. The path winds downhill toward the river.

"I've been working on it all week."

"So this is what you've been doing in the woods." I brush my hand against rain-glistened ferns that border the rocks. "I like it."

An honor guard of rhododendron bushes stretches overhead across the path, their boughs intertwining in a natural canopy twenty feet above us. We step through the archway into a small oval clearing overlooking the river. The clearing is rimmed with more small boulders like the ones Ben placed along the path. The river, a gentle stream at this point, sparkles in the morning sun, glinting like diamonds float on its surface. The water murmurs soothingly as it pours downstream.

A cardinal lands on a branch directly across from us on the opposite shore. It chirps and bobs its tail as it turns this way and that on the branch. It looks at me with one shiny black eye, cocking its head as if thinking it might know me. I wonder, can people come back as animals when they die? If so, could Dad have been reincarnated as a cardinal? The bird flits away without answering my unspoken question.

"I feel like I'm in a holy place when I come here," Ben says softly. "A sanctuary for man and beast."

"Mm-hmm. It's so tranquil."

"I did it for you," he says.

"For me? Really?" I reach up and peck him lightly on the cheek. "You knew I'd get more peace in a place like this than at Dad's funeral. You're the best."

The rhododendron arch that forms the doorway to the little clearing makes me think of the archway – the lichgate – at the churchyard where Dad's casket will pause later today before proceeding to the gravesite. I would much rather have Dad's funeral here than in town. I think Dad would have liked it better, too.

A psalm, Dad's favorite, chimes through my head, and I sing a few words: "All creatures of our God and King…."

Ben takes my left hand in both of his. "Lani, you know how I feel about you."

"Sure. We're best friends. Even better than me and Billie Mae, right?"

Billie Mae Wrenfield and I used to be tight. We taught ourselves how to shave our legs together, got our periods on almost the same day, shared the same taste in boys. That was probably the first crack that started the rift in our friendship. That we both liked Johnnie Barton, and Johnnie chose her.

"I know you're worried about Child Protective Services," Ben says, jerking my attention back to the present. "If we was married, the state wouldn't have any claim to you."

I shake my head. "That's no reason to get married. Besides, I'm fifteen years old. I've never even thought of marrying anybody." *Except that crush on Johnnie Barton, but that was third grade.*

"You'll be sixteen soon. You need a man to protect you. You need me."

"Ben, you're barely sixteen yourself. We're not old enough to get married."

"Tell me the truth, Lani. Are you in love with

someone else?"

"No! That's not it at all."

Ben grins mischievously. "Then I still got a chance."

I smile too. "Let's just promise to be best friends forever, no matter what."

"We can wait till you're sixteen," Ben says. His brow is furrowed and he's deep in thought, talking to himself as much as to me.

"Or seventeen or eighteen or twenty-three," I point out. I immediately regret saying it, thinking it might give him the wrong impression.

He jerks his head up and looks at me, wide-eyed. "No, you can't risk that."

"Risk what?"

His eyes dart around as if he's searching for an answer. "You'll be an old maid by then."

I shove his shoulder. "Maybe by hillbilly standards."

"Now, Lani. I'm not your regular hillbilly." He sits on the mossy bank and pats the grass. His worried look is gone, replaced by the impishly crooked grin I know so well. "I kind of like old maids."

I cross my legs and sit down beside him, laughing, glad that the mood has shifted.

We laugh light-heartedly, then he turns quiet. "I don't ever want anything bad to happen to you. No one else knows you like I do. No one else can protect you like I can."

We sit quietly and watch the water. Between the river's endless song and the warm blanket of sun, I'm lulled into a trance. In my mind, the babble of the river becomes the giggles of a little girl – me as a four-year-old. In my daydream, Dad twirls me around and around in my favorite game of airplane. "Fly me again," I squeal.

But then Dad's face grows old before my eyes. He morphs into an old man, just the way he looked in the days before he died.

"Remove the curse," the daydream Dad says, his voice becoming garbled as his face morphs into a wolf's.

"Wake up, Lani." Ben shakes my shoulder gently. I open my eyes and realize I have fallen asleep with my head in his lap. I jerk upright and smooth my rumpled hair.

"Sorry," I mumble groggily. "I didn't mean to fall asleep like that. In your lap, I mean."

Ben shrugs. "You ain't slept right since your father passed," he says. "You needed it."

"I guess we should go."

We climb the gently sloping path through the woods back to Ben's house.

At the front door, I turn suddenly. "I didn't bring any good clothes!"

"I'm sure Ma kept some of Jolie's dresses," Ben offers.

"I thought she gave them all to the church when Jolie died."

"She was Ma's favorite," Ben says without a trace of jealousy. "I know she done kept something to remember her by."

But the thought of wearing a dead girl's clothes to a funeral sends a shiver down my back. "I'm sure her clothes wouldn't fit me." His face falls and I quickly add, "But thanks for offering. I'll run home and get something. It won't take ten minutes there and back."

"I'll go with you, then," Ben says. "Ma would switch me good if something happened to you."

"What could happen? I've gone up and down that road by myself a hundred thousand times."

"If it's all the same to you, I'll come along anyway."

I remember about the hiker. "Okay, thanks."

All at once a mischievous feeling takes hold of me. The days of worrying about Dad, and then mourning for him, lift like a sheet on a laundry line, blowing in the breeze. I know the breeze is temporary, and make a snap decision to accept what it offers. "Race ya!" I holler.

I dash past Ben before he knows what's happened. I bullet down the gravel road, laughing with the rush of adrenalin I always get when we race.

He's fast, though, and it doesn't take long for him to catch up. "You'll never get away from me!" His voice comes from just a step or two behind me.

I squeal with excitement and the pseudo-fear of a make-believe chase – the hare and the hound.

When I turn the corner at our driveway, I stumble to a stop. Ben flings his arms out and grabs my shoulders so he won't knock me over. He can't stop his momentum and plows into Dad's trellis of moonseed bushes, pulling me on top of him.

"Why'd you stop?" he sputters as we emerge from between tall stalks. "You know the finish line is the top of the driveway. Not that I mind stopping here.

Boulder Man kind of freaks me –."

"Look," I interrupt. I point at a car in the driveway – a metallic-green Mercedes SUV that I don't recognize.

"Huh. Who do you know drives a Mercedes?" Ben asks.

"Nobody."

"Well, let's find out who it is."

"I'm sure it's just someone coming to pay their respects." Then it strikes me. "Oh, god. Maybe it's Child Protective Services."

"I don't think state workers drive Mercedes. And why would Tennessee government employees drive cars with Florida license plates?"

He's right. The vanity plate has the word REALGAL in capital letters, printed over an orange silhouette of the state of Florida.

Ben starts up the stairs to the porch.

I grab the back of his overalls and follow.

"The door's open," Ben says, stepping in to the living room. "Holy night. What a mess."

"What? What is it?" I push around him into the living room.

It looks like a tornado has struck the inside of my house. The coffee table is overturned. The sofa cushions have been shredded and tossed to the floor. The place reeks of urine.

"I can't believe it." I step gingerly through the mess. "What kind of jerk not only robs a dead man's house but pisses in it too."

"Stay behind me," Ben says, holding his arms out like a crossing guard. "It could be a wild animal. An ape-like predator."

"Driving a Mercedes?"

I push Ben's arm down and walk around him to the kitchen. The drawers and cupboards on the china hutch are all ajar. The kitchen cabinets and drawers all hang open as well, and the silverware tray is turned upside down on the counter by the sink, all its contents dumped in a clutter on the counter.

"This wasn't done by an animal." I pick up a ceramic dog head that had belonged to a Lady and the Tramp figurine my parents got me at Disney World when I was little. This more than the general mess of the room breaks my heart. It reminds me of happier times, now in shambles. "Who would trash my house when my father just died?"

"Maybe they didn't know he passed," Ben says.

"Ben, everyone in town knows he passed. Whoever that Mercedes belongs to has some nerve coming in and turning the place upside down."

I hear a door creak open. I grab a cast-iron skillet from the hanging rack over the stove and hold it like a baseball bat. I march back to the living room, not bothering to sneak quietly. "Who's there?" I demand.

A woman stands in the doorway to my Dad's room, silhouetted in the shadows. As she steps into the light, I notice that her face is hollow, almost skeletal in its severity. Yet there is an allure about her kohl-lined brown eyes, bright red lips, and glossy black hair bouncing in curls around her shoulders that makes me certain she can have men groveling at her feet like dogs at the snap of her fingers.

As if to prove my point, Ben brushes past me,

gawking at the woman. "Hello," he says.

Ignoring Ben, the woman steps toward me. Her shiny black high heels click on the hardwood floor. She wears a cream skirt suit that I can tell is expensive. A lacy black camisole peeks out at the neckline, and double swoops of a thick gold necklace drop into her cleavage. A small leather purse hangs from a gold chain draped over her shoulder. Not what I imagine a case worker from the state would look like.

"Melani?" the woman blurts.

I'm surprised but I don't loosen my grip on the skillet.

"I'm Lani," I say cautiously. "Melani was my mother."

"Of course she is," the woman says. She shoves her hand into her purse.

I raise the skillet instinctively. "What are you doing?"

She barks a fake-sounding laugh. "Please. I'm not going for a gun." She holds up a set of car keys and fiddles with the key chain, a digital mini-photo frame. "See? I would recognize you anywhere."

"How did you know Mama?" I ask.

I lower the skillet, but keep a tight grip on it with one hand as I reach for the keychain that she holds out to me.

Two little girls smile at me from the digital photo. The smaller girl, a pigtailed brunette, holds a lop-eared rabbit that looks like it's squirming to escape the girl's death grip. She looks just like me when I was about four years old, the age I was in the photo Dad kept by his bed.

Standing a head taller than the first girl, the second girl has shiny black hair that flows over her shoulders. Peaks of small breasts seem to fight the confines of her sundress with as much success as the unhappy rabbit trying to wriggle away from the littler girl.

"That's your mama," the woman says, tapping the tiny image of the shorter girl with a perfectly manicured pink-and-white fingernail. "And that's me. I'm your Aunt Romelia."

Did Dad say Aurelia or Romelia? I try to remember. The woman I remember, the one who wore a purple turban, was much older than this stranger, but I guess when you're little, everyone looks old.

"I didn't know I had an Aunt Romelia."

"Don't tell me you've forgotten me? I know I wasn't around much when you were growing up, but surely your father's mentioned me?"

I shake my head. I can't remember much about Mama's family before we left Georgia, and Dad never wanted to talk about them after Mama died. "You're not from Child Protective Services?"

"From the State?" Romelia makes a derisive noise through her nose. "Not hardly."

I twirl my fingers over my head. "Did you used to wear, like a purple turban thingy?"

Romelia laughs, a nervous, high-pitched sound that echoes around the room like gunfire in a canyon. "I wouldn't be caught dead in something like that."

That I can believe, judging by her Fifth-Avenue suit and designer heels.

I glance around the topsy-turvy living room and kitchen. "What were you looking for in my house?"

"I was looking for your father."

"What, you thought you'd find him in the cupboards, or under the sofa cushions?"

"No, no. Of course not." She makes the noise with her nose again, a quick burst of air.

I tighten my grip on the skillet. "Then why did you trash my house?"

"You think I did this?" Romelia flips her hands like birds fluttering on tethers. "How preposterous."

The way she says it makes me feel like *I* am the intruder. I grit my teeth together and glare at her.

"I think we should leave," Ben says.

"This is *my* house!"

"And who is your handsome friend?" Romelia asks as if seeing Ben for the first time.

She extends her hand, her long, delicate fingers posed like royalty awaiting a kiss from a commoner.

He shakes her hand like a lumberjack shaking loose a logjam. "Ben Stoat, ma'am."

"You'll not find my father here," I say. I put down the skillet so I can pull Ben out of her grasp.

"Is that right," she drawls. She plucks the keychain from my hand and twirls it so the keys clink against each other. "Then where might I find him?"

"Try the funeral home."

I can tell I shocked her. "Franzl is dead?" she asks, a quiver in her voice.

"Franzl? His name is Frank. Dad's name was Frank."

"Yes, of course," Romelia mutters. "Franzl was my nickname for him, back when we were in college together. He called me Romy."

"If you'll excuse me," I continue through clenched teeth, "I have to get my dress."

I don't like this woman, even if she is my aunt – which I doubt.

"Your dress…." Romelia's thoughts seem far away.

"For the funeral? It's in an hour and a half."

"Let's just get it and go," Ben whispers in my ear. "She scares me."

"Don't let me scare you, *dragul meu*," Romelia says.

Ben's cheeks turn red and I know he didn't expect her to hear his comment.

I turn and march to my bedroom.

Ben stops in the doorway.

I toss the skillet on my bed and look around.

I've always thought how cozy my room is, not like the house we lived in back in Georgia. My upstairs bedroom had been creaky and drafty in the winter and suck-the-breath-out-of-you hot in the summer. The floor tilted so steeply it threatened to dump me out the window.

Once when I was real little, maybe three or four, I asked if I could move my bed into the breezeway between the house and the carport out back. But Mama and Dad wouldn't let me. They said my room was the best place in the house for me.

One great thing about my bedroom here is the arch of moonstones embedded in plaster around the door frame. I vaguely remember a similar mosaic in my room in Georgia.

I'm both surprised and relieved that my room appears undisturbed. Maybe whoever ransacked the rest of the house got scared off before they had a chance to search my room for money or jewelry or whatever they thought they would find. Maybe they had even been in the house when Romelia arrived, and slipped out the back without her noticing.

I open the chifferobe and pull out my best dress. It's red satin with a black velvet faux bustier jacket sewn in.

"For a funeral?" Romelia asks. She and Ben stand side-by-side in the bedroom doorway.

"Red was Dad's favorite color."

With the dress draped across one arm and my only pair of good shoes hooked on my fingers, I march out the front door and down the steps.

"Aren't you going to lock up?" Ben asks.

"What for?" I say, not slowing down.

"What –," Romelia calls after me.

Halfway down the steps, I wheel around and glare at her.

"What did he die from?" she asks, her hand at her throat.

"Heart attack."

"Heart attack? But he was so young. And he stayed so fit, at least when I knew him."

"It was the accident, when Mama died. All the stress of being a widower, raising a child by himself. He went grey a long time ago. I guess his heart was going bad the whole time, too."

"Died? Melani didn't die."

"She did. I was there."

"You were five. You didn't understand what was going on."

I step toward her, fully intending to slap her in the face and maybe strangle her to death, right there on the deck. But Ben pulls me back.

Romelia taps her index finger on her chin. "She must have bitten him. That would explain it."

"Explain what? I think you should explain about my mother. Are you saying she's still alive?"

"Oh, yes, she's still alive. Franzl was supposed to tell you all this, plus the fact that I would be here."

"I guess he forgot to mention it. For ten years."

"No, no. We just made plans for me to come within the last month or so. He was going to –." She breaks off in mid-sentence, as if another thought has just occurred to her. "Tell me. Did Franzl ever go out at night? By himself? Come home late, without an explanation?"

I stare at her, incredulous. "Are you asking me if he had a girlfriend?"

"No, nothing like that." She floats past me on the stairs and steps carefully across the gravel driveway to her SUV. She presses a code into the entry pad on the driver door. "He … didn't have a girlfriend, did he?"

I roll my eyes. "Come on, Ben."

I stomp up the mountain road.

Ben skitters a few strides behind me like a puppy dog. "Do you believe her? About your mother?"

"No. Yes. I mean, I don't know." I pant with the exertion of trying to talk and run uphill. "Dad wouldn't've told me Mama was dead if she was alive, right? Why would he lie to me?"

Ben shrugs. "Dunno. Did they have a big fight and break up?"

We've reached Ben's house and I plop down on the front porch swing. "No. I think I would remember any big fights. We were all happy, until Dad and me left, and the accident."

Ben leans against the wall and pulls the chain to rock me gently. "If you were all so happy, why would he up and take you away?"

"I don't know. I don't know." I rub my eyes and press my finger and thumb against the bridge of my nose.

"Look, you can think about all this later. Talk to this Romelia gal, ask her about your ma. But for now, just set it out of your mind. Let's go inside and get ready to go."

Back in Jolie's room I slip the red dress over my head and smooth it out. It still fits, although it's a little tighter across the chest than I remember. I brush my hair, and do my make-up in the mirror over Jolie's dresser. My jacket lies on the bed where I threw it. I pull the envelope out of the pocket, sit on the bed and stare at Dad's writing, "Melani." My hand trembles as I trace my fingertips across my mother's name. My mother, whom my father believed in his dying delirium to be alive. Who apparently had a sister, who also declares Mama's alive. Could it be true?

There's a knock on the door and I hide the envelope behind my back.

"Lani? You about ready, child?" Mrs. Stoat opens the door.

I feel like a kid caught with my hand in the cookie jar, but why should I? The envelope is addressed to my mother, but my father wanted me to find it. Yet I keep it hidden.

Mrs. Stoat points at the shoes I have left at the foot of the bed. "Well, I declare. Those your shoes?"

I nod.

Mrs. Stoat picks them up as delicately as if they were ancient relics instead of plain old Sunday School shoes. She hooks her fingers in the heels and turns them this way and that.

"Jolie had a pair of Mary Janes when she was a little girl. They was just like these, only smaller, of course. I always thought they was so classy, but she hated them. She surely did. Don't think she wore them more than once or twice, to a wedding or a funeral or something. Oh!"

Mrs. Stoat slaps her hand across her mouth and her eyes brim with tears. I can't tell if she thinks she offended me, or if she has reminded herself of Jolie's funeral.

A whistling sound comes from down the hall.

"My water's boiling," Mrs. Stoat says. "Making a Jello for later. Hurry with your shoes, now."

She shoves the shoes into my lap and rushes out to the kitchen.

I slip my shoes on and wiggle my cramped toes. I'm much more comfortable in flip-flops or my soft, suede dingo boots. Jolie was the same, from what I remember.

I wish I had gotten to know Ben's big sister better, but she died when she was twelve years old. That was only a year or two after Dad and I moved up to the mountain. Ben never talks about how Jolie died. I've heard some crazy stories from kids at school and folks at church. Some say it was a bear attack, others say she was killed by an escaped convict.

When I asked Dad about the rumors, he said you can't trust everything you hear in a small town. He said it was a freak accident, but refused to give me any details.

All I know for sure is, Mr. Stoat left shortly after Jolie's death and never came back. Just up and deserted his family. Mrs. Stoat was left to raise Ben by herself.

Like Dad had to raise me by himself.

But the stress of being a single parent hasn't taken such a heavy toll on Mrs. Stoat as it took on Dad.

Maybe Ben was easier to raise than I was.

I thought for years that if I had been Mrs. Stoat, I would have taken Ben and moved somewhere else, somewhere new, where I wouldn't be reminded every day of the pain of losing a daughter and a husband.

But now, I feel differently. I don't ever want to leave the home that Dad and I shared. It's all I have left of him. I will always be able to visit his grave, which they've probably already dug in the little cemetery by the church. But I know that I'll always feel closer to him in the house we shared, tending the garden he tended, feeding the cardinals and chipmunks he fed.

Is that even possible? I wonder. *Will the State just let me live by myself?*

A stone seems to have landed in my gut. When Child Protective Services comes for me, they'll probably take me away to some group home down in Knoxville, and I'll never see my home again.

CHAPTER 5

We pull into the grass parking lot in front of the church. The tiny chapel that Dad helped build when he was a teenager gleams white as a sail on an emerald sea. Jesus and Mary, doves and mountain sunrises shine down on us from the tall, narrow stained-glass windows that line the chapel walls.

Ben, dressed in a chocolate-colored blazer over a cream shirt and jeans, escorts me up the whitewashed brick steps and through the double oak doors.

I stop just inside the chapel and stare at the transformation. The simple chapel, usually a reflection of my father's down-to-earth personality, has been decked out like a parade float. Every spare inch of the chapel is crammed with flowers. Vases of white lilies and roses and pale yellow mums crowd the window sills. A dozen wreath-style floral arrangements adorn the steps leading up to the altar where my father's body rests in a black mahogany casket. The scent of lilies and roses hangs sweet and noxious in the tight air of the chapel.

Everything blurs, my mind is in a haze.

Not just because Dad died so suddenly, before I

was prepared for him to go – as if you can ever be prepared for the death of someone you love.

And it's not just that I'm alone now and don't know what will happen to me. Sure, those thoughts have been swirling around in my head.

On top of all that, as Ben noticed, I haven't slept well for a long time.

But the main reason I'm in a fog is because of that letter. *Werewolves like you and me,* Dad wrote.

Dad never told me that *he* was a werewolf. But what did he say? "Your mother is a werewolf, *for one."* Was that what he was trying to tell me then? That he was a werewolf too?

Now I'm not even making sense to myself. He was delusional, that's all. My mother is dead. And now, my father is, too. I'm an orphan.

My chest feels like it's in a vice, my ribs squeezed almost to the point of cracking. *This is aloneness,* I think. *I'm alone.*

A soft voice whispers in my ear. "How are you holding up?" It's Billie Mae. Her breath smells like wintergreen gum.

Johnnie Barton stands close beside her. His black hair, normally shaggy as an Old English sheepdog's, is slicked back away from his face. "Sorry about your father," he says.

"Don't worry about your plot," Billie Mae says. "Me and Johnnie been taking care of it, three days a week."

"My plot? In the cemetery?" I'm confused. My father is the one being buried, not me.

"Uh, no?" Johnnie says, his voice a question. "She

means the garden down in Knoxville."

I bop myself on the forehead. "I forgot all about our garden."

Last year Dad bought four plots in the community garden. One for the two of us to grow vegetables and sunflowers. The other three plots, he donated to the Boys and Girls Club.

"We have so much," he told me. "We have each other, our beautiful home on the mountain, Boulder Man to keep us safe. Some of these kids share one bedroom with four or five sisters and brothers, and when they go to sleep at night, they don't know if they'll be safe all night or if they'll have anything to eat the next day. The community garden is something that can be theirs, something that they can be proud of. A way for them to contribute to their family's well being."

I thought about the day just this past spring when one little boy snipped an eggplant from the bush in the B&G's raised garden bed and presented it to me like it was made of gold – his treasure. I looked over at Dad and he nodded his head. In exchange, I gave the boy the biggest zucchini I could find on our vines. He hugged me and ran to show his prize to Ms. Parramore, the B&G sponsor.

So Billie Mae's been thinking about me, I realize. *And trying to help after all.* "Thanks for looking after it for me and Dad."

"What are friends for? And you know what? I think some of the other folks who have plots have been helping, too."

She gives me a quick hug. "Besides, you've had a lot on your mind, and Johnnie and I have been going into Knoxville a lot anyway."

She bounces on tiptoe and sings in my ear, "We're looking at rings."

"Oh." A lump lands in the pit of my stomach. I don't know if it's because she and Johnnie are getting engaged, or because my life seems so bleak at this moment in comparison to her happiness. I decide it's because I resent anything that takes the focus off my father at this uniquely personal event. A wedding is for two people, but a funeral should belong only to the person who died. "I'm so happy for you," I say, clinching my teeth so as not to choke on the words.

"Thanks, Lani. You know you're going to be my maid of honor, right?"

Johnnie scuffs his feet. "She don't want to talk about all that right now, Billie Mae."

At least he *understands.*

"Sorry, Lani. It's just all I can think about."

Johnnie leads Billie Mae to a pew near the front of the church. They scooch close and whisper with their heads bowed together.

Ben wraps his arm around my shoulders. I forgot he was there. He guides me up the aisle toward Dad's casket.

Mrs. Stoat chose an ornate, mahogany box with brass handles and matching brass curlicue accents. It's a work of art; the craftsmanship is undeniable.

Dad would have hated it.

He would have preferred a plain pine box, made from planks fresh hewn at the saw mill in Ivy Gap. *I should have told Mrs. Stoat what Dad would have liked. How was she to know?*

I clench Ben's arm as we stop in front of the casket. The top half is open, its satiny white lining poofed and darted like a fancy party dress. I concentrate my gaze on the big white flowers piled on the foot of the coffin. I don't want to look at my father, once so self-sufficient, so *alive,* now lying here, vulnerable, unable to do anything about his situation.

"He looks real natural," Ben whispers.

I shut my eyes tight. I don't want to look. I'm afraid if I look, it will mean he is truly dead.

But this is the last time I will ever see him. I force myself to open my eyes.

Dad looks like he fell asleep, right there in the chapel. His snowy-white hair has been neatly trimmed, the way he used to keep it before he got sick. His normally ruddy complexion, paled by weeks of lying in bed, has an eerie blue tint, as if the chill of his last few days of life has followed him into death. His skin looks like a plastic mask that they created at the funeral parlor.

"Very peaceful," I choke out, but I'm thinking, *What's so natural about sleeping in a box, in front of a church full of people, in a skin of plastic?*

I look more closely at Dad's fresh-shaven, blue-plastic cheek. There's a smudge of red. *Is that lipstick?*

I stand there staring, wondering, *Who would kiss a dead person?*

My hand shakes as I reach out to wipe away the mark.

Ben clears his throat and I jerk my hand back.

The mourners, waiting for their turn to pay their respects at the casket, shuffle and cough behind us.

"Oh," I murmur. "I guess we should sit down."

Ben indicates a pew up front that's marked with a gold cord and a red velvet *Reserved* banner.

"I can't sit way up here." I pull Ben further down the aisle and duck into a row about half-way down.

Ben sits down beside me and wraps his arm around my shoulders. "Are you okay?"

Inhaling his familiar, earthy scent of ginseng root and hemlock needles, I want to curl into his side for comfort. But would he think I'm teasing him, after I basically refused his proposal just hours ago? Part of me wants to let him take control, get married and let him take care of me. Part of me knows that would be wrong. Ben deserves to marry out of love, mutual love, like my parents.

"I guess."

I look around the chapel at all the floral arrangements. I spot the deep red gloxinia on a stand at the foot of the coffin.

Dad would have liked it. It's a living plant, and after the funeral, I'll plant it on his grave. It will live and bloom instead of wilt and die in a matter of days. Plus, red was his favorite color, and Dad always said gloxies reminded him of my mother.

Your mother is alive.

How could Dad have said something like that, then gone and died without giving me an explanation?

Of course, he left the letter, but that was even more confusing.

But the thought tickles at the back of my mind, refusing to go away.

Your mother is alive.

A deep, booming voice breaks into my thoughts.

"Thank you all for being here today." Preacher Wrenfield, Billie Mae's father, is a large, pink man. He wears a dress shirt and slacks. No robe, no Methodist stole. His shirt collar is open; no strangulation device, as Dad used to call neckties.

Dad would have liked the informality.

The preacher dabs at his brow and wipes his neck and under his chin with a cotton handkerchief. "It's a scorcher out there, so I'm sure you're all happy to be in the air-conditioned house of the Lord, even for such a sad occasion. Praise God for the blessing of air conditioning."

A few "Amens" rise from the congregation, along with a sprinkling of respectful laughter. Preacher Wrenfield's light humor is meant to ease the tension from the situation, but it only tightens the knot in my throat.

Two men with slicked-back hair, black suits, and skinny black ties shut the casket lid. They slip as silently as apex predators to either side of the apse and stand like soldiers carved of stone.

"Frank Morgan was a beloved member of this community for many years," Preacher Wrenfield begins.

"Cloud Pass was his home growing up and straight through his years at the University of Tennessee. It wasn't long before a Lady Volunteer track star caught his eye, and when he chased her, she didn't try to run away." The preacher pauses to appreciate the soft chuckles from his audience of mourners.

"After graduation, Frank followed the beautiful Melani to her hometown of Lafayette, down in Georgia, where the young couple wasted no time starting a family."

The preacher knows how to pull the congregation along with his story. He pauses again for the quiet laughter to subside. Then he kicks up the melodrama.

"Alas, tragedy struck the young family when Frank's beautiful bride Melani was killed in a horrific traffic accident." Preacher Wrenfield casts a meaningful glance my way and exhales a deep and mournful sigh.

This is such a show, I think. *Who is all this supposed to help? Dad? Me? The people in the pews salivating like peeping toms, getting a peek at our lives? Like the wolf at Dad's window, spying on him.*

"Frank returned to Cloud Pass with his young daughter, Melani, named after her lovely but ill-fated mother."

Every head in the church – at least the ones in front of me – turns to look at me.

"That same little Lani is now a young woman, and the spitting image of her mother. So Mr. Morgan – Frank – often said."

A hand squeezes my shoulder and I flinch involuntarily.

I turn to see Mrs. Stoat, in the pew behind me. Her sad eyes remind me of a homeless dog. She gives me a half-smile, then presses her hand to her mouth and hiccups, trying to hold back tears.

Looking past her, I notice that everyone sitting behind me in the church is staring at me as well.

I turn back around and stare at my hands as if my

alternating orange-and-pink nail polish is the most fascinating thing in the world.

As the preacher drones on, I stroke my moonstone ring with my thumb. I spin it in a slow orbit around my index finger like the moon around the Earth: a day, a night, day, night.

I wonder if any of what Dad had said was true.

Is my mother alive?

Are my parents werewolves?

Am *I* a werewolf?

"That is life's mystery," the preacher says.

I look up and see he is staring right at me, as if he is reading and answering my thoughts. *My* life's mystery.

"I knew Frank for many years," he says, "and if I might humbly opine, I knew him better than most members of this flock ever did. So I can tell you, with utmost certainty, that Frank Morgan is happy now. He has shed his worn-out body and replaced it with angel wings. He is free of his mortal weakness and joyfully embraces our heavenly father. Let us pray."

The swoosh and clap of bibles and hymnals closing echoes through the chapel. My ears buzz and I don't hear anything else until the preacher says, "Forever and ever, amen."

Everyone stands up. The two men in black suits skulk to the coffin. Joined by two others, they take hold of the fancy brass handles and lift the box.

Ben pulls on my elbow and I follow him into the aisle. The pallbearers fall in behind us with the box that holds my father. Behind them, the rest of the mourners join the procession, emptying the church row by row.

Clinging to Ben's arm, I walk out of the chapel into

the bright mountain sunlight.

The cemetery is a short walk across the parking lot. I pause at the lichgate, take a deep breath, and step onto the grounds of the graveyard.

Beside a fresh pile of rich black dirt, a green canvas tent shades several rows of folding metal chairs. We step to one side so the pallbearers can bring the casket through the lichgate. They set it on scaffolding over the grave at the front of the chairs.

Ben leads me to the tent. I pick my way carefully across a carpet of royal blue Astroturf to a chair in the middle of the front row. I might be able to feel eyes boring into the back of my head, but at least I won't see everyone gawking at me like in the chapel. I won't have to look at the pity-filled eyes of my Dad's friends and the curious faces of people I barely know.

The preacher stands in front of me and pets my head with his doughy hand. I look at my lap so I'm not staring at his crotch.

The cicadas sing in the trees all around, and the drone of the preacher's words melt into their hum. Even in the shade of the tent, I feel beads of sweat trickle down my back. The satin dress sticks to my body like a glove.

I look longingly at a hydrangea bush a few feet away. Its mop-head clusters of lavender blooms bob in a puff of wind. This isn't a bad spot, I tell myself. I wish I could have buried him by Mama. A tear trickles down my cheek. I don't even know where Mama's buried. Or if she's buried, now.

My eyelids droop with the close heat under the canopy. I wish I could feel the breeze that ruffles the hydrangea blooms. I wish I could splash some cool creek water on my face, wash away the buzzing in my ears and the tightness in my throat. I wish Dad and I were sitting in the yard at home, weeding the flower garden and laughing about ladybugs.

I fan my face with the funeral program for Dad's service.

A movement behind the hydrangea bush catches my attention.

A skinny, long-legged dog with sleek, reddish-brown fur stares at me through the hydrangea blossoms. She turns and trots away, weaving through the tombstones, and disappears into the woods.

Only it isn't a dog.

I stand bolt upright and the funeral program flutters to the ground. "Did you see that wolf?" I blurt.

Ben coughs as if he's choking, and thumps his fist against his chest. "What wolf?"

Preacher Wrenfield stops eulogizing in the middle of a word. He stares at me, then looks over his shoulder in the direction I'm pointing. "Lani, maybe you'd best sit back down," the preacher says. "I think the heat is getting to you."

I glare at him.

Ben tugs my arm. "Sit down," he says.

When I don't sit down, he stands and pushes my shoulders until I slump into the chair. "I know how hard this is for you," he whispers. "But it will all be over soon."

I look at his earnest face beneath the jet-black hair, his clear blue eyes and straight, fine nose.

"No," I say. "It's just beginning."

CHAPTER 6

After the funeral, we go back to Ben's house. It seems like the whole town is crammed into the front parlor. When the parlor can't hold any more people, they overflow into the dining room, living room and kitchen.

The dinner table is heaped with serving bowls offering the massive amounts of comfort food you only see at funeral receptions. Three different kinds of potatoes, plates of sliced ham and turkey, baskets of rolls and cornbread, and at least four green bean casseroles.

I have no appetite.

The jumble of perfume, cologne, and aftershave makes my head spin. I slip out to the front porch and sit on the swing, my refuge since Dad died.

The evening is warm, clammy even. A heavy mist swirls low on the ground.

Four older ladies sit around a table under a hemlock tree in the yard, the mist licking around their ankles. A young woman hovers over a baby who toddles up and down the front steps.

A few minutes later, Ben plops down beside me.

He holds a plate piled high with mourning food in one hand, a cup of steaming hot tea in the other.

He hands me the tea and I hold it an inch below my lips, inhaling the clove-and-honey aroma.

"Want some food?" He slops a thick slice of turkey breast in cranberry sauce and shoves the whole thing into his mouth.

I grimace and shake my head.

"I knew you would want hot tea," he says around his mouthful of meat. "Even on a warm evening like this." He grabs a half-empty bottle of Mountain Dew that someone has left on the porch rail and takes a long swig.

"It's my weakness," I agree.

"Mmmph," Ben replies, shoveling more food into his mouth.

"How can you eat like that?" I ask in wonder. "You act like you haven't eaten in a week."

"I'm a carnivore," he says.

"Yeah, you're a carnivore like the Grand Canyon is a slight erosion issue."

"Glad you're feeling better," Ben says, popping a whole yeast roll in his mouth. "That's the most you've talked in days."

I shrug my shoulders and sip the tea.

"I thought you were going to pass out in the graveyard," Ben adds.

"I'm okay. It's just seeing that wolf, so close to everyone, and in broad daylight."

"You sure you weren't just seeing things?"

"I wasn't seeing things. It was a full-grown, reddish-brown wolf. It had a scar along its right cheek.

I think it was the same wolf I saw at the house."

Ben swallows the yeast roll with a gulp. "You saw a wolf at your house?"

"The night before Dad died. She got up on her back legs and looked in his window."

He shrugs and licks his fingers. "Okay, I get it. You were dreaming."

"Didn't you see it? At the cemetery? It was right there behind the hydrangeas." I blink at him, disbelieving. "You have to have seen it."

He shakes his head. "I guess all that heat was too much for you. Sure sign of heat exhaustion, when you start seeing things. Classic case. It was so damn hot, plus you haven't slept or ate hardly anything lately."

"You just said I was dreaming. Wouldn't I have been asleep if I were dreaming?"

"You can dream without getting good sleep. Nightmares, fatigue. Man, I had some intense nightmares for about a month."

"What about?"

"Doesn't matter. I better keep an eye on you for a few days, make sure you're okay."

"I feel fine, now." I cross my legs under me on the swing and shift so I am looking directly at him. "Maybe it wasn't the heat. Isn't there a phenomenon, where you hear about something and then think it's happening? Power of suggestion?"

"Yeah, I've heard of that. Like whenever I find a tick on my leg, I feel like I got ticks crawling all over me."

"That's right. Do you think that could be it?"

"You've been watching the news about that hiker,

haven't you? That's what's got you seeing wolves behind every bush. Those people on the news? They sensationalize everything, so you'll watch their show and they can sell more commercials."

"It wasn't on the news. It was a note my father wrote."

Ben pauses with one fingertip in his mouth. He pulls it out with a pop. "He wrote you a note about wolves?"

"Well, technically he wrote the note to my mother. But I found it and read it."

I look into his big blue eyes, trying to tell what he's thinking.

All I see is deep concern, and at that moment I think I might be able to fall in love with him.

"You're going to think I'm crazy," I whisper, "worrying about something so – so silly and unbelievable."

"You're not crazy, Lani. There *are* wolves around these parts. More than you might imagine. You let me know if you see one, and I'll let you know if it's a real wolf or some dog."

"Not regular wolves." I pause and take a deep breath before I blurt out, "Werewolves."

Ben sprays Mountain Dew through his nose and lips. "What?"

"I know it's crazy. Poor Dad. He must have been hallucinating there at the end."

He wipes his sleeve across his soda-spattered five-o'clock shadow. "So, he wrote a story about werewolves. What's so crazy about that?"

"It wasn't a story, like a novel or anything. He

really thought *he* was a werewolf. My mother, too. He told me he'd seen her recently."

"Uh-huh." Ben rubs the back of his neck, his nervous habit. "It's terrible what happens to people's minds."

"Yeah." It's hard for me to talk about it, but I need to confide in someone about the information overload that's been dumped in my lap. I pull the envelope out of my purse and withdraw the letter. "Here."

He carefully unfolds the letter. "You want me to read it?"

I nod.

"'My dear Melani.'"

I slap my hand over the letter. "Not out loud!"

"Oh. Sorry."

I watch his facial expression change from mild interest to astonishment as he reads silently.

"Jaws of death," Ben murmurs. "Sounds like he was planning to send you someplace dangerous. You think it was foster care?"

I shake my head. "I don't think so. Keep reading."

His eyes open wide and I know he has reached the word "werewolf." When he finishes reading, Ben folds the letter slowly and hands it back to me.

I slide it into the envelope and rub the wax seal like a blind person reading a Braille message. "What do you think I should do?"

"I'll tell you what you should do." He grabs the envelope from my hand. "You should set it out of your mind and not let it bug you. In fact, I'll light a fire in the fireplace and burn this for you, right this minute so you don't have to think no more upon it."

"No!" I snatch the envelope back and hold it against my chest, my hands clutched together like Dad's in the coffin.

Ben's hand hovers in the air as if he is deciding whether to grab the envelope from me again, but he pulls back and runs his fingers through his hair. I can tell I've hurt his feelings.

"I mean, it's the last thing Dad ever wrote to me," I say in my own defense. "Even if it is loony."

Ben drops his hand and goes rigid. "Oh, no."

I follow the direction of his gaze.

A tall woman with glossy black hair slams the door of a Mercedes SUV that I last saw parked in my driveway. Wearing the cream skirt suit and black high heels that accentuate her long, muscular legs, Romelia walks up the stone steps to the house.

"Crap," I say under my breath. "She gives me the creeps."

"Is that any way to greet your Aunt Romy?" the woman says.

"Sorry, I didn't mean for you to hear that."

"Apology accepted." Romelia – I can't bring myself to call her "Aunt Romy," or "Aunt" anything – leans against one of the front porch pillars, swinging her key chain round and round on her index finger. She tosses the keys up and snatches them out of the air. "You know how to drive?"

I don't know what I had expected her to say, but that question comes completely out of the blue. "I have my learner's permit," I say.

"Oh, good. It's such a long trip. It'll be good to split up the driving."

I unwrap my legs and set my feet on the floor to stop the motion of the swing. "What trip? What are you talking about?"

Romelia gives me a look of innocent misunderstanding, not that I trust her expression any more than I trust the woman wearing it. "Why, Lani! Didn't Mrs. Stoat tell you? Or I thought the preacher might have mentioned it?"

"Tell me what?"

I reach with trembling fingers for Ben's hand. He entwines his fingers in mine and clutches my hand tightly.

"That I'm taking you home," Romelia says nonchalantly. "You're going to live with me now."

"I don't think so," I scoff.

"I'm your nearest family now. It's my responsibility to raise you."

"You're not my family," I snarl. "You claim to be her sister, but you're nothing like her."

When I was little, Mama always made me feel calm, protected, treasured. Romelia has the opposite effect on me. She makes me feel like a wild animal with its foot caught in a trap.

"I never said we were twins," Romelia says in the mocking tone that makes me feel five years old.

"Whatever. She's alive. You said so yourself."

"Oh, so you think she'll raise you."

"That's right."

"I guess your father didn't tell you. Your mother's in the mental institution. Down in Lafayette?"

"Mental institution? You mean Hunt House?"

Romelia grins at the shock that I know is etched on

my face in that instant. *Karma can be lightning quick,* I think, remembering my twinge of pleasure at seeing how news of my father's death had shaken her, just hours earlier.

"That's right, Hunt House," she says. "So, you do know about it."

"Dad had to go there after the accident. When I stayed with that old voodoo woman for a while."

"The woman with the purple –." Romelia swirls her finger around the top of her head.

"The purple scarf-thingy, yeah."

"I'm afraid you've got your facts mixed up. The fact is, your *mother* is in Hunt House, and that's no place to raise a child."

"Why didn't my father tell me she was alive?"

Of course, he did *tell me.*

"Maybe it was easier for Franzl to tell you that she died, rather than to tell you the truth about her."

"I think I would have rather known the truth," I grumble.

"Don't be so sure," Romelia says. She shifts her position, jutting out a narrow hip.

"So she's in a mental institution. At least she's alive."

Again, bitter resentment rises in my throat. Resentment at having been lied to all these years, by my own father. I swallow my hurt, reminding myself how much Dad gave up to raise me. He did the best he could. If he lied about my mother, it was only to protect me from a truth he thought I was too young to handle. I wish I had acted more grown up, so he would have felt I was mature enough to handle the truth.

Romelia gives me a pout and a puppy-dog look that I guess is meant to convey heartfelt concern. "Look, let's start over, okay? We shouldn't be adversaries."

I look at Ben and roll my eyes.

He shrugs. "Sounds reasonable," he whispers.

"What? You're on *her* side?"

"*Thank* you, young man," Romelia says, flashing a TV-quality smile. "One thing I can say about you, Lani. You certainly have good taste in men."

I look over at Ben again, and this time, I swear he's blushing.

"So if Mama's at Hunt House, obviously I can't stay with her," I say, trying to sound less adversarial. "But why can't I stay here, with Ben and Mrs. Stoat?"

"That would be awesome, Lani," Ben chimes in. "I'm sure Ma would let you!"

As if she has been waiting for her cue, Mrs. Stoat elbows the screen door open, wiping her hands on a dish rag. She stands with her back against the screen door, holding it open.

"Well hello, Ms. Marks," Mrs. Stoat says to Romelia. "Missed you at the funeral."

"I sat in the back," Romelia says. "I didn't want to intrude. And please, Sally, call me Romelia."

"Why don't you come on in and have something to eat?"

"That's very kind of you, Mrs. Stoat." Romelia saunters up the steps and across the porch, her high heels clicking on the boards. "We need to chat more about my plans for Lani."

"We surely do." Mrs. Stoat guides Romelia inside

like some long-lost sister.

Romelia tosses me a look over her shoulder. "You and I will talk more later."

"Sounds like she's already discussed it with your mother," I say when the two women have gone inside.

Ben waves a barbequed chicken leg at me. "Don't mean nothing."

I nibble my fingernail, something I haven't done since I was little. "I don't know. I have a bad feeling in my stomach."

"That's just 'cause you ain't had nothing to eat." Ben shoves his plate at me. "At least take a carrot stick. God knows I ain't gonna eat it, and you wouldn't want it to go to waste."

After a while, the guests begin to leave, most stopping to say a few parting words.

"He's in God's arms."

"I'm praying for you, dear."

"Here's my card. Let me know when you're ready to list the house."

Eventually all the cars are gone except Mrs. Stoat's mini-van, Ben's vintage Chevy Bel Aire, and Romelia's Mercedes SUV.

"I wonder when she's going to leave," I grumble.

"Don't let her upset you," Ben says.

We sit on the porch swing until the fireflies come out and dance across the lawn. I rub my arms against the breeze that sweeps in when the sun goes down.

"Chilly?" Ben asks.

"Mostly just nervous." I get up and kick off my funeral shoes. I pace the length of the porch, barefoot, looking out at the mountain crest across the way.

Ben comes to my side and tries to wrap his arm around my shoulders, but I shake him off and hop down the stairs to the yard.

"Be right back," he calls behind me. He dashes into the house.

In the deepening night, I listen to the crickets sing.

A few moments later, Ben is back, carrying my jacket. He drapes it across my back, and gives me a quick squeeze on the shoulders.

"Shouldn't the moon be up by now?" I ask, wiggling my arms into the jacket and zipping it up as I search the sky over the mountain crest.

"It's there." Ben points at a dark circle in the sky. He shoves his hands in his jeans pockets, I guess to assure me he isn't going to try to touch me again.

The thought that he is too scared to touch me gives me a pang of guilt. He had only been trying to comfort me, and maybe get some comfort from me for himself in return. After all, Dad was about the closest thing to a father figure in Ben's life. He would invite Ben to go with us into town, when we went to Knoxville for a movie or for dinner. I slip my hand through the crook of Ben's arm.

He presses my hand against his side. "It's a new moon tonight. My favorite. Know why?"

"No werewolves?" I ask.

"Yeah, right." He gives me a hip bump and points his face to the sky. "It's 'cause you can see so many stars on a night like tonight. And all the fireflies look like starglow on a lake."

"Why, Ben, you're a poet."

"That didn't rhyme," he says with a self-conscious

little cough.

"I know."

We stand together, looking at the stars in the ink-black sky and the fireflies twirling around the yard.

"Do you really think she'll make me go with her?" I ask.

"You know, Lani, if we was married, she couldn't take you."

"I'm serious, Ben."

"Me too." He touches my chin gently, turning my face to his. "You know I am."

"Ben, you know that wouldn't work. I'm only fifteen."

"Almost sixteen. My ma was only sixteen when she married my pa." He nudges me and I see him smiling in the starlight.

"If she makes me go, I'll text you every day."

"And I'll dream of you every night."

"I hate to break up this little love fest," a voice close behind me purrs.

Startled, Ben and I jump apart.

"Romelia. I didn't hear you come up," I say.

"I *do* wish you'd call me Aunt Romy."

I refuse to give her the pleasure. "I *do* wish you'd quit sneaking up on me."

"Please!" Romelia scoffs. "I can't sneak up on anybody in these heels! They are *not* meant for mountain climbing."

"Isn't it time for you to be headed home, Romelia?" I ask.

"It is late, in fact." Romelia walks in a slow circle around me, her arms crossed, cutting Ben outside the circle like a wolf cutting a lamb away from the flock.

"I'm staying down at the Orange Knight Inn tonight," Romelia says. "I want to get an early start in the morning. Have your bags packed by eight AM, 'kay?"

"No, not okay." I clench my fists at my sides and glare at her. "I'm staying here."

Romelia exhales and shakes her head. Her shiny black curls bounce the way models' hair does in shampoo commercials. "Oh, Lani," she sighs. "It would make things so much easier if you'd accept the fact that you'll be with me for a while."

"I haven't had a chance to talk to my mother," Ben says. "She'll want Lani to stay with us. I'm positive."

"She and I have already discussed this." Romelia stops her pacing and whirls to face me. "Tell you what," she says in the fake-excited tone adults often use with five-year-olds. "I'll take you to visit your mother."

I'm pretty sure this isn't her spontaneous idea, but clever bait that she's kept in her mental tackle box, waiting for the right moment to dangle it in front of me. "We're going to Lafayette?" You'll take me to see Mama?"

"You'd like that, hmm?"

"Well, yeah. If she's really still alive."

"It's settled then." Romelia fishes her keys out of her purse and twirls them around her finger. "See you at eight – no, make that nine o'clock in the morning. I'm still on Central Time."

As Romelia backs her SUV into the road and heads down the mountain, the twin beams from her headlights bathe Ben and me in light. I feel like the proverbial deer caught in the headlights.

"Do you believe her?" Ben asks. He snuggles close again, but the fireflies are gone and so is the mood.

I step away. "I don't know. After thinking my mother was dead for all these years, it's strange to think she's alive."

"What about the stuff your pa wrote? The werewolf curse and all?"

"I guess I'll figure that out later." I sigh and gaze at the horizon, the shadowy treetops jagged like wolves' teeth along the ridge.

"I'll tell you this," Ben says. "If ever anyone was a werewolf, it's Romelia."

"Why's that?"

"Sharp hearing. Sneaks up on us. And her attitude. What a bitch!"

I have to laugh. It's been a long time since I've laughed. It feels good. I know it's Dad's funeral day, but I don't think he would mind me sharing a laugh with my best friend, especially since it looks like Ben and I will be saying goodbye to each other soon.

Later, as I pack the few things I had brought to Ben's house, I think about my mother. Dad hadn't mentioned her being alive until he got sick.

And then this stranger shows up, saying she's my aunt and telling me the same things Dad had told me. If she isn't my aunt, how does she know about the things Dad had confessed? About Mama being alive? About Hunt House?

Dad had also claimed there was a curse on our family, and that he and Mama were werewolves.

Romelia hasn't mentioned that.

Of course, if she did, I would think she was hallucinating too.

Wouldn't you have to be, to believe in werewolves?

I try to put thoughts of the curse out of my head and concentrate on the part of the story I want to believe: *Mama is alive,* I tell myself. *Mama is alive!*

That night I dream of werewolves and moonstones and a woman in a purple turban.

I wake up missing both Mama and Dad, my chest hurting and my cheeks smeared with tears.

CHAPTER 7

You'll need a whole new summer wardrobe," Romelia chirps as we zip down Interstate 75 out of Knoxville.

"I've got plenty of clothes," I say, only half-listening. I'm trying to read *The Host* on my Kindle, but the curvy road makes me start to feel carsick. I switch off the Kindle and rub my eyes with my thumb and forefinger.

"So you think. But you've never spent the summer in Pensacola. It's not so much the heat; it's the humidity!"

"Pensacola?" I sit up straight and slap my Kindle against the center console. "You said we were going to Lafayette."

"We'll drive through, but there is no *way* I'm staying in Lafayette. I escaped that backwater town years ago." Romelia pushes her shades down on her nose and looks at me over the tortoise-shell frames. "Same as anybody with brains between their two ears."

"You said we'd go see my mother at Hunt House." I hesitate before adding, "And I want to go by our old house."

"I promised about Hunt House, and I'll keep that promise," Romelia says. "But why do you need to go by your old house?"

"I just want to see it, that's all," I answer carefully.

I can't explain – even to myself – exactly why I want to go there. Dad had said *go home.* But did he mean literally go to the very house where we used to live? If Mama was in Hunt House, what was the point of going to our old house? I don't know the answer, but something inside is urging me to go there. "It isn't too out of the way, is it?" I ask in my sweetest voice.

"You don't remember much about Lafayette, do you? Nothing's very far from anything else. It's just all far away from anything resembling civilization."

"So can we go? I kind of promised Dad I would. If I ever got to Lafayette, I mean."

Romelia sighs like it's a big sacrifice. "I suppose it wouldn't hurt to drive by. Especially if it's for Franzl."

A moment later, she arches her eyebrows. "You know, it's probably not a bad idea to check out Melani's old haunts, the house included. But not tonight."

We drive on in silence, until Romelia wakes me from my road-coma by jerking the steering wheel erratically.

I crash my elbow onto the console, knocking the Kindle to the floorboard, then lurch the other way and wince as my right side slams into the arm rest.

"All righty, then! Here we go," Romelia says.

"Where are we?"

"North of Chattanooga. It's a little rest stop I like. I

figure we can both use the facilities and freshen up."
She pulls to a stop next to the only other vehicle in the
graveled parking area, a big, black Harley Davidson.

I eye the concrete block restroom facility with
suspicion. It looks clean but primitive.

"Couldn't   we   just   find   someplace   in
Chattanooga?"

"I want to avoid the traffic. This place will do
fine." She hops out of the SUV and walks briskly to the
restroom   building.   "Check   out   the   view.   It's
spectacular. Your father used to love it."

The rest area is at a scenic overlook, so I zip up my
hoodie, shove my hands deep into my jeans pockets,
and walk to the aluminum-rail fence that separates
highway   travelers   from   a   steep,   rhododendron-
carpeted drop-off. Green, heavy-duty garbage cans are
chained to the rail about every ten yards. A ragged-
looking man in baggy clothes peers in to the can at the
far end of the parking area. He doesn't look like he
belongs to the bike.

The damp morning mist clings to the ground and
swirls around the rhododendrons as I gaze out at the
mountain ridges on the other side of the fog-shrouded
valley. I imagine Dad stopping here, standing in this
spot and looking across this same valley. I can see why
he would have loved this view, as I do, but I wonder,
Why would he have stopped here with Romelia?

Missing my father has become an ache rooted
deep in my chest. It started the day Dad died and has
grown with each change I experience. Discovering that
my house has been ransacked. Meeting an unknown
aunt. Burying my father. Leaving my home and my

best friend. The ache deepens and swells.

A cardinal lands on a steel fence post and chirps his staccato call. It makes me think of the cardinal at Ben's clearing on the Garnet River, the way it cocked its head as if it recognized me. This cardinal, too, cocks its head and bobs its tail before darting away.

I swallow hard and wipe my face with my jacket sleeve to clear the blurry view of the valley.

"Awesome view," a deep voice beside me says.

I will myself not to flinch, although I'm startled to realize that I'm not alone. I've been joined at the railing by a not-bad-looking guy, maybe eighteen or nineteen years old. He has shaggy, dark brown hair and ocean-blue eyes.

"If you like wild, unspoiled beauty and that sort of thing," I say.

"I'm Jace," he says, extending his hand for a shake. "Jace Lovari."

He wears black skinny jeans and a plain white t-shirt that shows off his biceps. He has a thick leather cord around his neck with some sort of pendant tucked inside his shirt, where it makes an oval bulge.

With his lanky build, muscled arms, and shaggy hair, he reminds me of Johnnie Barton. Only Jace is much more sure of himself. He acts like he starts conversations with girls all the time. As an added attraction, he doesn't have Billie Mae Wrenfield hanging on his arm.

I look at his outstretched hand but leave mine shoved in my pockets. I'm not in the habit of introducing myself to strangers, even if they are over-the-top cute.

A hurt look flits across his dark eyes, but it's gone in a flash. "My hands are kinda cold too. When it's overcast like this, I wish I had a nice hot cup of tea."

"Tea?"

"Uh-huh. Strong, hot tea for a strong, hot body."

"That . . . that's so weird," I sputter.

"I know, I know," Jace says, holding up his hands to stop me from protesting. "I didn't mean to imply I think I have a hot body. Or that you do. Not that you don't. It's just, you're probably more of a coffee drinker."

"No, I like tea." I laugh lightly. So he's not as self-assured as he makes out to be. "It's just weird that you would say it makes you strong, when just yesterday afternoon, I told Ben it was my weakness."

"Ben? That would be your boyfriend?"

"No, we're just friends."

"But about your boyfriend," Jace drawls. "Would he be jealous of you, say, going out for a cup of hot, strong tea with a hot, strong guy?"

"You're very smooth." I take my hand out of my pocket and wag my finger at him. "I guess that's your way of finding out if I have a boyfriend."

He grabs my hand. "Nice ring. Moonstone, right?"

Romelia suddenly appears beside me, slaps my hand out of Jace's and grabs my elbow. "Get away from her!" She pulls me away from Jace, back towards the SUV.

"What's wrong?" I ask, digging my heels in like an obstinate child.

Jace follows at a trot. His eyes are wide with concern, or at least surprise. "Do you know her?"

"Unfortunately, yes." My cheeks burn with embarrassment. "She's my aunt."

"Don't talk to him," Romelia growls.

"What did I do?" Jace asks.

"Go away," Romelia says. "*Pleaca*!"

Jace stops as if shot. "Nice knowing you," he calls. He waves and shakes his head as he turns away.

"Are you *crazy?*" I shout as Romelia drags me across the parking area. "Why didn't you just push him off the cliff, while you were at it?"

"Talking to strangers at rest stops is not a smart idea. No telling what that Roma boy wanted."

"What's Roma?"

"Roma. You know, Gypsy."

"He's a Gypsy?" I stare over my shoulder at Jace. He swings his leg over the Harley. "How can you tell?"

"Just look at him."

"I was *trying* to look at him. Maybe even talk to him. But you came along and dragged me away."

"You let him grab your arm. He might have dragged you away. How would I explain that?"

"Explain to who?"

She stops at the passenger side of the SUV and opens the door.

I wrench my arm away from her. I think about running away, but she has me cornered between the SUV and the door. *I can push right past her, but what then?* I look around at the rest stop. It's deserted except for the bum digging in the trash bin, us, and Jace, who's straddling the Harley and snapping his helmet strap under his chin.

The motorcycle rumbles to life and Jace slowly

cruises by us. He waves and steers the bike out onto the highway.

"I thought Gypsies were just in Europe."

"They're like ticks," Romelia sneers. "They wander around until they find someone to latch on to, then they suck you dry."

"He wasn't trying to latch on to me. We were just talking."

"Oh, they're harmless enough, as long as they keep to themselves. Trouble comes when –." She shakes her head. "Never mind. Get in the car and I promise I'll tell you everything."

"Everything about what?"

"Everything about your mother and the Gypsy curse."

CHAPTER 8

"Your mother was not your father's first love." We're back on the road, speeding southwest toward Chattanooga. Romelia gives me a glaring sideways glance as if judging how much her statement hurts me.

I won't give her the satisfaction.

"Doesn't surprise me. They didn't meet till college."

Romelia arches her brow and turns her eyes back to the road.

"Franzl was in love with a Roma girl, a Gypsy." She looks at me again and smiles a smug little grin. She has my attention now and she knows it.

"Oh, yes. They met in college, and they were instantly smitten with each other. But the girl's mother was against the relationship. The girl was going to transfer to another school for a track and field scholarship, and her mother thought Franzl would meet someone else."

"Which he did. My mother."

"You know, the preacher had it wrong at your father's funeral. Your mother wasn't the track star."

"It was the Roma girl?"

"That's right. And when she left UT, Melani was right there to take her place."

Realization dawns on me. "You had a crush on Dad too."

She shrugs her shoulders. "Everybody did."

"But you never called, or wrote, or came to see him after we moved to Tennessee."

She doesn't answer right away. I've hit a tender spot.

She takes a deep breath, staring straight ahead at the road. "No," she says softly.

"Why not? You were in love with him. Your sister was institutionalized."

She stares straight ahead.

"He needed friends," I press, my voice rising. "He needed family."

"Lani, why do you think Franzl told you your mother was dead?"

I twirl my moonstone ring; the silver setting glints in the sun coming through the windshield but the stone itself seems cold, opaque.

In my mind, I see my mother's fractured face against the car window. I have replayed that scene in my dreams more times than I can count over the last ten years. *How could she have survived that?*

"I don't know." I search the vast blue waves of mountains as if the answer might be out there somewhere. "He told me right before he died that he was protecting me from a nightmare. He said he should have told me the truth sooner."

"Well, we'll go to Hunt House, and you'll see the nightmare that your Dad didn't want you to know about."

"And the curse? You said there was Gypsy curse."

"Oh, yes, there's a curse, all right."

"Dad said there was a curse, too."

She turns to me, then quickly looks back at the road. "What did he tell you?"

"You tell me." I don't want to give her information that she might later pretend was her own knowledge, like a fortune-teller saying *I see a troubled past. Has someone close to you recently died?*

"Melani brought Franzl home from college, back to Lafayette. Seeing them together broke the Gypsy girl's heart. Her mother didn't want her to be with Franzl, but she couldn't stand to see her daughter so broken-hearted. The daughter begged her mother to do something. So, the woman gave her daughter a curse to put on Melani."

"What a nutcase. Putting a curse on someone for revenge. As if that would work anyway."

"She's not a nutcase," Romelia says, a note of testiness in her voice which she quickly erases. "And like I told you, the curse worked."

"Is that common?" I ask. "For Gypsies to put curses on people?"

"Oh, yes. Some Roma charge a lot of money to put curses on rich women's cheating husbands." She blows air through her nostrils. "I doubt many of their so-called curses are more than mumbo-jumbo. Not that they couldn't do it. But why bother when you can get the money without the work?"

"Yeah, I've heard that about Gypsies. That they're con artists. Thieves."

Romelia's knuckles turn white as she grips the steering wheel. "That's not true. The Roma are hard working people. Loyal to their families. True to their word."

"You call that hard work if they pretend to put a curse on someone and take their money as if they really did?"

"It's like the old saying goes, 'work smarter, not harder.'"

"If Roma are such upstanding citizens, why did you freak out about that guy at the rest stop?"

"Strangers are strangers, Roma or no."

You're a stranger, I think.

"Are there a lot of Gypsies – Roma – in Georgia?"

"Hard to say. Roma try to blend in with the neighbors. But there's a community of Roma in Lafayette. Part of the reason I had to get out of that place."

"How could you tell Jace is Roma?" I scan the traffic ahead of us to see if I can spot his bike.

"I've been around them a lot. We lived in Lafayette till your mother and I went to college. After that, thank God, I got the hell out of Lafayette and moved to Pensacola. Quite a good market for beach-front condos. Now, I'd much rather talk about real estate than Roma."

We pass a large green highway sign that reads ROCK BLUFF, 1 MI. "Let's take a break and get some lunch."

We take the exit and cross a river, and it's like we've gone back in time. The main street through the town is lined with old clapboard houses, some of them converted into stores with hand-painted signs reading "Mamie's Quilts 'n' Such" and "Puckett's Buckets – Live Bait and Fine Art."

We pull into a fresh-paved parking lot in front of a single-wide trailer. I can smell the creosote through the air conditioning vents and it makes my nose tingle. A plywood board in front of the trailer reads "Rock Bluff Café," and a red neon sign in the front window glows with the word, "Open."

When I open the door, a whiff of smoke from a stove pipe on top of the trailer replaces the creosote smell with the aroma of char-grilled steak.

Bells attached to the door frame tinkle as we walk in.

"Howdy, folks," a large woman with a gravity-defying blonde beehive hairdo greets us. "Y'all just grab yourselves a seat anywheres. I'll be with you in a sec."

There are only four tables, plus a row of stools along a counter. A man in overalls with a napkin the size of a tablecloth tucked in his collar sits at one table, shoveling beef stew in his mouth like he hasn't eaten in a week. From the looks of him, though, he hasn't missed any meals lately. He has that mountain-man frame that seems to be shared by ninety percent of males in Tennessee who are over thirty.

He eyes Romelia hungrily as we walk by.

Romelia and I slide into vinyl-cushioned chairs at the table furthest from Mountain Man.

The waitress slaps two laminated menus in front of us and fills our water glasses. "I'm Cary, y'all. Bring ya somethin' to drink?" she drawls.

I ask for a root beer.

"I guess cabernet is out of the question," Romelia says.

"This ain't the Ritz Carlton, hon," the waitress says with a smile. I get the feeling she has handled bigger snobs than Romelia without ruffling a single hair in her huge hairdo. "We got Sam Adams, Rasputin Stout, and Stone India Pale. Also got coffee from this mornin' that'll put hair on your chest."

Cary jabs her pencil toward Mountain Man. "That's what he's been drinking for the last ten years."

"Glass of Stone India, hold the hairy chest."

"My pleasure, hon." The waitress winks and sticks her pencil in her hair. "Be right back with those drinks."

As Cary leaves, she swishes her ample backside within a whisper of Mountain Man.

"Hey, Cary," he says, "I got a hairy chest you can hold."

"I know you do, hon. I know you do."

As soon as the waitress is out of earshot, I ask Romelia to tell me more about the Gypsy curse.

"Oh, that. Well, the Roma girl turned your mother into a –." Romelia leans in across the table.

I lean in too. "A what?" I whisper. Gooseflesh prickles my arms and the back of my neck.

"A werewolf," Romelia mouths, barely breathing any sound into the word.

I lean back in my chair. "You have got to be kidding me."

"Shhh! Not so loud!"

Mountain Man pauses with his spoon in his mouth

and his cheeks full like a chipmunk's.

Romelia fixes him with a laser stare and he looks away.

"You and Dad must have been sniffing the same glue," I whisper.

"So, he told you!"

"Oh, yeah. He said Mama was a werewolf, and that he had been cursed, too. That he was a werewolf, and he was afraid I'll become one too. A family of werewolves. But he was delirious."

"You're wrong, Lani. I've seen your mother change with my own eyes."

"Yeah. Sure you have."

"But how could he have been cursed too?" Romelia taps her finger against her chin. "She must have bitten him. It's the only explanation for how old he looked."

I bristle at her remark. "How do you know how he looked?"

"I was at the funeral.""

"I didn't see you."

She waves away my skepticism. "I came in early to pay my respects. Then I sat at the back."

"Do werewolves age fast?" I ask calmly, as if it is a perfectly normal question and we are having a perfectly normal conversation.

"They age like dogs, seven years to one year of human life. Normally, they rejuvenate themselves. But under certain circumstances … well, it's the only explanation."

"So Mama is old, too."

"Oh, no-no-no. She's hardly aged a bit."

I try to ignore the chill that creeps over me. "Why would Dad age but not Mama?"

"Because she fed. Franzl must have defied the curse. He must have suppressed his animal cravings for human flesh."

"She fed on human flesh?" I shiver, not really wanting to hear the answer, but knowing I need to.

"She isn't eating Alpo, that's for sure." Romelia clicks her fingernails on the vinyl tablecloth. "Werewolves crave human flesh like I crave Versace shoes."

"How can she – feed – on human flesh, I mean, if she's at Hunt House?"

"Inside sources," Romelia answers, flipping her hand in the air.

"You mean she attacks the other patients at Hunt House? Or the staff?"

Romelia shakes her head, tossing her curls. "That would attract too much attention. She has her meals delivered."

I wonder, *How safe is it to travel with this stranger?*

She thinks my mother is a werewolf. Seriously believes it.

She thinks Mama turned my father into a werewolf, too. That I was raised by one werewolf who took me to a whole other state to keep me safe from another werewolf. I would laugh at the irony if it wasn't my life we were talking about. My parents.

"Listen, I'm not Little Red Riding Hood, okay? I think I would know if Dad was a werewolf."

"What if I were to tell you," Romelia starts to say. Then she clears her throat and pats her hair as the waitress returns to the table.

"One root beer, one Stone India." The waitress puts a straw on the table next to my root beer. "I'll be right back to take your order."

She grabs a coffee pot from the counter and pours coffee for Mountain Man. She sits down at his table and launches into testimony about the bumper tomato crop in her vegetable garden.

I feel my chest squeeze tight like it does when I have to take a test in school. The only difference is, today the subject is *werewolves* and I haven't studied. If ever there was a day to play hooky, it's today.

I scrape my chair back and sling my backpack over one shoulder.

"Where are you going?" Romelia asks.

"Could you order for me while I go check out that art gallery across the street?"

"Oh. Okay, sure. What do you want?"

I haven't even looked at the menu, so I scan it quickly. Beef stew or steak and gravy. "I don't care. Whatever you're having." I hustle toward the door.

"Lani, wait!"

I try to stay calm as I turn to see what she wants.

"I know you're not stupid enough to try to run off. I want you back here in ten minutes."

"Right." I dash out the door and scurry across the street. I take the gallery's front steps two at a time.

Inside, I hear crickets chirping. A grizzly bear of a man stands on a step ladder, dusting a shelf of miniature clay vases with an old-fashioned feather duster.

A girl my age sits behind the counter, punching

keys on an adding machine and smacking gum. A shock of purple hair flops over her black elastic headband.

"Welcome to Puckett's," the girl says. She pops a huge pink bubblegum bubble. "I'm Lisa."

She adjusts her headband so its decoration – a rhinestone skull-and-crossbones – is centered over her forehead. Her black, sleeveless T-shirt has a picture of Johnny Depp as the pirate Jack Sparrow.

"Hey," I nod. I open my cell and text Ben.

When I don't get a response in a few seconds, I punch in his number, but can't get a connection.

I end the call and hit "call last number." The call connects, and I think I hear Ben's voice, but the call drops almost immediately. I look at my phone in disgust.

"No bars?" Lisa asks. She pops another bubble.

"None." Frustrated, I type in another text message.

At first an envelope icon twirls over the words "sending message," but it blinks out, replaced by "message failed."

"Won't get good reception in here," the grizzly bear says. He climbs down from the ladder and kicks it closed. "You could try the front porch."

Lisa jabs her pencil in the direction of the man. "That's my dad, Stan the Man."

"Can I interest you in some art or some bait?" Stan asks. "Or some bait art?"

I look up from my futile attempts to reach Ben on my cell.

"Did you say, 'bait art'?"

Stan leans the step ladder against the counter. He

winks at Lisa. "She's hooked."

"That's not where the ladder goes," Lisa scolds.

"I'm just parking it for a while so I can help the young lady. Isn't that right, Miss, um?"

"Lani."

Stan taps the ledger Lisa is entering information on. "Go back to cookin' the books, LP, while I show Miss Lani around."

"You're gonna cook your goose if you don't watch it, SP."

Stan takes my elbow and guides me from the reception area into the main room of the gallery. "Know what 'SP' stands for?"

"I thought it was your initials."

"SP stands for 'short play,'" he confides. "Like an old single record?"

I stare at him blankly.

"Probably before your time, but they was short and sweet. Now, LP, that stands for 'lo-o-o-ng play. An LP record goes rooooouuuuund and rooooouuuuund forever." Stan twists his wrist to make the feather duster spin tight circles. The circles get bigger and bigger until he is pointing the feather duster at a huge canvas that takes up almost the entire back wall of the gallery. He spreads his arms wide to express the grandeur of the scene before us. "Voila!"

At first glance, I think the picture is composed of blobs of glossy paint – a school of shiny black fish undulating through a garden of reddish-brown seaweed. Interesting, but not breathtaking.

I push the buttons on my cell. "I've really got to get a text to my friend," I explain.

But something makes me look at the canvas more closely. "Those black blobs. Are those . . . crickets?"

"Good eye, little lady," Stan says. "And the sea grass? Dried-up worms."

"Wow. That's uh, I mean I've never, um."

"I know," Lisa says. When I look back at her, she is grinning and smacking her gum. "There just ain't words for it."

"It's my best piece," Stan says with unmistakable pride. "I call it *The Bait-iful Sea.*"

"You made this?"

"Beauty of combining a live-bait business and an art gallery," Stan says, his large white teeth gleaming in the middle of his bushy beard. He brushes his feather duster lightly over the scene. "The bait that ain't so lively becomes found art."

"Reduce, reuse, recycle," Lisa chants.

One of the cricket-fish drops off the canvas.

"Oopsy-doodle." Stan plucks the cricket off the floor, licks it, and repositions it in the school of fish.

"How much does something like this go for?"

"This one's not for sale." He points at a sticker on the frame with the letters NFS. "Unless you're interested. Wanna make me an offer?"

"Um, tempting, but no thanks. What I really need is some help."

"What kind of help?" Lisa asks.

I walk back to the counter. "I'm traveling with my aunt, only I'm not sure it's safe to drive with her. I'm not even sure she's my aunt."

"Well, girlfriend?" Lisa asks. The headband has slipped and she pushes it higher on her forehead with the eraser end of her pencil. "If she ain't your aunt, why are you traveling with her?"

"She *said* she was my aunt." I shrug my shoulders. "Maybe she is. I just never met her before yesterday. She showed up right before my father's funeral."

"Oh my god, your dad just died? I'm so sorry," Lisa says. "My mom passed away a couple years ago, so I know how you must feel. But at least I've got Stan the Man. Do you still have your mom?"

"No, she's, well, I'm not exactly sure what happened to her. That's why I agreed to go with Romelia. She promised she'd tell me about my mother."

I haven't talked this much with anyone but Ben. It feels natural to talk to Lisa and Stan. I have to remind myself that I don't know them. That I have to be careful how much I tell them.

"Why are you worried, then?" Stan asks. "Do you think your aunt is dangerous?"

"I don't know. But I can tell you one thing: She is seriously weird."

"You're how old?" Stan asks. "'Bout fifteen?"

I nod.

"Every fifteen-year-old thinks their family is weird," Stan says, swishing his hand like he's shooing a fly. "Even LP."

"Well, duh," Lisa says. "Hey, Dad, remember when Carson was fifteen?"

Stan chuckles through his wild and woolly beard. "Lisa's older brother. There was that time …."

I'm getting nervous. It won't be long before Romelia comes looking for me. "Sorry to interrupt, but do you guys have a land-phone I can use? I need to call a friend to pick me up. It's long-distance, but I can give you money."

"Sure," Lisa says. "Phone's in the office, in the back."

"Great, thanks."

Lisa comes out from behind the counter and I follow her toward a door at the back of the gallery. "Can I maybe hide out here for a couple hours till my friend can come get me?"

"Long as you like," Stan answers. "You know, it's a really funny story about Carson."

"SP won't let you get a minute's peace until he tells you about it," Lisa warns.

"What'd he do?" I ask, hoping the story is short.

"He once called 9-1-1 on me," Stan says, scratching his beard. "Told 'em I was abusing him."

"How … how were you abusing him?" I'm suddenly leery about who I've gone to for help. The phrase, *out of the frying pan, into the fire,* runs through my head.

"You see, darlin', it wasn't *really* child abuse," Stan says with a laugh. "I just wouldn't let him turn on the TV till he'd done all his math homework."

"Brutal," I laugh too.

Then I pause, reminding myself that this homey scenario – where kids not doing their homework is the biggest problem – is not my life.

My life involves people who believe in werewolves. It involves strangers who may or may not be related to me, and who may or may not be psychotic. "Lisa, can you show me that phone now?"

"Sure."

Just as Lisa opens the back door, the bells on the gallery's front door tinkle. The crickets stop chirping.

"Welcome to Puckett's Buckets," Stan says behind me.

"There you are!"

Without turning around, I know it's Romelia.

Why did I tell her where I was going? So much for hiding out here till Ben can come get me.

Romelia barges right past Stan, swinging a plastic bag of take-out on one elbow. "You took so long, I finally asked the waitress to box this up," she says. "How long does it take to look at art?"

CHAPTER 9

Stan rushes to greet her. "Can I interest you in my day-glo homage to William Walmsley?"

Romelia cocks an eyebrow at the larger-than-life painting. "Is that *bait?*" she asks.

"Why yes, yes it is," Stan answers proudly. "If you think that's something, I'd be happy to show you my exclusive collection in my, er, private studio."

"Awful sweet of you to offer, but we've wasted enough of your time already." Romelia grabs my elbow and steers me toward the front door.

Lisa quickly blocks her way. "Your niece was just signing up for our email newsletter," she says. She slides back behind the counter and thrusts an index card and pen in front of me.

I shake free of Romelia's grasp and scribble my name, cell phone number, and Gmail address on the card.

"Don't forget to fill out all the information, including any of your friends that you think would like to hear from us. Ten percent off any one item for each person you refer who buys a piece of art."

Taking the hint, I add Ben's information.

Lisa slips the index card into a purple plastic file box by the register. She winks at me and chomps her gum. "Thanks for dropping by. We'll take care of everything from here."

As Romelia and I walk across the road to the café parking lot, she twirls the key chain on her finger. "Here, catch," she says, tossing me the keys. She escorts me to the driver's side.

"You should've eaten before we got on the road," Romelia says as I get in and buckle my seat belt. "You can't drive and eat at the same time. It's dangerous."

"I'm not really hungry anyway." It's hard to have an appetite when your stomach is in knots.

"I'm going to try to take a little nap," Romelia says with a yawn.

I stare at the instrument panel. "I don't know how to drive this thing."

"Brake on the left, gas on the right. Lights on the left, wipers on the wand. Ignition where it always is." She turns off the radio and cuddles into the plush leather seat.

"Where am I headed?"

"Just stay on the Interstate till you get near Atlanta. I'll be awake by then.

I pull out on the road and follow the signs back to the Interstate. Traffic is light, and once I get the feel of the steering, acceleration, and brakes, I relax. I'm not nervous about driving. Dad has let me drive a lot since I turned fifteen and got my learner's permit. The road is hypnotic, and I find myself thinking of werewolves and wacky relatives.

At least Dad had an excuse when he was talking

about werewolves and curses. He had been delirious, close to death.

Romelia doesn't have that excuse. I decide she must be seriously disturbed. I think about kids you see on the news sometimes. They hitch a ride with a seemingly normal person and wind up dead, their body parts scattered across multiple states. Is traveling with Romelia any safer than hitchhiking with a stranger?

I glance quickly at Romelia. She's nestled in a little ball with her eyes closed, legs tucked in, and high heels cast off.

Sure, she showed me a picture of herself with my mother when they were little kids. But she could have Photoshopped her image next to Mama. Or that might not even have been Romelia in the photo, although I'm positive the smaller girl in the photo is my mother.

Dad always told me how much I reminded him of Mama. With his arm snuggled across my shoulders on the couch, and a huge photo album spread open across my lap, he would show me photos of our family when I was a baby, a toddler, a kindergartener.

"You are so beautiful," he would say. "The spitting image of your mother."

I remember one photo. It was taken on my fifth birthday, not long before Dad and I moved to Tennessee. I wore a necklace that Mama had just given me. A moonstone ring – the one I now wore on my index finger, dangled from the gold chain.

"This ring will keep you safe," Mama said as she slipped the ring onto the necklace and fastened the clasp behind my back. "Promise you'll always wear it."

"I promise, Mama. Even in the bathtub?"

"Yes, Lani. Even in the bathtub." Her tinkling laughter sounded like notes plinked out on my toy xylophone.

I held the necklace in my fingers, swinging the ring back and forth like a hypnotist's charm. Mama squeezed my hand shut around the ring and kissed the back of my fingers. Her lipstick left a bright red imprint across my knuckles.

The thought brings on another memory.

Mama and I were playing dress-up. I had on a pair of her high heels and dangle earrings. Mama wore a floppy hat, an emerald-green feather boa, and her moonstone earrings. I watched in awe as she applied bright red lipstick without looking in a mirror. I tried to do the same thing.

"Maybe a little more practice," she said. We looked in the mirror and laughed at the clownish grin I had painted on my face.

"What flavor is this lipstick?" I asked.

Mama giggled. "The color is called Sizzle. It's your Dad's favorite."

I said the name over and over in my head, Sizzle, Sizzle, to help me remember. "When I'm old enough to wear lipstick for real, I'm going to wear Sizzle, too."

Dad loved red.

"Romelia?" I ask. "Does Mama still wear lipstick?"

She's slumped against the passenger window, mouth breathing and sound asleep.

I drive and drive with the thoughts of my family swirling through my mind.

Then it starts to rain. I search the dash for the controls and switch on the headlights and wipers.

The rain comes down harder, pounding the windshield so insistently that the wipers barely have any effect. I hunch over the steering wheel and squint at the road, but I still can't see very well. I take the first exit ramp I come to.

The change in the rhythm of the road beneath the tires wakes Romelia. Surfacing from a dream, she mumbles something that sounds like, "Zamoon out?"

"It's raining real hard," I tell her. "I think I should pull over."

"Drive toward the moon," she mumbles without fully waking.

She curls into her seat sideways with her back toward me. Her hair is pulled away from her neck, exposing a tattoo just below and behind her ear.

I stare at it, mesmerized: a paw print.

I look back at the road and swerve, missing a small deer by a few inches. "Whoa!"

Headlights glare on the windshield. I wrench the steering wheel to the right and fishtail back into my own lane a heartbeat before a semi truck whooshes past, blasting his horn at me.

"The hell?" Romelia is suddenly wide awake.

My heart pounds in my throat. I can hardly breathe. "I can't see! The rain's too hard."

"Where are we?"

"I don't know! I got off the interstate. I need to find someplace to pull over."

I veer off the road onto the gravelly shoulder and stomp on the brakes. The SUV slides in the gravel and jerks to a halt.

Romelia unbuckles her seat belt and looks all around. "What happened? You're driving like a maniac!"

"There was a deer. I was scared I was going to hit it."

Romelia growls through gritted teeth. "How do you expect to get anywhere if you're scared of every little thing? A little rain, a little deer. Hah! Maybe it was a little *reindeer*."

"Have you looked out the window? That is not a *little rain*."

"Oh, for heaven's sake. Just let me drive. If I want to get where I'm going, I can see I'll *literally* have to take the driver's seat." She dashes out, holding her hands over her hair, and scampers around to the driver's side. She opens the door and motions for me to scoot over. I half-crawl, half-tumble over the center console, slouch against the seat and put my feet on the dash.

Romelia jumps in and slams the door. She shakes her head like a wet dog, spraying drops of rain from her hair around the leather interior.

Speckles splatter the windows, dash, steering wheel, console, and me. I watch droplets that appear on my jeans and fade into nothing.

Romelia puts the SUV in gear and spins out onto the highway.

All I can think is, *Did she* growl *at me?*

CHAPTER 10

A cool breeze blows across my face, half-waking me from my nap. In my half-awake, half-asleep dream state, I'm lying on the slanting hardwood floor of my room in Georgia, a bit scared that I'll roll out the picture window, but wanting to hear the rhythmic *tick tick tick* of the metronome that means my mother is downstairs, teaching piano lessons.

I sit up groggily and look around. My first thought is that Romelia has parked us inside a barn. The car windows are down and the driver's seat is empty.

Gradually I realize Romelia has stopped the SUV in an old covered bridge. The whole thing is made of wood, and almost every board that I can see in the glare of the headlights – the lattice-work supports on the walls, the cross-ties supporting the roof – is covered with graffiti. *Sup Dog. Rednecks Rule. Cathy Lovz Tony.*

The place is familiar somehow, comforting even.

A shape passes in front of the car. It's Romelia, pacing and talking on her cell phone. I realize the ticking sound from my dream is Romelia's high heels, clicking on the wooden planks of the bridge.

Whoever she's talking to is getting a verbal shredding.

"That's not the point," Romelia says. "I need it in Lafayette by tomorrow. I don't want to stay in this hellhole one minute longer than necessary."

On her next pass, she glances at the car and sees me watching her.

"Sleeping Beauty's awake," she says. "Gotta go." Her heels tap-tap-tap as she walks to the SUV and leans against the driver's side door.

"Who were you talking to?" I ask.

"Mother." She says the word as if it leaves a bad taste in her mouth.

"You must have great phone service," I say. "Grandma's dead."

"Right, um, ha, ha, very funny. Did I say *my* mother? I meant, um, my ex-husband's mother." Romelia hops in the SUV, cranks the engine, and drives slowly out of the covered bridge.

"I didn't know you were married."

"There's lots you don't know about me."

"I'll say."

"Don't worry," Romelia chirps as the SUV rolls slowly off the bridge. "We'll have lots of time to get to know each other."

As we emerge from the bridge, I see stars in the night sky. The storm has either rained itself out or we have driven through it.

"Tell me more about the curse."

She takes a deep breath. "Mothers always want to protect their children, Lani. Whether physically, spiritually, or emotionally."

"But isn't it dangerous to turn someone into a werewolf? I mean, wouldn't Mama have wanted her own revenge against the Roma girl?"

"In matters of the heart, Lani, rational thought sometimes gets buried like a bone."

Matters of the heart. I know my parents were deeply in love. How can I blame them for not thinking rationally when they let me think my mother was dead instead of telling me she was a werewolf?

Wait, is that a rational thought?

I worry Mama's moonstone ring in its orbit around my finger.

"That ring, for instance," Romelia says. "Moonstone, isn't it?"

I nod.

"Your mother gave you that for protection, didn't she?"

"That's what she said, yes."

"How rational is that? Everyone knows there's only one way to protect yourself from a werewolf."

"And that is?"

"Kill it."

"Sounds like the cure is worse than the disease." A shiver races down my spine.

"I suppose so," Romelia says, blowing air through her nostrils. "From the werewolf's point of view."

We drive on without talking until we get to a town that looks a lot like the town where we stopped for lunch, except that the houses and shops are more run-down. I recognize a two-story stone building with a green-roofed turret like a fairy-tale castle.

"That building we just passed. That looked like the

library in Lafayette."

"That's right. You remember it?"

The last of my drowsiness evaporates. "Mama would take me there when I was little. Once when we were there for story time, a lady was reading *Little Red Riding Hood*. She was dressed like Little Red. Someone else in a wolf costume sprang out from behind a cardboard bed. Little Red screamed, 'Eek! The wolf,' and some of the other kids hid behind their moms and dads and cried."

"What did you do?"

"I stood up and said, 'Wolves don't really eat people.' I asked Mama, 'Right?'"

"What did she say?"

"Usually."

Romelia grins at me. "I remember that day."

"You were there?" I try to remember seeing her at the library, or visiting us in Georgia, or meeting her ever before the day of Dad's funeral.

If I can remember a long-ago trip to the library, why can't I remember my own aunt.

If she is my aunt.

But I'm too excited to think about it.

"So if we're in Lafayette, does that mean we're going to see my mother, like you promised?"

Romelia pats my thigh. "You can trust me, Lani, to do whatever I say I will."

We drive through town, but it doesn't look the way I remember. Time has not been kind to my hometown. Most of the buildings on the main road are dilapidated, their tiny yards choked with weeds. The sign for Trickels Jewelers still hangs from the eaves of what used to be my mother's favorite store, but the windows are boarded up and a bunch of trash and twigs have piled up against the door.

And then I see a neon sign, shaped like an ice cream cone, glowing in the window of one store. "The Kremy Kone! Dad used to take me there on Saturdays. Can we go there?"

"It's closed," Romelia says.

"I bet it'll be open in the morning. We could stop there on the way to Hunt House tomorrow."

"Can't you just get some ice cream from whatever restaurant we go to tonight?"

"I want to get a cup of chocolate ice cream with red sprinkles for Mama, just like Dad and I used to bring her after we went to the Kremy Kone on our 'ice cream dates'."

"I doubt they allow 'outside' food at Hunt House."

"If they allow certain patients to have human flesh delivered, do you seriously think they'll have a problem with some ice cream?"

Romelia flexes her fingers while she steers with the palms of her hands. "You might not even get to see her," she says slowly.

"Why not?"

"Well, she might not be ... receiving visitors."

"I'm her daughter. I haven't seen her in ten years. I don't think she'll turn me away."

Romelia says nothing, just stares straight ahead.

I glare at her. "The reason I came with you is to see her. You said I could trust you. You said–."

"I said I'd take you," Romelia snaps.

One block off the main road, Romelia turns up a

long gravel driveway lined with palm trees whose trunks are wrapped in miniature white Christmas lights. Lights sway on their fronds as well. At the end of the driveway stands a gingerbread house, complete with icicle lights hanging from the eaves.

"What is this place?" I ask. "Winter Wonderland in July?"

"It's a bed-and-breakfast. You like?"

"It's cute," I allow. I yawn, road-weary. "As long as it's got beds and a shower, it could look like a prison and I'd still like it."

"I think you'll find it a notch or two better than a prison."

A woman sits behind a tall mahogany counter in the miniscule lobby. She is so short that at first, all I can see is a bright floral scarf wrapped turban-like around her head. I immediately think of the old woman who took care of me in the weeks after the accident.

I'm still not sure who that long-ago woman in the purple turban was, but now that we're back in Lafayette, maybe that question will be answered – along with lots of others.

The woman behind the counter looks up and smiles, displaying big yellow teeth. She slaps a paperback on the counter, splayed open. "Weary travelers, welcome to Nelson Cottage!" she says, her accent heavy on the *r*'s. Feathers dangle from her gold hoop earrings. Her eyes are rimmed in kohl, like Romelia's. She has the same exotic air, deepened rather than dampened by age. "You will be wanting one room or two?"

"Two," I say quickly. I want a locked door

between me and Romelia. Actually, I'd feel better with a couple time zones between us, but that isn't in the stars.

"Two would be fine if you have them," Romelia tells the woman. Her brusque tone makes me look at her questioningly. She seems repulsed by the woman, as if she smells bad or something. I don't notice anything gross or unpleasant, though.

"Only one guest room is taken tonight, and that is my grandson, a weary traveler himself." The woman winks at me. "You would be liking my grandson, I am thinking."

The woman plucks two keys off a pegboard on the wall behind her.

"I want to see the owners," Romelia demands.

"I am Natasha. Me and my husband are owners here."

"Owners? What happened to the Nelsons?" Romelia asks.

"Old owners? They move to Miami. Me and my husband, Ivan, we bought inn three years ago." She pronounces the name *Yvonne.* She slides a guest register across the shiny mahogany counter and offers Romelia a pen. "You know old owners?"

"They were old family friends." She signs the register and flips a credit card out of her purse.

"Then you will be happy to know they are enjoying retirement. I get postcard from Mrs. Nelson just a week or two ago."

The woman turns the register around and, with her hawk-like nose an inch from the page, peers at Romelia's signature.

She swipes Romelia's credit card through the router, punches in a code, and when the paper tape curls from the top of the machine, she tears it off with a flourish and holds it on the counter for Romelia to sign.

Natasha wears a large, chunky silver ring with a milky white stone. "That's a pretty ring," I comment. "Is it your wedding ring?"

"No, this is wedding ring." She shows me her right hand, which has a narrow gold band around the third finger. "In old country, we wear wedding ring on right hand and shield ring on left hand."

"Shield ring?"

"I'm not sure is right word. Costume, maybe that is word?"

"I don't think that ring's costume jewelry. It looks even nicer than mine." I show her my ring.

"Ah, moonstone, same as mine," she says, patting my hand. "Quite lovely."

"Thanks. It was my mother's."

"Breakfast starts at five, but we serve until ten if you like to sleep in. Ivan will make you delicious omelet, cooked to order."

"Sounds great," I say with a smile. "Where are our rooms?"

"Upstairs, rooms Six and Five. First and second doors on left." She hands us each a key.

"Thank you."

"Ms. Marks, is it?" Natasha asks, watching Romelia closely. "I think I know this name. Do you have relatives nearby?"

"It's a common name," Romelia says brusquely.

"Yes, I suppose in many places this is so. Do you

need some assistance with your luggage?"

"No, we can manage." Romelia grabs her suitcase, a hard-case roller model with an abstract heart design in bright colors. *I'd like that design, if it wasn't Romelia's,* I think to myself.

"Very good, Madame. If you need anything before morning, please to dial zero on your phone."

As we turn toward the staircase, Natasha calls after us, "My grandson has only one flaw. He snores like sawmill. He is across hall from you, young miss. I will whack him with broom if you do not sleep well tonight."

"Thanks again," I say, feeling my cheeks burn.

Romelia wheels her suitcase to the stairs. "I'm expecting a delivery," she says to Natasha. "Let me know as soon as it gets here, no matter how late." She clumps up the steps and stops in front of Room Number Six. I crab-walk past her to the next door.

Snores resonate from the door across the hall.

"I rise early," Romelia says. "Be downstairs for breakfast by seven."

"Will Hunt House even be open to visitors that early?"

"They'll open for me."

I unlock my door and reach in to flip the light switch. "Romelia, why don't you like Natasha?"

"Roma," she growls. "They're taking over this town."

"So? Do all Roma go around casting werewolf curses on people?"

"They are all the same," Romelia scoffs. "Sweet dreams."

The room has a huge, four-poster bed covered with an heirloom quilt. It has the same wedding ring pattern as Dad's quilt. I trace the interlocking circles, lost in thought for a moment. Then I reach for my cell phone.

It isn't in my jeans pocket.

I check my jacket pocket and rummage through my backpack, but it's not there. *It must have fallen out in the SUV when I was sleeping.*

I grab the room phone off the bedside table and plunk it on my lap. It's an old-fashioned rotary phone and it weighs a ton. I dial Ben's number. It takes forever for the dial to spin back around after each number. I listen to a rushing sound through the receiver like when you hold a seashell up to your ear.

After about 30 seconds, I get a three-tone signal, followed by a robot voice. "We're sorry. The number you have dialed is a long distance number. Please hang up and dial the toll-free number provided by your carrier, then follow the directions for completing your call. We're sorry, the number you have dialed – "

I hang up and flop down on the bed. In the morning, I'll check the SUV for my phone. If I can't find it, I'll ask Natasha how to make a long-distance call from the house phone.

My stomach growls and I think briefly about the bag of take-out from the Rock Bluff Café, but I'm too exhausted to care.

The bed is soft and cushy, and as soon as I kick off my shoes and lay my head on the pillow, I fall into a coma-like sleep. Except that I don't know if you dream when you're in a coma, and I am dreaming like crazy.

My dreams are tormented, but not by Natasha's grandson's snoring.

I'm running through the woods, as fast as I can go. I stumble over a root and fall to the ground. I can even smell the damp leaves covering the forest floor. I scramble to my feet and start running again. Dogs bay behind me. From the sound of their voices, I know that they are hunting. I am the prey. I look over my shoulder to see if they're catching up, and that's when I run right into a man. He grasps me by both arms to keep me from falling, or maybe to keep me from running away. I'm scared to look at him, but I look anyway. He's younger than I thought at first, not much older than me. His hair is dark brown, his eyes the deep blue of a stormy sea, his face tanned. "I know you," I say. "You're Jace. The Roma boy." He holds his finger to his lips and whispers, "Beware the hounds at your heels."

I wake up to the howl of a wolf that crosses out of my dream and into my reality. I lie perfectly still in the bed, the way I did when I was a kid and my nightmares woke me up.

With child-like logic, I know that if I stay under the covers and don't move, the monster won't see me.

But I'm on top of the quilt, unprotected.

And besides, there's no such thing as monsters, no such thing as werewolves. And I'm too old to be scared by nightmares.

I take off my hoodie, wriggle out of my jeans, and crawl under the covers in my tank top, undies, and socks. I sleep the rest of the night with no more dreams.

CHAPTER 11

I wake to the tangy smell of onions cooking. After a quick shower, I put on a fresh tank top and the same jeans that I wore yesterday. The room is a little chilly so I put on my hoodie and zip it half-way up.

Following the aroma of onions and peppers, I find the kitchen. The room is bathed in sunlight from a bay window with filmy lace curtains that dance in the breeze from the open window. Rich hardwood floors and Tuscan-red walls pull me in like a grandmother's welcoming embrace.

A tall teenage guy in a tight t-shirt stands at the stove, his back to me. He has a dishrag slung across one shoulder and frilly pink apron strings tied around his waist.

"Breakfast smells good," I say.

When the guy turns around, his eyebrows raise and his smile broadens into a grin of recognition.

I recognize him, too. *Jace!* "Hi."

I feel like a giddy schoolgirl who unexpectedly comes face-to-face with her summer crush. I know how ridiculous I must look, a mouse like me, starry eyed over someone like Jace. I strafe my fingers through my damp hair.

"Hey, Wolf Girl!" he says.

My schoolgirl giddiness is yanked back down to earth like a choke chain at my throat. "*What* did you call me?"

Jace holds a spatula in one hand, a sizzling-hot frying pan in the other.

He points the spatula at the front of my hoodie. "That's the same jacket you had on yesterday. It used to say 'Genius,' right? The album by Zevon?"

I stare at him blankly, trying to sort through the information. *He's calling me Wolf Girl because of my jacket?*

"You know, *Werewolves of London?*"

"Oh. Right." I try to sound casual, but I'm thinking, *How could Dad give me Mom's old jacket and never tell me it had a reference to werewolves?*

Jace takes a step toward me and instinctively I back up a step. "Don't you remember me? I'm Jace? I met you at the rest stop in Tennessee?"

And you visited me in my dream last night.

"I remember you," I manage to say. "It's just so weird to run into you again."

"I know, right?" He laughs and turns back to the stove. "Do you like Southwestern omelets?"

My growling stomach reminds me that I haven't eaten in twenty-four hours. I shake off my agitation. "That's what brought me downstairs. It smells amazing."

"Do me a favor. Grab a couple plates out of the cupboard." Jace points with the spatula to a row of cabinets above the counter.

I stretch on tip-toes to reach the shelf and notice him admiring me. He quickly looks away.

"You can sit in the dining room." He nods in the direction of an archway leading to a formal dining room. It's what Dad would call a "company room," as in you only use it when there's company.

Jace motions to a white porcelain table with black metal legs and a pair of straight-back wood chairs that crowd the corner by the bay window. "Or you can eat in here with me."

"In here's fine." I grab the nearest chair.

"Not there!"

I yank my hand away from the chair. "What?"

"You'll step on Buddy." He points to a black-and-tan coonhound that's asleep under the table. "You have to keep your eyes open around here. There's always a dog underfoot."

"Better a dog underfoot than hounds at your heels." I laugh nervously.

"Uh, yeah," Jace says. He puckers his lips and makes a smoochie sound followed by a soft whistle. The hound dog scrambles out from under the table and sits in front of Jace, his tail wagging so hard his whole body wiggles.

I slip into the chair by the wall, which gives me a view of the kitchen and everything in it, including Jace and the dog. The only thing I can't see is the screen of a small TV that's mounted on the wall behind me. A quick glance tells me I'm not missing much. The local news is on, close-captioned with the volume muted. The big news in Lafayette on a sunny summer morning is the 4-H hog report.

Jace jerks the pan to flip the omelet. "Ever meet a dog who can count?"

"Can't say I have."

"Buddy," Jace says, "How many eggs in the pan?"

The dog thumps his tail against the floor and gives three quick "woofs."

"That's right! Good boy!"

"How did he know it was three?" I ask. "Since they're all stirred up together."

Jace folds the omelet and slides it onto my plate. "Well, it's really canine ESP, but he'd be embarrassed if I told you he can't count."

"But canine ESP is so unique. I've never heard of a dog with ESP."

"That's another thing. He doesn't want to seem different or special. The other kids might pick on him."

"Poor puppy."

Buddy's ears prick up at my voice. He pads slowly to my side and lays his head on my lap.

Jace brings two china cups and a Kodak yellow, porcelain teapot to the table. "If I remember right, you're a hot tea kind of girl."

"Yeah, that's right."

He fills my cup and then his own with steaming hot tea. "So what brings you to Lafayette?"

I stroke the dog's silky head, rubbing the bump in the center of his skull. "I could ask you the same thing."

"Right," Jace says with a laugh. "You don't give out your 411 to strangers. Maybe if I tell you a little about myself, we won't be strangers any more."

"I'm all ears." I dump two heaping spoonfuls of sugar in my tea, then offer the crystal bowl to Jace.

"No, thanks, I take mine black."

"I'll need more information than that."

"Okay, let's trade. I'll give you a piece of info, you give me one."

"Deal." I cut into the omelet with my fork and take a bite. Gooey cheese dangles from my chin and I lick it off. "Oh my god, this is delicious."

I'm so famished, I suck in half the omelet like a vacuum. I wash it down with a gulp of Jace's tea. It's strong and hot, just like he said it would be when we were talking at the scenic overlook. The memory brings a fresh burst of heat to my cheeks.

Jace watches me with a satisfied grin on his face. "You've got an impressive appetite for someone so skinny."

"I haven't had much of an appetite lately. But why are *you* cooking? When we checked in, Natasha said her husband is the omelet maker."

Jace nods. "My grandfather, Nicu Ivan. He's the one who taught me to cook. He even helped me get a temp job at a five-star restaurant up in the mountains."

Jace takes eggs out of the refrigerator and breaks them into a bowl. "But Buni, my grandmother, Natasha? She's the one who taught me about tea."

The word has a familiar ring to it, but the thought flies away as something Natasha told me clicks in my head. "So you're the grandson who snores."

"Vicious rumors! I don't snore. Don't believe anything that woman tells you."

"Your grandmother seems honest to me." I sip the

steaming hot tea. "And she must be a good person to share with you the secret ways of tea."

Jace grins. "Yeah, she's all right. When I was little, she and Nicu lived with us. I always loved being in the kitchen with them, either helping them cook or just watching the two of them together. You haven't met Nicu, have you?"

"No, just your grandmother."

"They are a pair of lovebirds." He shakes his head. "Even after all these years."

He whisks the eggs and pours the mixture in the skillet, creating a burst of steam accompanied by a sizzle. "Buni told me to only make one cup of tea per bag, or if you have loose tea, use twice what the tin tells you to use. Strong tea makes strong bodies."

"I remember."

"It's your weakness," he answers.

"*You* remember."

I feel heat spread downwards from my ears to my navel.

Jace's ocean-blue eyes bore into mine.

I pick off a sliver of omelet and feed it to Buddy as an excuse to break eye contact.

"So why isn't your grandfather in the kitchen this morning?"

"He got in late. He works at the hospital, and there was a big wreck on the interstate last night. I told him he could sleep in and I would make breakfast."

Jace dumps a small bowl of sliced mushrooms, diced jalapeño and red bell peppers, and slivers of onions on top of the eggs in the bowl. His muscles flex under his shirt as he whisks the mixture and pours it into the pan. Steam bursts from the pan with a sizzle.

"But don't try to sidetrack me," he says. "It's your turn to divulge some classified information."

"Like what?"

"Tell me your name, for starters."

"Lani. Lani Morgan."

"Jace. Jace Lovari." He flips the omelet, creating more sizzles.

Sizzle is Dad's favorite.

Dad's favorite.

"Your turn," Jace says.

"Doesn't count," I say as Jace slides the omelet out of the pan and onto my plate.

"I already knew your name. You have to give me a new piece of information."

"So, ask." He breaks three more eggs and stirs them in the pan.

"Where do you live?

"I live here most of the time. With Buni and Nicu."

"Your grandparents?"

He nods.

"Not with your parents?"

"They moved … overseas. I decided to stay."

"My aunt says you're Roma." Another bite of omelet.

He drops the skillet into the sink with a clatter. "She should know."

"What do you mean?"

"Takes one to know one. Isn't that what they say?"

I can't hold back my laugh, and along with it, egg and jalapeño particles spray across the table. "You mean she's Roma? Sorry, but that is just too ludicrous."

I pick up tiny pieces of egg debris and wipe them on the edge of my plate. "She's my aunt. That would mean I'm Roma too."

Jace snorts. "Hah! You're no more Roma than the Queen of England." He deftly turns his omelet onto itself and slides it onto a plate.

"How can that be, oh wise Roma Boy?"

"Hey, I kinda like that. At least the wise Roma part. But I'm hurt that you think of me as a boy."

"You can quit with the pouty lip and fake sniffles." I polish off the last bite of my omelet. "To be treated as a man, you must prove yourself a man. For I am the Queen of England and I command it."

"Oh, no! I didn't say you *were* the Queen." He slides into the chair next to me and points his fork at me. "I said your so-called aunt is Roma."

"'So-called?' You don't think she's my aunt?"

"Do you?" He raises an eyebrow.

I look out the window to avoid his penetrating gaze that makes me feel naked. "What's that supposed to mean?" I try to take a sip of my tea, but my hand shakes so badly that I slosh the scalding liquid all over my fingers and the back of my hand. "Damn it!"

Instantly, Jace whips the dish towel off his shoulder. "Give me your hands."

He wraps the towel around my hands, blotting gently. "Lani, I don't know why you want to insist she's your aunt. It doesn't really matter to me. There's just something about her that gives me the creeps."

I guess he's immuned. Unlike Ben.

"I hope I'm not out of line for asking this. But are you sure it's safe to be traveling with her?"

A shiver races down my spine at the touch of his hands on mine, but at the same time, my instincts shout at me to be careful; I barely know this guy and he's getting way too personal.

"Who are you, my guardian angel?" I pull my hands away, but he tightens his grip. I pull harder and he spreads his hands wide, like he's releasing a bird.

"Holy crap," Jace says.

I feel my face burn at his reaction. "I'm sorry; I shouldn't have said that. You were only trying to help."

"No, it's not you. Look." He's staring at the TV.

"What is it?"

He stands and reaches for the volume button. His torso is inches from my face. I catch a whiff of his body odor and find it oddly pleasant.

"I was just there yesterday," he says. "I stopped for lunch at that diner on the way home."

"Where?" I have to stand and turn around to see the screen.

Jace is behind me now, with one hand on my shoulder. He points at the TV. "See the sign, behind the news guy? The Rock Bluff Café."

"I think Romelia and I stopped there for lunch, too." I scoot out of my chair and stand beside Jace, my eyes riveted on a very familiar scene on TV.

The reporter on TV steps inside a shop.

"That's the art gallery I visited," I tell Jace. "Puckett's Buckets."

"Yeah, me too."

A shiver runs down my spine again, but for a different reason this time.

The reporter walks backwards through the gallery

as he talks to the camera. He waves his hand at a pile of wreckage. The camera pans over to the mess that, less than twenty-four hours earlier, had been Stan's bait-art masterpiece. Now the mangled canvas has been torn off the wall and lies on the floor in a crumpled heap.

As the television camera zooms in on the rubble, the reporter explains what happened. "The gallery owners appear to have become victims of the same lunatic drifter that struck a highway rest station last night."

"My god, what is that?" Jace asks, pointing at Stan's torn and twisted bait-art canvas.

"Crickets and worms, mostly."

"I mean, what's that sticking out of it?" He points at what used to be the bottom left-hand corner, where the cricket-fish swirled in the sea of red wigglers.

"Oh, god." My voice chokes with horror as I begin to comprehend what I'm seeing. "It can't be."

But it is: A hairy, bear-like human arm, the hand tightly gripping a feather duster, pushes through the canvas in seeming defiance of the attacker. A woman wearing a white lab coat puts her hand in front of the camera to block the view.

"Lisa Puckett, age eighteen, and her father, Stanley Puckett, forty-five, are missing and presumed dead," the reporter continues. "The severed arm which you just saw here on Action 5 News and which is now being removed by the medical examiner's office is assumed to belong to Stanley Puckett. The man who was killed in the earlier incident on I-75 just north of here appears to have been homeless and remains unidentified. Anyone with information –"

Suddenly the kitchen feels as hot as Dad's bedroom with the fire raging.

Jace puts his hands on my waist as my legs buckle. "You don't look so good. I think you need some fresh air."

He guides me out a back door and down a brick walkway to a secluded garden. He "Sit here," he says, helping me to a wrought-iron bench that rests between an ivy-covered wall and a large concrete fountain.

Birds sing in the garden around us. I sit on the bench and hold my head in my hands.

"Are you okay?" Jace asks. He sits beside me and I can feel his arm against mine. "You looked like you were going to pass out."

"It's such a shock. Those people at the gallery? Lisa and her dad. I just met them and now they're … they're …."

"I know. It's hard to believe." Jace clasps his hands between his knees and bends forward. The dog has come outside, too, and paws and licks Jace's face and hands.

"Yesterday, they were happy and friendly." I swat away tears that dribble down my cheeks. "They had no idea that they were about to be attacked. Killed. Why them?"

"Sounds like some maniac just strolled through town and picked his victims at random," Jace says. "It could have been anybody, any town."

The birds go quiet and the only sound is the water splashing in the fountain.

The dog growls.

Romelia emerges from behind the fountain. "What a macabre coincidence," she says.

"God, Romelia. Why are you always sneaking up on me like that?"

"I'm sure I don't know what you mean." She walks around to where Jace and I are sitting, her high heels clacking on the bricks.

Buddy growls again and slinks behind the bench.

"Did you see the news?" she asks. "A lunatic at the very same gallery you just visited, Lani."

Jace looks up and Romelia's eyebrows shoot up.

"You!" Romelia snarls through clenched teeth.

"Talk about macabre coincidences," Jace says.

"What are you doing here?"

"I live here."

"He's a chef, Romelia." I don't have the strength to sit through another one of Romelia's tirades about the Roma in general or Jace in particular. "Why don't you let him fix you an omelet?"

"Those awful murders. I'm afraid I've lost my appetite." Romelia's heels click on the brick walkway as she paces in front of the bench. "And they seemed to be such nice people."

Romelia squints her eyes at Jace. "You were at that gallery, too."

Jace squares his jaw. "That's right."

"*And* you were at the scenic overlook where that hobo was killed."

Jace yanks at the apron strings and throws his apron in a wad on the ground. "I was at *a* scenic overlook. Same one *you* were at."

Romelia taps her fingertip against her chin.

"Maybe I should call the police in Rock Bluff. They might want to question you."

"The girl and her father were both alive and well when I left the gallery," he says. "Can you say the same?"

My head spins. *I've got to get out of here! I've got to call Ben!*

"Romelia, can I have the keys to the car?"

"We're not leaving yet," she says. "I'm still waiting on my delivery."

"I just want to look for my phone. I think I left it in the car."

"Oh, yes, your phone. I forgot to tell you." Romelia reaches into the pocket of her crisp linen jacket.

I hold out my hand, expecting her to give me the keys, and instead she dumps several mangled pieces of plastic and wire onto my palm.

"My phone?"

"I'm afraid I backed over it," she explains.

I stare at the rubble. "How could you back over my phone?"

"I had an errand to run last night. I didn't notice your phone on the ground until I got back."

"My phone."

"Let's go back to my room where you can rest and we can talk – privately." She grabs my elbow and steers me back toward the door of the B&B.

I am too numb to argue.

"Young man," Romelia snarls at Jace. "Make yourself useful and let me know when my package arrives. Otherwise, we're not to be disturbed."

CHAPTER 12

Flopping into a pale-pink wing-back chair in the corner of Romelia's room, I stare at the pile of rubble in my hands that used to be my phone.

Romelia paces the length of the room, from the window to the door and back. The room is crowded with a huge, four-poster bed, night stand, dresser, the chair I'm sitting in, and a 1950s-era table with a pole lamp sticking through the middle of it. Romelia is left with a narrow space which she covers quickly with strides that would be long and fluid if not for the confinement of her narrow skirt. Instead of looking like a graceful model, she looks like a caged animal.

"These deaths are a bad sign," she says.

"Ya think." I turn the pieces of my phone this way and that and press the two biggest remnants together like Legos, hoping they'll fit.

"I'm serious," Romelia says. "You and I were at both murder scenes, mere hours ahead of the killer."

"If you're trying to freak me out, it's working."

"I'm trying to prepare you." Romelia stops pacing and turns to face me. "I don't think it was coincidence that we were there."

I feel the hackles rise on the back of my neck. "What do you mean?"

"I think these murders were committed by someone who was following us. Your mother."

"As in, my mother, the werewolf?"

Romelia nods.

"Who's supposedly locked up at Hunt House?"

Romelia doesn't answer except to exhale as if I am intentionally exasperating her. She snatches her tiny, designer purse from the dresser and paws through it.

I press her for a response. "Do you know how crazy that sounds?"

"Yes, it must sound like something out of a horror movie."

She dumps the contents of her purse on the bed, forming an amazingly large pile for such a small purse.

"Especially since, for you, it's brand new," Romelia continues. "For me, it's been reality for years."

I think of standing under the stars with Ben, just two nights ago, waiting for the new moon to rise. I feel a sudden, overwhelming rush of homesickness, but I tamp the feeling down because I have come across an obvious flaw in Romelia's logic.

Other than the fact that werewolves aren't real.

"It wasn't even the full moon. Explain that."

"Werewolves get more active on the full moon, it's true," Romelia says, pawing through the pile of debris from her purse. "But they can attack at any time of the month, and it doesn't even have to be at night."

I throw the fragments of my dead phone onto the table. "You seem to know all about werewolves."

"That's right. You might call me an expert on the

subject."

"So enlighten me."

"Werewolves prefer darkness, but are not limited by it. They can be active in their wolf form any time of the day or night. They feed on human flesh as often as multiple times a day, or as rarely as once a month. Those with enough control go as long as possible without killing anyone, and then do it under cover of darkness, in remote areas, where they are least likely to be caught or bring suspicion to themselves."

"How do you know all this?"

"I studied. After all, with a werewolf in the family, well, it's a little more complicated than paper-training a puppy." Romelia zips open a compartment in her purse and pulls out a miniature black handgun.

"What. The hell. Is that?" I jump to my feet and look anxiously from the gun to the door. *She's nuts. Can I get past her?*

"It's a Baretta." Romelia admires the shiny black gun with its stubby barrel and wooden grip.

Run, my mind screams. I should run out of this room and straight out of the B&B and keep running as long and as far away as I can. But Romelia is standing directly between me and the door.

The second time she has cornered me.

I weigh my options. If I push past her, will she shoot me in the back as I dash out the door? If I stay, will she shoot me in cold blood?

Romelia suddenly seems to become aware of my state of alarm. "Oh, don't worry. It's not loaded."

"Is that supposed to make me feel better?"

"Have you ever fired a gun?"

"No," I say flatly. "Have you?"

"Yes, I have," she answers matter-of-factly.

"Oh." My throat feels tight.

"Come here," she says, sitting on the bed. "You'll need to know how to use this one."

"Why?" I stumble toward her. I don't totally believe that the gun is not loaded, or that she won't use it against me if I bolt for the door.

"You have to shoot the werewolf."

"You want me to shoot my own mother?"

"To get rid of the curse, yes." Romelia opens the gun's chamber and peers inside.

"Forget it."

She snaps the gun barrel closed. "You have to. If you don't do it, the killing will continue, and the curse will find you, too."

"Why now? Why after all these years?"

"Because up until about a month ago, I didn't know your mother had hurt you. I thought you were safe, as long as you were far away from her. Then I get a call from … from the Roma woman who tended your wounds after the accident."

"The lady with the … ?"

We both swirl our fingers over our heads to indicate the turban-like scarf that I remember.

"She's Roma?"

Romelia nods. "Aurelia."

"*That's* Aurelia?" A long-ago memory nudges the door of my mind, the haunting idea that I might once have called her "Grandma." Or another word, *Bunica.*

Running to her with an armful of wildflowers I had picked.

"Bunica, the purple daisies reminded me of you."

"And you, dulce nepoata, *remind me of your beautiful mother."*

Before he died, Dad said, *Aurelia can help you end the curse.*

I realize Romelia is talking. I remind myself I should pay attention to someone who is holding a gun.

"I had to escape this town long ago," Romelia says. "For my own sanity. But I've stayed in touch with Aurelia. That's how I know it's gotten worse. Day by day, year by year, the werewolf part of Melani has grown stronger and the human part has grown weaker. She can no longer control her werewolf instincts. Her appetite for human flesh is . . . ravenous. Insatiable."

She pauses, lowers her head. "Your wounds from the accident? Aurelia finally told me, they weren't all from shattered glass. Some of your injuries were from an animal."

"Why would she keep something like that secret?"

"Maybe she didn't want to admit to herself what had happened."

I shake my head in denial. "Besides, Mama didn't bite me. She didn't. She wouldn't!"

Or did she?

NO! I argue with myself. *It's a nightmare! It's not real!*

"Bit you, clawed you. Intentional or an accident. Either way, it means you are running out of time to end the curse."

My heart pounds. I take a deep breath and step toward the door.

As quick as a rattlesnake, Romelia grabs my arm, but it's her words that hold me in place.

"What I said, about the curse finding you?"

"I'm listening." I pry her fingers off my arm.

"If the werewolf who bit you is still alive when you turn sixteen, *you* will become a werewolf."

My mind flashes to Ben. What did he say about being sixteen? Whatever it was, I don't have time to think about it now. I have to focus on getting away from Romelia. I slip closer to the door.

"Franzl should have told you," Romelia continues. "He was supposed to tell you."

"Tell me what?"

"How to end the curse."

"So we agree on wanting to end the curse, if there is one. But I want my mother to live through it."

She shakes her head. "Not possible."

My muscles tighten in defiance of what she's saying. "Then do it yourself."

"I would, if that would end the curse," Romelia says. For once she doesn't look as sure of herself. "It's all my fault, anyway."

"Why is it your fault?" I ask.

She looks up and I see clownish streaks on her face.

"Are you crying?"

She swipes at the teary streams of mascara on her cheeks with long, delicate fingers.

Then realization dawns on me. "It was you! You're saying *you* put this so-called werewolf curse on my mother because you were jealous."

She doesn't say anything. She doesn't have to. I

can see by the weary look on her face that it's true.

Suddenly, my fear is gone, replaced by rage so fierce my eyeballs burn. "Even if that was possible, how could you do something so heartless? To your own *sister*?"

"A woman scorned, Lani. You're too young to know what that feels like." Romelia points at me with the hand that holds the shiny black gun.

"Um, Romelia? The gun?"

She places it in her lap but does not let go.

"In the story about the Roma girl, you said her mother – *your* mother– gave you the werewolf curse. My grandmother's been dead since before I was born. How could you be my aunt?"

"It's a long story. The point is, after the curse, your father left Melani." Now Romelia is consumed by that long-ago fury, her rage matching mine. As if talking about the past has re-opened old wounds. "He knew what she would become. A murderous animal."

"*You're* the animal," I snarl. "No, you're worse than an animal. You're evil."

"I know it was wrong, but remorse won't change anything. The curse worked. All we can do is end it. And believe it or not, I don't want you to become a werewolf. That is why *you* must kill her, and kill her now."

A thousand thoughts swirl through my head. *What have I gotten myself into, agreeing to leave with Romelia? My home isn't in Georgia any more. It's in Tennessee, in the house where Dad raised me.*

I tell myself not to panic. It's like Romelia said, regretting what I've done won't help me out of this situation. I try to think of ways to escape.

Maybe I can make her think *I'm going to kill Mama. She'll show me how to use the gun. Then, when she takes me to kill Mama, I won't do it. I'll take the gun and call the cops.*

Not much of a plan, but it's the best I can come up with for now.

I clear my throat and try with everything I've got to sound convincing.

"When will we be facing, um, the werewolf?" I won't call the werewolf *Mama* any more than I'll call Romelia *Auntie.*

"Tonight, if Aurelia comes through with the bullet."

"You need a special bullet?" I ask. "Let me guess. It's gotta be a silver bullet."

"Of course it must." She laughs, a high-pitched, hysteric little sound.

I walk over to the window and gaze at the horsetail clouds high above us. "Just for curiosity's sake," I say slowly, "how do you plan to convince me my mother is a werewolf?"

"You'll see for yourself."

"Is she going to be a werewolf when we get to Hunt House? Or will she change while we're there?"

Romelia looks around the room, like she can't look me in the eyes.

"What?"

"I don't even think she's there."

"Oh, right. You think she's on the loose, wreaking death and destruction across two states."

"That's right." Romelia pushes herself off the bed.

Her whole body tenses and I wonder if *she* is about to morph into a werewolf. She seems ready to spring on me and rip out my throat.

I automatically back up a step and knock into the little table. The pieces of my phone rattle to the floor. "If she's not there, how are we going to find her?"

"First we'll go to Hunt House," Romelia says, "just to verify my suspicions."

"And if she's not there?"

Romelia steps closer to me, and I back up until my heels scrape against the wall by the window.

"I've been thinking. If she's escaped Hunt House, which I'm sure she has, then it would be natural for her to return to the old house."

I grip the window sill, afraid Romelia is going to push me right out the window. Glancing out at the ground below, I wonder what my chances of survival would be if I jumped out. I might be able to get away if I didn't break any bones.

"It's like her den," Romelia explains. "Her canine instincts would lead her there, to rest after her murder spree."

"She's not a dog, for god's sake."

Romelia snorts disdainfully. "Not a registered breed, anyway."

"Just take me to see her." Acting braver than I feel, I squeeze past Romelia and walk quickly toward the door. "I'm ready when you are."

"Aren't you listening? First we need the bullet. Otherwise she will shred us both where we stand."

"I think my mother will be too happy to see me to want to murder me."

"Are you willing to bet your life on that?"

"Yes. Yes, I am."

Romelia's voice trembles with intense emotion. Hatred? Fear? Or both. "Promise me that if she is a werewolf, you will kill her."

"I promise, okay?" Behind my back I touch my moonstone ring.

Romelia's shoulders relax. She holds up the gun and stares at it. "I suppose I had better teach you how to shoot this thing." She laughs again, that humorless, nervous laugh that makes me think *she* is the sister who needs to be in an institution. "But you gotta promise not to use it on me. Don't want to waste a silver bullet. They're hard to come by."

Another promise. One to Dad, two to Romelia.

I make a fourth promise, this one to myself and to Mama.

I'll sort this mess out. I'll find a way to save you. I'll save us both.

CHAPTER 13

"Make sure the safety is on," Romelia says.

I'm sitting on the bed next to her, holding the Baretta.

I can smell her floral perfume, and it makes me sneeze.

"Careful." Romelia points to the safety flip and I rotate it down.

"Like that?"

"Good. Now slide the clip in."

I push the clip with the butt of my palm until it clicks into place. We've been practicing over and over for an hour.

"I feel like I'm in a marksmanship class."

"No marksmanship class is going to train you to kill a werewolf."

"Not even in the third degree advanced machine-gun level?"

Romelia trains a cold stare on me. "This is serious."

"I guess you can tell I'm still not convinced my mother is a werewolf."

"You will be," Romelia says. A small grin, more

like a snarl, plays across her lips.

I shiver involuntarily.

A knock on the door brings us both to our feet.

"Who is it?" Romelia asks in a chirpy, sing-song voice. She casually takes the gun from my hand and crooks her elbow so that the gun is pointed at the ceiling.

"Lani?" the visitor asks in a voice I recognize.

"Ben!" Relief floods over me.

I leap to the door, Romelia on my heels.

"Don't open that," she shouts as I fling the door open.

She quickly hides the gun behind her back.

I run into Ben's arms.

He picks me up and twirls me once, then, still holding me off the ground, gives me a big kiss right on the lips.

My heart pounds and my throat constricts. Is it just relief at being rescued, or does my reaction to his kiss mean something more?

I don't care. It feels right, right now, and I kiss him again.

"Oh my god, Ben! I'm so glad you're here. How did you find me?"

Ben drapes his arm around my shoulder. I snuggle into his side, breathing in the familiar piney-woods-and-topsoil smell of him. I like it a hundred times better than I like Romelia's designer perfume.

"I got a call from your Goth friend at the art store," Ben says. "I came as fast as I could."

"So, Ben, what brings you down here to Georgia?" Romelia sashays close to him. "Is there a special someone you couldn't live without?"

Ben blushes all the way to his ears.

"I came for Lani."

"Did you really?"

Ben inhales deeply as she steps close to him.

Even in three-inch heels, Romelia is a head shorter than Ben. She tugs on the front of his shirt and he leans down obediently. With her lips a micro-inch from his ear, she whispers, "It's Chanel, darling. Only the best for Romelia."

"It's very nice, ma'am."

A second ago you were ready to help me ditch her, I think. *Then she whispers in your ear, and you're a goner.*

I feel my face turn red. *What is this?* I ask myself. *You can't be jealous!*

But I am.

I pull Ben away from Romelia and give him a sharp look.

Ben squares his shoulders. "I'm taking her home."

"I don't think that's a good idea," Romelia says. "She could be in danger."

"Oh god, Ben! Did you hear what happened to Lisa?" I ask. "The girl at the gallery?"

Ignoring my question, Ben gently lifts my chin with his fingertips. "You're not in danger as long as you're with me. How long will it take you to pack?"

"I'm ready now."

"Lani, wait," Romelia says. "You can't find your mother without me."

"Your mother?" Ben cocks his head quizzically.

"She says Mama's living here in Lafayette."

"Don't tell me your aunt's as delusional as your

father was."

"There's more, Ben. She says Mama's a werewolf."

"Be careful, Lani," Romelia warns.

"It's okay. He knows my father thought Mama was a werewolf."

"C'mon, Lani. Let's go."

"You can't leave," Romelia says. "You made a promise."

"What promise?" Ben asks. "What's she talkin' about?"

"I promised her I'd go with her to see Mama, so she can prove she's a werewolf."

"You know that's insane! What proof has she shown you that your ma's even alive?"

I cross my arms and cock my head at Romelia. "Come to think about it, she hasn't actually shown me any proof of anything. Not that Mama is still alive, much less that she's a werewolf."

"I thought it might come to that." With the gun still hidden behind her back in one hand, Romelia sifts through the pile of things she dumped out of her purse onto the bed. She finds her car keys and clicks buttons on the digital photo frame. "There," she says, tossing me the keys.

The image is small, but in the background is what looks like a highway and the fender of an SUV with a Mercedes emblem. Beyond the Mercedes, another car is flipped on its side.

In the foreground, a woman crouches over a man's body in tall, weedy grass. The woman is staring up at the camera, a wild look on her face like a rabbit caught in a snare.

I don't recognize the man, but it would have been hard for his own family to recognize him. His face is covered in bloody gashes, his clothes are bloody and torn, and his arms and legs are splayed at unnatural angles.

I recognize the woman, though. It's my mother. Definitely.

My hands shake as I hold the digital photo frame, making the keys rattle together. "Wh-when was this taken?" I ask.

"I took that last week," Romelia says. "See the date?"

Small amber numerals in the corner of the screen read "14 July."

"The day Dad died." I hand the key chain to Ben.

"I was on the way up to Tennessee. I passed an accident. It was pure luck that I saw her."

She takes her keys from Ben and swings them around on her finger. "Ask me what you really want to know."

"Is the man in the photo – dead?" My voice trembles but I force the words out. "Did – did she kill him?"

"He's dead all right." Romelia slaps her fist shut around the keys. "He had wrecked his car, crashed it into a tree, probably not more than ten minutes before I drove by. Was he alive when your mother found him? I don't know. I pulled off the road and ran back to the scene. I pointed the gun with one hand and took the photo on my cell phone with the other."

"But you didn't shoot her."

"I wanted to shoot her then and there, but it

wouldn't have done any good."

I know why. "No silver bullet?"

"That's right."

"You really need a silver bullet?" Ben asks, scratching his head. "I thought that was just in the movies."

"As I explained to Lani, werewolf lore is often misrepresented in the movies. The part about a silver bullet being the only way to kill a werewolf, though – that's accurate."

"Holy shit," Ben says. "This is too freaky. Let's just go now, Lani."

But I have too many questions. I can't leave without the answers. "What happened after you took the photo? If you didn't kill her, did you just let her go?"

"Well, more like she escaped, but she left these behind." Romelia walks to the nightstand and pulls open the drawer. She tosses me a small grey velour pouch. "Open it."

I loosen the drawstring and dump the contents into my hand.

Ben gasps suddenly and springs away from me, bumping his head against the wall.

"It's just earrings." I show Ben the oval moonstones. They're set in silver filigree, identical to the setting of the moonstone ring I wear.

Ben rubs the back of his head, obviously embarrassed. "I, uh, thought it was going to be, um, body parts. A finger or something."

Romelia barks a laugh. "Big guy like you? I wouldn't think a little blood would bother you."

I study the earrings, entranced, observing their eerie radiance.

These were my mother's.

An image stirs in my mind from long ago: Mama slides the moonstone ring onto a silver chain and fastens it around my neck. As I cup the ring in my palm, she puts my hand to her lips, then to her cheek. The moonstone earrings – these that I now hold in my hand – peek out from the curtain of her wavy chestnut-brown hair. They glow in the moonlight as if emitting their own luminosity.

"This ring will keep you safe," Mama's voice echoes in my mind. *Had the earrings kept* her *safe?* I wonder.

"Look at the photo again," Romelia says.

Ben hands me back the keys.

When I peer closely at the photo, I see one of the earrings dangling from Mama's ear. Her other ear is covered by a swirl of hair, but I have no doubt the matching earring is hidden there.

"Do you believe me now?"

"How … how did you convince her to give them to you?"

"The gun was very convincing," Romelia says. "I didn't have a silver bullet, but she didn't know that."

I tilt my head and put the earrings on. "You don't mind if I keep these, do you? Since they were my mother's."

"Fine. Take them. They served their purpose, didn't they? You believe me now."

"I . . . I don't know."

"How can you not believe me?"

"Lani, what's the point of all this jewelry talk?

Let's get out of here," Ben pleads.

"I can't," I say with a deep sigh. "If I don't go with her, I won't ever know for sure if my mother's alive."

"That's right," Romelia gloats. "And don't forget, I've still got this."

She pulls the gun from behind her back.

"What in hell is that?" Ben asks.

"It's a Baretta," Romelia and I say together.

Ben grips my arm. "In that case, I *really* think it's time to go."

I put my hand over his and gently loosen his fingers, entwining them in mine. "No, Ben. Not yet. After I go check out Romelia's story – or more likely, disprove it – wild horses couldn't keep me from going home with you."

"Oh, it'll check out, all right," Romelia says.

"If that picture hasn't been Photoshopped, my mother could still be out there." I sweep my arm toward the window. "She could be anywhere."

"She'll come home. She's too … domesticated to stay away for long."

"Come on, Ben. Let's go for a walk. I need some fresh air."

I duck out the door into the hall, dragging Ben behind me.

"Remember your promise, Lani," Romelia calls.

"I'll be back."

"Girl, I'm warning you."

The tone in her voice stops me in my tracks. I hold firm to Ben's hand.

"I'm leaving at eleven o'clock," Romelia says. "That's one hour from now. If you want to go to Hunt

House, you had better be back."

"What about your silver bullet?"

"If Aurelia hasn't brought it to me, I'll have to go get it from her. Either way, we're out of here at eleven."

"You won't leave without me." I hope I sound braver than I feel. "You need me, remember?"

CHAPTER 14

I slam the door, getting a last glimpse of Romelia standing there, stunned, the gun held limply at her side.

I lead Ben downstairs, so absorbed in thought that I don't see Jace until I bump into him.

"Lani! I was just coming to ask you –." His voice trails off as he notices Ben.

"Ask me what?"

"I was going to ask if you wanted to take a walk downtown. I didn't know you had company." He narrows his eyes at Ben.

"Actually, Ben and I were just going for a walk. Why don't you come along?"

"I'm sure he doesn't want to be the third wheel," Ben says.

"Last time I checked the dictionary, I'd only be the third wheel if you were Lani's boyfriend," Jace says. "And I heard she doesn't have one."

"Maybe you heard wrong." Ben drops my hand and pushes in front of me, going toe-to-toe with Jace. Ben's about four inches taller than Jace, but Jace is more muscled and doesn't seem to care.

"Who are you, anyway?" Ben growls.

If I didn't know better, I'd think *he* was jealous. But of Jace? Jace isn't interested in some girl who has to answer to her aunt like a second grader.

"Ha-ha, don't I have horrible manners." I laugh nervously. I disentangle my hand from Ben's. "Ben, this is Jace. His grandparents own this bed-and-breakfast. Jace, this is my best friend, Ben. We're neighbors up in Tennessee."

"Ben," Jace says. "Yeah, Lani told me about you when we were sharing a lovely thermos of hot tea at the romantic little outdoor spot where we met."

I try to correct Jace. "Technically, we didn't –"

"Funny, she hasn't mentioned you," Ben snarls.

"So did someone mention going downtown? That sounds good to me."

"There's an ice cream shop that opens early on Saturdays," Jace suggests.

"The Kremy Kone?"

"You've heard of it?"

"My Dad used to take me there every week when I was little. It was our favorite thing to do."

Somehow, a trip to the ice cream shop where Dad and I used to go is exactly what I need. I've lost my father, and the current direction of my life is impossible to wrap my mind around. But the Kremy Kone is still there, an emblem of my childhood stability.

"They make a wicked chestnut-honey ice cream," Jace says.

"That's new." I shrug. Even new flavors won't ruin my trip down nostalgia lane, I decide.

As we walk through the B&B's lobby toward the towering, carved mahogany front door, Natasha looks up from the counter she's polishing and arches an eyebrow. "Heading out, *copii*?"

"Back soon, Buni," Jace says. He gives his grandmother's cheek a quick kiss.

Natasha swirls her hands in the air. "Watch out for –."

"I'll be careful."

"What did she mean by that?" I ask Jace as we walk outside. "Some sort of Gypsy warning?"

"Only if Gypsies are more in tune to rain than other folks. I think it's supposed to storm later."

He squints at the white-blue sky.

The wispy clouds I saw earlier have been blown away, much like my fears, now that Ben is here.

"Not on my parade." I hook my arm through the crook of Ben's elbow.

Jace slips my other arm through his. "Let's get some ice cream."

We walk three abreast down the brick walkway.

"Look at us," I say with a smile. "Dorothy, the Scarecrow, and the Tin Woodsman."

"One has no home, one has no brains, and one has no heart," Jace remarks.

"Are you saying I'm stupid?" Ben snarls.

"Not at all."

"Good, because I'm not stupid."

"Of course you're not."

"Ben, what's gotten into you? Can't we just enjoy the walk?"

Ben pokes his bottom lip out like a pouting little

boy.

With a jolt I realize he's *not* a little boy. He's a teenager with maturity beyond his years. How many boys would marry me just to keep me out of foster care? How many boys would travel for hours when I asked them to come for me?

I feel a surge of affection for him that goes beyond our life-long friendship. I admit to myself that I *was* jealous over his apparent crush on Romelia. But I think her holding a gun on us crushed that crush. I'm glad to have Ben focused on me instead of Romelia.

I breathe in the sweet scent of the tea olive that grows in a hedgerow at the end of the driveway. The intense aroma reminds me of Dad's funeral. I brush that thought away and replace it with a pleasant memory, one of Dad and me working in the community garden in Knoxville.

"The lilies' flowers get all the attention," he told me one glistening spring morning, "because they smell so intoxicating. But smell this." He grabbed two fistfuls of the dark soil and held his hands out to me. "Never forget where you come from, Lani. Where you plant your roots, how you take care of your home and your family, these are more important than how you smell."

I sniffed under my arms. "That's good, Dad, because right now, we both smell pretty rank."

We both laughed, and I smile now at the memory.

We walk in silence except for the voices in my head. Dad saying my mother's alive. Romelia saying she's my aunt. Ben saying he loves me. *Well, technically, did he say he loves me? Or just that he wants to marry me? Does he love me? Do I love him?*

"So, Lani. You're from Lafayette," Jace says. "Why on earth would you ever leave this paradise?"

"Family business," Ben responds.

"Where do you live now?"

"None of your concern," Ben says.

I roll my eyes at him. I might not have told Jace anything about me when I met him at the rest stop, but now, it's not top-secret information.

"Cloud Pass, Tennessee. It's a little town up near Knoxville."

"You're kidding, right? I worked in Knoxville last summer. This summer too, until last week when Nicu asked me to come home. I was a cook at Guy L'Orange."

"Ghee what?" I ask.

"Seriously?" Jace releases my arm and grabs his chest like he's having a heart attack. "You don't know Guy L'Orange? The Orange Man."

"No. Should I?"

"Five-star restaurant." He kisses his fingers. "Best food in Knoxville. Especially when I was cooking."

I shake my head. "Dad and I don't, um, didn't go to ritzy restaurants much. We're more barbeque kind of folks."

"Me too," Ben says. "Me and Lani and Mr. Morgan always went to Big Bob's Bar-B-Que Palace."

"I've been to Big Bob's," Jace says, bobbing his head. "It's not bad. But when you're in Lafayette, Georgia, the place to go for fine cuisine is the Kremy Kone. And here it is."

The familiar ice cream cone sign glows neon red in the front window.

Jace holds the door open for me, and Ben ducks in right behind me. They bump shoulders as they try to fit through the doorway at the same time.

The place looks just the way I remember. Even the Felix the Cat clock on the wall is the same. Tiny wrought iron tables and chairs evoke an outdoor Parisian café. Watercolor prints of the Eiffel Tower, the Arc de Triomphe, and a tour boat on the River Seine add to the ambiance.

We order our ice cream – Jace and I both get the honey chestnut and Ben gets chocolate. Jace pays for all three cones and we go to a table by the window. There are only two chairs at each table, so Ben pulls an extra chair over from the next table. He squeezes in between Jace and me, forcing Jace to slide a little further away.

Jace licks his cone once all the way around. "Tell me," he murmurs dreamily, almost to himself. "Is this the best ice cream you've ever had, or what?"

I lip a bite of ice cream off the top of my cone. As it dissolves on my tongue, I can almost pretend that I'm a normal· little girl again. The Kremy Kone is a tiny island of peacefulness and normality in the river of craziness and uncertainty that my life has become.

"Ohmygod. Dad would have loved this if they'd had it when I was little."

Ben bites the top off his ice cream. "I'll stick with plain old chocolate."

"New flavors keep you from getting into a rut," Jace says. "You know, like the rut you get in when you choose the same, plain old flavors you see every day."

Ben looks like he might shove his plain old chocolate cone right in Jace's eye. "One rut Lani and I are getting out of is this town. Sooner. The. Better."

So much for peace and normality.

"I guess Ben's right," I sigh. "Not about this town being a rut. I love Lafayette. But I should be thinking about what to do after we go to Hunt House."

"The mental institution?" Jace asks. "Why're you going there?"

"To see my mother, hopefully."

"Does she work there?"

"No," I answer slowly. I watch Jace closely for his reaction to my next words. "She's a resident there. According to Romelia, anyway."

"According to Romelia? You don't sound like you believe her."

I shake my head. "I don't, really. Not completely. But she has some pretty strong proof."

"What about your father? Doesn't he know where your mother is?"

I swallow hard. "He passed away a few days ago."

"I'm sorry," Jace says.

Ben pokes him in the chest. "Didn't see that one, huh."

"Cut it out, Ben."

"Were you close?" Jace asks.

Ben jumps in with his answer. "No duh. He only raised her single-handed since her mother died."

Jace's eyebrows scrunch together. "But you just said your mother was in Hunt House."

"She might be dead, she might be in Hunt House." I wrap the rest of my cone in a tiny napkin. I no longer have the appetite for it. "She might be . . . somewhere else."

"So you don't know for sure if she's even alive?"

"It's a long story."

Jace gives me an intense look that is charismatic, sympathetic, hypnotic. "I've got time."

Ben leans across the table and cocks his head so he is directly between Jace and me. "Here's the story," he says. "Once upon a time, Lani had a best friend named Ben who came down to Georgia to rescue her from an obnoxious guy she has absolutely no interest in."

"Ben! I don't need to be rescued from Jace."

"I think you do," Ben growls.

I feel the heat radiating off Ben, he's so angry. It's how he had acted when we saw Romelia's SUV in my driveway. He had been in protector mode then, same as now, ready to rip the intruder to pieces. That is, until he got a look at Romelia, and the boy hormones took over. Maybe if he'd been a little more attentive then, I wouldn't have wound up all this way from home, traveling with a woman who wants me to kill my own mother.

Jace is waiting for me to respond. I take a deep breath and tell him the short version. The version where hopefully I don't come across as a lunatic.

"My father told me my mother died in a car crash when I was little. But Romelia says he made that up to protect me from the truth. That Mama was in an institution."

"Tell him the rest," Ben taunts. He knows if I tell Jace the part about my father claiming my mother is a werewolf, Jace will say *adios* and that will be the last I hear from him. Ben's competition, as he apparently sees Jace, will be history. There's no way Jace is interested in me, but I like him, and I don't want him to think I'm a lunatic.

"Not now, Ben."

"Go on, Lani. Tell him how you had that Goth girl at the gallery send *me* a message that you were in trouble. How you needed *me* to rescue you."

I study Jace's face. Can he see how uncomfortable this conversation is making me? Can he tell how screwed up my life is? He knows I'm upset about the attacks at the art gallery and the rest stop. Now he knows that my father died recently, and that I'm not even sure if my own mother is dead or alive. And just a day ago, I wouldn't even tell him my name.

"Listen, Lani," Jace says. "I already told you that you don't need to be rescued from me. But if Ben's here to rescue you from Romelia, that's different. I'm all for it."

"See?" Ben smirks.

I rub my hand across my eyes. "At least we agree on one thing. I seriously don't know what I was thinking, coming with her."

"I don't know what her problem is, but she definitely has issues," Jace continues.

"She seemed nice enough to me," Ben says, "until she pulled out that gun."

"Ben, shut up! I think we should go."

"Now you're talking," Ben says.

"No, wait," Jace says. As he reaches across the table to grab my hand, he bumps Ben's arm, knocking the chocolate ice cream off Ben's cone and into his lap.

Ben jumps up. "Crap!"

"Gee, dude, sorry about that," Jace says.

"Sure you are." Ben stomps off to the counter and paws at a napkin dispenser, shredding several tiny napkins before he manages to remove a handful. He swipes them over the mess on the front of his jeans.

Jace whispers, "Quick, while he's gone. Tell me what's going on. Did she really pull a gun on you?"

I shake my head. "If I told you what was going on, you'd think I was nuts. And there's nothing you can do to help, anyway."

"Try me."

Felix the Cat chimes the top of the hour.

"Oh, god, it's already eleven. I've really gotta go!" I scoot my chair out and take my napkin and cone wrapper to the trash can.

"Let's go," I tell Ben.

He's still wiping the chocolate goo off his jeans. "First you're Dorothy, now all of a sudden, you're Cinderella?" he snipes.

"You heard Romelia. If I'm not there at eleven, which is now, she's leaving without me."

The only way I can keep Romelia from killing my mother – if Mama's still alive – is to be with her when she goes to Hunt House.

"I can take you on my bike if she leaves before you get back," Jace offers.

"That won't be necessary," Ben says, shoving the sticky, wadded up napkins at Jace's chest. "If Lani needs a ride, I'll take her."

"You sound like a bodyguard," Jace says flatly.

"Yeah. That too." Ben pokes Jace's shoulder.

"Let's just get back so she doesn't leave without me, okay?"

"What kind of crazy is your mom, anyway?" Jace asks as we file out of the Kremy Kone.

I stop dead in my tracks. I feel the hackles rise across the back of my neck. "*Excuse* me?"

"Oh, jeez," Jace says, holding his hands up apologetically. "That didn't come out right."

"Obviously." I take off at a quick pace, almost jogging back toward the B&B.

Jace trots up to my side and matches my stride, step for step. "All I meant was, what's her diagnosis?"

The term *lycanthropy* pops into my head, but I can't exactly say that out loud.

"I'm not sure," I admit. "But she's *not* crazy."

"It was a bad choice of words," Jace says. "A horrible word. *I'm* crazy for saying that. Please forgive me."

I stomp a few more angry steps, then slow my pace.

Jace sees the chink in my armor. "Pleeeeease?"

I exhale a deep breath. "Apology accepted."

A smile of childlike relief spreads across Jace's face, and I have to pull my gaze away from his mesmerizing blue eyes.

"The ice cream was a brilliant idea, wise Roma Boy." I smile at the nickname. It captures his exotic charm.

"Anything for you, Wolf Girl."

Ben grabs my elbow roughly. "I can't believe you told him!"

"Told me what?" Jace asks.

I tell Ben, "It's just a joke."

Then to Jace, "Seriously, you have *got* to come up

with something better to call me."

He shakes his head and scratches his chin. "But 'Wolf Girl' fits you so well."

My hair whips in the breeze that has come up while we were in the ice cream shop. I hold the most annoying strands behind my ears. "What. The hell. Is that supposed to mean?" I spit the words out like bullets.

"I just meant, I think you've got a wild side, that you're intriguing. And that there's something. Don't be offended, but something a little bit tragic about you, I guess." Jace looks down at his shoes. "What with your family troubles and all."

"Everybody's got some sort of tragedy in their lives," I say. "I'm no different from any other teenage girl."

"You're different to me," Jace says softly. "In a good way."

"Give me a break," Ben says contemptuously. He puts his arm around my waist and pulls me toward him, away from Jace. "You don't know anything about her. You need to just give it a rest with all your wild-side talk."

"Can you both just give it a rest?" I bark at them. "Maybe a walk wasn't such a good idea after all."

When we get back to the B&B, Romelia's SUV is still in the driveway, along with Ben's Chevy and Jace's Harley.

"Thank god, she hasn't left."

I run up the steps. Romelia opens the door just as I reach for the door knob.

"Romelia! Thanks for waiting for me."

"As you pointed out," she says icily, "it wouldn't be much use for me to go without you."

She sashays down the steps, barely glancing at Jace but throwing a flirty look at Ben and tweaking his chin as she struts past him.

Ben seems to be hypnotized, like an alligator when you rub its chin.

"Snap out of it, Ben!" I hiss under my breath.

"Let's hit the road," Romelia says. She jangles her keys for emphasis.

"Oh, yeah. Right," Ben says, shaking off the trance. "What am I supposed to do while you're gone?"

"Maybe you should go, too," Jace suggests.

"What?" I can't hide the surprise in my voice. "You *want* him to come with me?"

"I really didn't have a big welcome party in mind," Romelia says.

"Of course I should come," Ben says. He glares at Jace.

Romelia throws her arms in the air. "Well, Jace, would you like to come, too? The more the merrier, it would seem."

Jace straddles his bike and cranks the pedal. The engine rumbles awake and settles into a purr. "I'll pass." He pulls the helmet off the handlebar, snaps it under his chin and blows me a kiss. "Let me know how it goes."

I grab Ben to prevent him lunging after Jace as the bike serpentines down the driveway.

"So," Romelia says as we drive down Main Street, "the hour of truth is at hand."

Ben stretches out in the back seat and props his

boots on the center console between the front seats. "I hope this doesn't take long," he says. "For some reason, I've got a hankering for barbeque."

"Darlin'," Romelia drawls, "I'd appreciate it if you'd remove your boots from my leather console."

Ben immediately scrambles to sit up straight as a school boy with his feet on the floor. "Yes, ma'am."

Good boy, Ben, I think. *Another gold star for you!*

"So when we get to Hunt House," I ask, "do we just ask to see my mother?"

"That's the idea, yes."

"What if they say no? What if she's not there?"

Ben taps my shoulder. "Where else would she be?"

"According to Romelia, there's a high probability she's on a murderous, multi-state rampage."

He rubs his five-o'clock shadow. "You think she attacked those people at the gallery? And that hobo at the rest stop? Maybe it's not a good idea for you to go looking for her."

Romelia guns the SUV around a slow-moving truck full of cattle. "Let's not air dirty laundry around strangers," she says.

"Ben's not a stranger. He's like a brother to me."

Romelia yanks the SUV back into her lane just before a minivan buzzes by in the opposite direction, the driver laying on their horn. I watch the minivan through the rear window. Someone in the passenger seat waves a finger out the window at Romelia.

She deserves it, I think.

A few minutes later, we swing around a curve and I gasp. Up ahead, off to the side of a modern concrete bridge, an old covered bridge spans a small river.

"Mill Creek House!"

I think of the many times Mama and Dad and I drove through the bridge. Each time, I'd beg them to let us live there. The new bridge hadn't been there then.

"Can we drive through the old bridge?" I ask impulsively.

Romelia swerves the car off the paved road onto the dirt road that leads down to the covered bridge. She slows down as we bump over the joinings in the floorboards, creating a slow, rhythmic beat.

"This is where you parked last night, to talk on your phone."

"I couldn't very well stop in the middle of the real road."

"Oh, my stomach," Ben moans. "This is the bumpiest bridge I've ever been on."

"Come on, suck it up," I chide him. "The road we live on is worse than this, especially after it rains."

But suddenly, I wish I hadn't asked Romelia to drive through Mill Creek House. The accident that killed my mother happened right after Dad and I crossed the bridge for the last time. In my mind, Mama's death is indelibly attached to Mill Creek House.

"It's a pretty old bridge," Romelia says. "It affects some people more than others."

The next moment we're out of the bridge and light streams in the windshield.

"Did the air just change?" I crane forward to look up at the sky. It has taken on an eerie hue.

"Wasn't me," Ben says.

"No, I mean outside. Does the air look green to you?"

"I felt green back there," Ben moans with self-pity.

I give him my "grow up" look.

"Please," Romelia says.

"But I'm better now," Ben says when he sees he's not going to get any compassion from the front seat.

"There's a storm coming," Romelia says. "We better be quick at Hunt House or we'll get caught in it."

Ten minutes later, we pull through an ivy-covered archway onto a long gravel drive.

Roiling purple clouds hang low in the sky. "Those clouds sure came up in a hurry."

"Like I said, there's a storm brewing." Romelia pulls the car around a three-tier fountain in front of a brick building that looks like a mansion straight out of *Southern Living*.

Fluted white columns support a portico lavishly embellished with scenes of a fox hunt: Riders on prancing horses, hounds with their tails in the air.

Romelia pulls the SUV to a stop under the portico. "You can get out here. I'll park and join you in a sec."

As we wait on the brick porch under the portico, the wind whips around us and I shiver. "I thought it's supposed to be summer."

The tiny trees dotting the parking lot tremble as well, their leaves chattering in the wind in answer to rumbles of thunder that quickly are moving closer.

"I'm going to wait inside," I tell Ben.

"You scared of a little lightning?"

Just then a bolt strikes close-by with a loud *POW!*

"I think I better get you inside," Ben says, wrapping his arm around my shoulders and steering me toward the door. "Don't want you getting yourself struck by lightning."

"May I help you?" a plumpish woman in a tight tweed pantsuit asks. She has a friendly, grandmotherly smile and smells faintly of cookie dough.

"We're waiting on my, um, aunt to park the car," I say.

"Certainly. Let me know when I can be of assistance."

As the woman turns to walk away, I call after her, "Wait!"

She turns back to me with a pleasant smile. "Yes, dear?"

"I'm here to see my mother."

"Oh, that's lovely. Visits are so important to our residents. What's your mother's name?"

"Melani Morgan."

The woman makes a choking sound and puts her hand to her throat. "You're Mrs. Morgan's daughter! I thought you looked familiar."

She's alive! My mother is alive, and this woman knows her!

I follow her to a booth in the corner. An engraved sign affixed to the wall beside a sliding glass window instructs, *All visitors kindly check in here.*

The woman taps on the window, which slides open immediately.

"Tara, please call Nurse Alday. Tell her Mrs. Morgan's daughter is here."

"Yes, Mrs. Poole." Tara, a college-age girl in a candy-striper shirt-dress, speaks into a telephone, then reports, "She'll be right down."

I try to ignore the idea that gnaws at the back of my mind, *If Dad and Romelia were right about Mama being alive, were they right about her being a werewolf?*

I get a sick feeling in the pit of my stomach.

"So how is my mother? When can I see her?"

"Let's have a seat, shall we, dear?" Mrs. Poole directs Ben and me toward a brown vinyl couch and matching loveseat. "Nurse Alday will be here in a moment to speak with you about your mother."

"Mama *is* here, isn't she? She's all right, isn't she?"

"You'll need to speak with Nurse Alday."

Ben and I sit close together on the couch. Mrs. Poole perches on the edge of the loveseat.

I hear the soft squeak of nurse shoes. A professional-looking woman dressed in blue-green scrubs strides across the lobby in our direction. She holds a manila file folder.

"Mrs. Poole," the woman says. "I got an urgent call for my assistance. Tara mentioned Mrs. Morgan."

"Yes, Nurse Alday. This is Mrs. Morgan's daughter."

The smile on the nurse's face seems glued in place, but I notice her eye twitch slightly. "Pleased to meet you," Nurse Alday says, extending her free hand to me. "And what is your name, dear?"

"I'm Lani, and this is my friend, Ben Stoat."

"So good of you both to come," Nurse Alday says. "I'm Alisha Alday, Head Nurse here at Hunt House. We've been very worried about your mother."

Mrs. Poole clears her throat. "Excuse me, Nurse Alday. Perhaps we should wait for Miss Morgan's aunt to join us. She's parking the car."

"Is your aunt your guardian, dear?"

"No, my father is." I shoot a warning glance at Ben so he won't say anything about my father technically being unable to provide guardianship. "Why? What's wrong?"

Mrs. Poole wrings her hands and looks at Nurse Alday.

"I'll handle things from here, Mrs. Poole," Nurse Alday says.

The older woman wipes a trickle of sweat from her hairline and trots away as fast as her tweed-encased legs can carry her.

Nurse Alday flips pages in her file folder. "We've had a slightly embarrassing turn of events," she says, studying the pages intently.

I shiver involuntarily. I hold the ends of my jacket sleeves in my fingers and wrap my arms tightly around my chest. "Nurse Alday, please tell me what's going on."

A loud grumble of thunder echoes through the high-ceilinged room and I hear a barrage of rain on the roof.

"Well, we've never had anything like this happen before," Nurse Alday says.

"She's gone, isn't she?"

I can tell by Nurse Alday's wide-eyed expression that I'm right – that Romelia had been right.

The nurse nods once, quickly. "Yes."

Even with my hoodie on, I can't stop shivering.

"When?"

"Four days ago."

The automatic doors slide open and Romelia dashes in from the rain. Her hair dangles over her shoulders, bounceless and dripping wet. She peels off her jacket and shakes it, splattering raindrops on the floor around her, then prances toward us. Even sopping wet, she looks like a model on the catwalk. Her self-satisfied grin tells me she knows exactly what Nurse Alday is saying to us.

The head nurse stands up and smiles warmly at Romelia. "Ms. Marks, it is *so* good to see you again. It's been a long time. When Lani said she was waiting for her aunt, I didn't realize she meant you."

"Thank you Alisha. I believe you have some news for us about Melani."

"Yes, ma'am, and I am afraid it is not good news." Nurse Alday thumbs through her chart.

"Please, Nurse Alday, can you just tell us what happened to my mother?"

The nurse draws in a deep breath and exhales slowly before she responds. "Four days ago, Mrs. Morgan broke out of her room."

"She *broke out?*" I interrupt. "What is this place, a prison?"

"My dear Miss Morgan," Nurse Alday says, straightening her back. "This *place* is a highly regarded institution for mentally disturbed individuals. Some of them, such as your mother, have been judged a danger to themselves and others."

I can't sit still and listen to this. I jump up and pace back and forth, clutching my arms around my chest.

"Her room is locked," Nurse Alday continues in a muted tone that won't carry through the cavernous lobby. "A nurse monitors her and the other residents on the Level Red floor at all times via closed-circuit TV."

Dad loves red.

I whirl to face the prim and bony nurse. "Then how could she 'escape'?"

"She had apparently hidden a piece of beef jerky in her shoe. When the nurse closed the door, Mrs. Morgan slipped the jerky between the bolt and the latch. She waited until the duty nurse was distracted and crept unnoticed to the emergency stairwell. The video tapes show her emerging on the second floor, then walking down those stairs." Nurse Alday motions to a prominent stairway with mahogany rails and carpeted steps at the other end of the lobby.

Ben stands and points at the expansive stairs. "So she walked down *those* stairs, in plain view of *that* reception station, straight through this area here, and out the front door, pretty as you please?"

Nurse Alday clears her throat. "That's correct."

"Right in front of, what, half a dozen nurses?"

"Overnight, there are only two nurses on the lobby floor." A drop of sweat dribbles down the nurse's cheek. "She timed her escape at the shift change, when the overnight crew is giving the morning staff their update."

Ben towers over her as he snarls, "And she was never seen or heard from again."

"Not exactly," Nurse Alday says, gesturing toward the automatic door.

I notice she keeps a wide distance from Ben, whose presence seems to unnerve her. *Good. Ben will get the truth out of her.*

"The security guards were alerted by screams coming from the woods on the other side of the parking lot. They saw a large wolf run off, but found no trace of Mrs. Morgan."

"A ... wolf?"

"Why didn't you call me?" Romelia asks.

"We tried to call Mr. Morgan, but got no answer."

"Did anybody follow the wolf?" I ask, afraid to hear the answer. "Did they ... kill it?"

"I'm sorry, Miss Morgan," Nurse Alday says. "We called the police, and they brought out a pair of bloodhounds. But they weren't able to find the wolf, much less take a shot at it. Nor were they able to pick up your mother's trail, I'm afraid."

I breathe a sigh of relief. I sway back and forth, clutching my arms around my chest.

Miss Alday rushes to my side and holds me as if I'm about to faint. "Do you need to sit down, dear? I know this has been quite a shock."

"You don't know the half of it," I say. "But I think we should leave now."

Ben wraps his arm across my shoulders protectively, prying me away from Nurse Alday. "I'll make sure she doesn't fall," he says.

As we turn to go, the door slides open and Jace sloshes in, his motorcycle boots leaving watery footprints. He looks from face to face. "What did I miss?"

CHAPTER 15

Ben steers me past Jace, through the automatic door.

"What's wrong?" Jace asks.

"Nothing," Ben growls. "Family business."

"I didn't think you were coming."

Jace shrugs. "Changed my mind."

The sky is dark as night, the rain coming down in torrents. The wind whips the rain sideways so it lashes at us where we stand.

"Why don't you ride back with us, Jace?" The rain pounds on the dome of the portico so hard I have to shout to hear my own voice. "You can come back for your bike later, after it's stopped raining."

"Damn it, this is a linen suit," Romelia says. "This rain will ruin it."

I pull the hoodie over my head. "Give me the keys. It's no big deal if my clothes get wet."

"I'll go with you," Jace says. "I'm not afraid of a little weather, either."

"Then take your bike," Ben suggests.

I dash across the parking lot; Jace runs right beside me.

"Why did she have to park so far away?" he yells over the roaring wind and rain.

"Maybe she's afraid someone might key her car," I yell back.

I run around to the driver's-side door and fumble with the key in the lock. Suddenly a bolt of lightning streaks across the sky, turning the tree trunks silver in the woods a few feet away. *That's where my mom ran. Where she turned into a wolf and ran away from this place.*

I want to get away too, but the icy rain drizzles into my eyes, and every soaked inch of me shivers from the cold. In stark contrast, I feel warm breath on my cheek.

"Do you mind, Jace? You're making it hard to concentrate on getting the key in."

"What?" Jace yells from the other side of the SUV. He stands by the front passenger door, blinking the rain drops off his eyelashes.

Being as still as the day I saw the wolf in the back yard, I only move my eyes. Ben stands inches from me, huddled over against the rain. I flinch at his unexpected presence.

"What?" he asks.

I shake my head. "Nothing. I just didn't know you were there."

"So hurry up and unlock it, would you, sweetheart? Before we both catch pneumonia."

"Since you asked so nice." I turn the key and open the door, popping the button on the door panel to unlock the other doors as I jump in.

Jace hops in the front seat and shakes his hair. Water sprays the dash. "You know that key fob has a remote entry." He reaches for the keys dangling from the ignition. "Hey, is that a digital photo frame?"

"Don't touch it!" I warn. "I mean, I'm driving and all."

He flinches with surprise at my reaction. "What's got you so on edge? Was there a problem?" He squints his eyes at Ben.

"Family business," Ben snaps. "Keep your nose out of it."

I'm tired of secrets. "My mother's not here."

"Why would your aunt lie to you about her being there? I mean, what's the point of lying to you, and then bringing you out here, where you were bound to learn the truth."

"She didn't exactly lie. Mama *was* here, but they've lost her."

"How do you lose a full-grown woman?"

I drive over to the front of the building and pull under the portico.

Romelia opens the driver door. "Hop in back," she orders. "I'm driving."

I get in behind Jace, and before I can close the door, Mrs. Poole appears beside the car. She takes hold of my wrist.

"Miss Morgan, there's something you should know." She darts her eyes at the building's entry and I can tell she's afraid of getting caught. She glances at Romelia, obviously afraid of her, too.

"Go on," I tell her. "What is it?"

"This wasn't the first time."

"What do you mean?"

"It's not the first time that your mother . . . got

loose."

"It's happened before?" I feel blood rush to my ears and throat. "How many times?"

"Since I got here three years ago, it's happened three times."

"Oh my god!"

"But until last week, we always found her the next day, wandering around the campus in a daze."

"Doesn't the Health Department or somebody audit you? Why haven't they shut you down?"

"We called your father each time it happened," Mrs. Poole says defensively. "He always tells us the same thing: As long as she comes back, don't report it. Nurse Alday and the others, they're only too happy to oblige."

"Just as I thought," Romelia says as she drives away. She stares straight ahead at the road. "This weather is a *fiara* to drive in."

I've been watching Jace's reflection in his window, listening to him rapping his fingers on the console. The rapping stops and in his reflection, Jace's eyes catch mine.

"Don't know what fire has to do with all this rain," Ben says, "but personally, I think this storm's a bitch.

Romelia drives much more slowly than on the way to Hunt House. The rain makes it difficult to see much further than the area illuminated by the headlights. We go around a curve and through the blur of water on the windshield, I see the red tin roof of the covered bridge up ahead. "There's Mill Creek House. Can we pull over until the rain slacks off?" I suggest.

Romelia pulls onto the gravel road and heads for

the old bridge.

The water in the creek churns as it rushes by.

"Is it safe?" I ask.

"Mill Creek House is safe," Jace answers. "I wouldn't go for a swim in the creek, though."

Memories echo in my mind, the voices of both my mother and my father: *Mill Creek House is a safe place.*

"When the sun's out, I'll show you the high water marker from the flood of '72," Jace says.

"How bad did it flood?"

"Three-quarters of the way up the walls."

"That's a lot of water," Ben says. "Maybe we should stay on the new road."

We bump onto the bridge and the wipers scrape the windshield dry. The headlights flood the bridge housing, casting eerie shadows across the lattice patterns of the wallboards of the old structure.

"The bridge design is simple, yet very strong," Jace says. "The water's nowhere near the high mark now."

"Is that a fact," Ben says.

"Yes, that is a fact."

"Uhhh, here's another fact." Ben leans forward with his head between his knees, his fingers laced through his hair. "I think I'm going to throw up."

"I'd appreciate it if you didn't throw up in my car," Romelia says.

"He's really sick," I tell Romelia.

I stroke Ben's back. "Do you want to get out and get some fresh air?"

He sits up, limp and green. "Maybe – good – idea." He flings the door open and tumbles out.

I get out, too, and reach to help him to his feet, but he shoves me aside. He pinballs against the bridge walls until he stumbles out onto the road. He stands in the pouring rain for a moment. In the blink of an eye, he jumps down the creek bank.

"Ben, no!" I yell.

I run to the bank, ignoring the rain that immediately drenches my hair and clothes, but he has disappeared.

"Ben, come back!" I search frantically for a way to follow him. Just as I start down the bank, Jace grabs my arm.

"You can't go down there!"

"But Ben is down there. He shouldn't be near the creek. It's too dangerous!"

"I'll go," Jace says.

"He's my friend. He needs me."

"You'll fall in the creek and drown yourself. I know this place. I can find him and bring him back."

I search his eyes for reassurance. Rain streams down both our faces. He kisses me, crushing our lips together. It's over in a heartbeat, leaving me wondering if I imagined it. But my lips tingle so I know it was real.

Romelia steps to the edge of the bridge, staying dry. "We should leave," she yells over the clatter of the rain on the bridge's red tin roof.

"Don't leave yet," Jace tells her. "Wait here till I get back, or till it quits raining."

Jace takes my hand and leads me back to the bridge. We peer out into the rain. "How will you find him?"

Jace and Romelia stand side by side, illuminated by the headlights. They are ghostly twins; the same tall, slender build, the same wild, black-as-night hair.

"I don't know, but I will. I'm not going to just leave him out there, no matter how annoying he is."

Terror seizes my chest. "What if he fell in the river? He'll drown! What if you get swept in, too?"

"I'll be careful. I promise. Stay here. Don't leave the bridge."

"Nice knowing you," Romelia scoffs.

Jace pulls the collar of his motorcycle jacket up around his ears. He puts his hand on the frame of the bridge, winks at me over his shoulder, and jumps down onto the bank.

"Be careful!" I call. But the darkness of the storm swallows him and all that's left is the rain, pounding furiously on the metal roof.

CHAPTER 16

"Well, we're alone." Romelia sashays down one of the parallel rows of long wooden planks. "Do you want to ask me what happened to your mother? How she escaped Hunt House?"

"Why should I believe anything you tell me?"

"If you don't believe she's a werewolf, or that you'll become one, why are you wearing her ring? Why were you so intent on taking the earrings?"

I clutch my hands to my ears, feel the cold gemstones against my fingers. "Because they were hers. Don't you love your mother? Don't you want reminders of her?"

"My mother! My mother?" Romelia says with a huff. "If she really loved me, she would have told me no when I asked her to help me put a curse on Melani."

"What does my mother's jewelry have to do with her being a werewolf?"

Romelia laughs as she walks closer, her heels tapping on the floorboards. "You don't know? She didn't tell you when she gave you the ring?"

I clasp one hand around the other, now feeling the cool stone of the ring against my palm. I back up until my back presses against the wall of the bridge. Mama's words echo in my head. *This ring will keep you safe. Promise me you'll always wear it.*

"It's like a good luck charm."

Romelia stands directly in front of me now, her face so close I can feel her breath on my face. She puts her lips close to my ear. "It wards off werewolves," she whispers.

"How come she didn't keep the ring, then? To keep her from changing."

"Poor Lani," Romelia says, smoothing a wisp of hair from my eyes. "So confused."

I wrench my head away. "Don't touch me."

She steps away. "Ironic, don't you think? You would rather go back to thinking your mother is dead than admit she is a werewolf."

Romelia paces away, her heels clicking rapidly on the ancient boards, joining the cacophony of the rain on the roof. Suddenly, she rushes at me. I jerk backwards and bump my head against one of the X-shaped wooden supports on the bridge wall. I wince, close my eyes, rub the back of my head.

When I open my eyes a second later, Romelia is staring at me with such intensity that I feel like I have been dunked in ice. I shiver in my wet clothes.

"You will see with your own eyes, and you will kill her, before she kills you. If you have an ounce of humanity in you, an ounce of your father's humanity, you *will* do it. You're Melani's only blood relative. I have to do whatever I can to save you. To make it up to her."

"You're not worried about me. If my mother is a

werewolf, she's coming for you. She's been trailing you all the way back from Tennessee, leaving calling cards so you know it's her and you know she's after you."

"Do you hear yourself?" Romelia asks. "You are calling your mother a mass murderer, and I happen to believe you are right about that. Yet you refuse to do anything to stop it."

"*You* should stop it. Make her human again."

"I can't remove the curse. Only you can do that, and there is only one way. A silver bullet to the heart."

"Then do it yourself."

"Believe me, I tried it once. When I took that photo on the highway last week." She laughs humorlessly. "Only, no silver bullet."

"Where are you planning to get a silver bullet?"

"My mother has one," Romelia snarls. "She had it made back when she gave me the curse. She was supposed to bring it to me this morning, but she got lost. Do you believe it? She's lived in this town since her Roma band decided to end their nomadic days and settle down, before I was even born. And she gets lost? Idiot."

"Old people forget things sometimes." I don't know why I feel like I have to defend the woman who helped Romelia cast the werewolf spell on my mother. The woman who is going to supply Romelia a silver bullet intended to murder my mother. But for some reason, I don't blame Romelia's mother. I blame Romelia. "Why didn't we just stay with her instead of going to the B&B? Then she wouldn't have had to try to bring the bullet to you."

"She and I –.We're not close any more. I haven't

even seen her since I moved to Pensacola. Trust me. Staying at the B&B is a much better option."

"What makes you think you can find Mama? Or that she'll get near enough to let you shoot her?"

"She won't. She's too smart to let me near her."

"Unless you have some sort of bait."

"Yes, my shiny little cricket. Unless I have bait."

"You bitch."

"Because I figured out a way to save you? That's not very grateful."

"You're using me as bait and as your contract killer. Where's *your* humanity, Romelia?"

A bolt of lightning cracks close-by. I dart to the edge of the bridge and stare into the rain. "God, Where could Ben be? Jace should have found him by now."

"Speaking of your handsome friend from the mountains, I think you and I should share a room tonight. So the two of you don't get any funny ideas about running off together."

Standing in the headlights, I cast a long shadow across the rain-mudded road. "I'm not sharing a room with you."

"Well, I can't wait around in this ramshackle – building – any more."

I whirl to face her, but all I see is her silhouette, rimmed in gold from the glare of the headlights.

"What do you mean?"

"Those idiots are going to have to find another way home. Both of them."

I gape at her. "What if they're hurt?"

"Boo hoo. A no-good Roma and a love-sick redneck. I couldn't care less."

I cross my arms over my chest and plant my feet firmly, a shoulder width apart. "I'm staying."

"No, you're not." Romelia opens the door of the SUV on the front passenger side and bends over, looking in the glove compartment. When she stands back up she holds the Baretta, pointed at my chest.

"Is that supposed to scare me?" I say, calling her bluff. "I know it's not loaded."

She aims at the roof and pulls the trigger.

The gun explodes. I cover my head reflexively as sawdust from the wooden ceiling and support beams flutters down all around Romelia. The bullet has opened a hole in the roof, piercing straight through the wood and tin, and now rain dribbles on Romelia's shoulder.

All I can think of is how my father had wanted to save me, so he told me to go back to Georgia. I wanted to save my mother, so I let Romelia bring me here. Then I wanted Ben to save me, so he came down to Georgia.

And now look at us.

My father is dead.

My best friend might be dead.

Jace, an innocent bystander, might be dead.

My mother is a werewolf.

And Romelia is going to use me as bait so she can kill my mother.

I can either go with Romelia or try to help my friend.

"Nice knowing you," I whisper to Romelia.

Before she can stop me – before I can change my mind – I run from the bridge and slide down the bank.

CHAPTER 17

"Are you crazy?" Romelia shouts at me over the drumming rain. "You'll get yourself killed!"

The drone of the storm and the angry rush of the river drown her voice.

I keep going, sliding down the bank. I grab at branches to slow my forward motion. I call Ben's name, but my voice is broken into shards and scattered on the wind.

I must have lost my flip-flops somewhere on the bank. My bare feet are muddy and slippery. At the water's edge I lose my footing and fall on my butt. I'm up to my thighs in cold, mud-red water. I grab a willow tree by one of its rope-like tendrils and scramble out of the creek.

Sitting on the bank while I catch my breath, I wipe rivulets of rain off my face. "Ben! Ben, where are you?"

The only answer is the howling wind and rain and the churning creek. To either side of me, the bank is overgrown with brush and small trees, a tangle of vines and roots. In front of me, the river crashes through its slough, wilder than the Garnet River back home at its worst.

I have no place to go.

I crawl up the bank on my hands and knees until I reach the road. As I stand up, I feel eyes watching me. I look up. About fifty yards away, a shadowy figure stalks into the road. A big black wolf.

It bares its fangs and stalks toward me.

"Run!" Romelia shouts from the bridge. "Run to the bridge!"

I walk backwards so I can keep my eyes on the wolf, but it quickens its pace. I hate to turn my back on it, knowing that if I run, it will give chase. But if I don't run, it will catch up with me anyway. I turn and bolt to the bridge.

The wolf snarls and bays.

As I run, I look over my shoulder.

I step in a puddle-filled hole and lose my balance, tumbling onto the road. I'm sure this is the end. The wolf will be on me in a matter of seconds.

Then Romelia is there, pulling on my arm, helping me up. "Hurry! We have to get back to the bridge," she says.

The wolf is closing in.

I reach into my pockets and grab the moonstone rocks. I chuck the first one at the wolf, but it lands short, splatting in the muddy road. I throw the second one, and it hits the wolf square in the eye.

The wolf yelps. It paws its eye – distracted just long enough for Romelia and me to scramble toward the bridge. Then it's after us again. A second after I reach the bridge I hear another yelp and turn around. The wolf is sprawled in the road. As Romelia and I watch, the wolf lunges at us again. I stagger backward, but see the wolf leap and fall back as if it just ran into a brick wall.

"It can't come on the bridge," I pant. "It can't come after us."

"Get in the car." Romelia reaches into the SUV and grabs the gun. She wraps both hands around the pistol grip and aims at the wolf.

The gun goes off and the wolf spins in the air and lies still on the road.

"Did you kill it?" I ask.

"Doubt it."

The wolf rolls to its feet. It shakes its head and limps into the woods, holding up one front paw.

"Time to go," Romelia says.

"But Ben," I plead. "He's sick, he may be hurt. I don't want to think what could happen to him if he comes face-to-face with that wolf."

"We're leaving. Now."

When we pull into the gravel driveway at the B&B, I dash inside. I plan to go right to Natasha tell her everything, especially the part about Romelia having a gun. I will ask her – beg her, if necessary – to protect me.

But there's no one behind the reception counter. At first the lobby appears completely deserted, until I notice a woman in a flowing dress and a turban-like floral headscarf, slumped in an easy chair as if she fell asleep reading.

"Natasha!" I run to her side and shake her shoulder.

The woman looks up and flutters her peacock-like false eyelashes.

It's not Natasha.

Her dangling, gold hoop earrings glitter in the light from a floor lamp. She reaches a hand to me and I gasp at the long, curving fingernails painted blood-red, the moonstone ring on her index finger that is identical to mine.

"You ... you're Aurelia!"

She takes my hands in hers. "Yes, Lani. It is I. Your grandmother."

Romelia saunters up to the woman and kisses her cheek, a dry peck. "Mother. You finally got here."

CHAPTER 18

Other than the purple bags under her eyes instead of kohl, the woman hasn't changed much in all the years since I last saw her, when I stayed with her after the car crash.

"Lani, you are soaked to bone, child." Aurelia shakes her head. "No, you are not child. You are young woman. And so much like your mother."

"I remember you. But how could you be my grandmother? She died before I was born."

"Technically, she's not your grandmother," Romelia says.

I fix her with a cold stare. "And you're not my aunt."

"Not by blood, no."

"So you were lying. How much of your story is lies?"

"You mean, did I lie about the werewolf curse? Unfortunately, no."

I turn to Aurelia, my last hope for the truth. "What happened to my mother? You couldn't have given Romelia a curse to use against her."

Tears pool in her dark eyes.

I feel tears sting my own eyes as the depth of the betrayal strikes me. "Could you?"

"Mothers will do many things to protect their daughters, to make them happy." She extends her arms and wiggles her fingers at me to help her up. I pull her out of the chair and her exotic aroma – jasmine and cinnamon and orchid – washes over me.

"Then there's really a curse? My mother's a werewolf?"

"Is true." She covers her face in her hands.

"So to make Romelia happy, you gave my mother a horrible curse? How is that fair? How is that being a good mother?"

"Was wrong, I know." Aurelia looks up at me again. Her cheeks are streaked with tears. One of her false eyelashes has come unglued and dangles in front of her eye, bobbing up and down as she blinks. She pulls it the rest of the way off, then removes the other one as well. "But do not think Romelia was untouched. She has been, I think, even more unhappy than Melani."

"How can you think that?" I storm about the room, my cold, wet feet leaving muddy tracks on the polished hardwood floor. "Look at her. She has a life. She got married, right? It wasn't as if Dad was her only love."

Aurelia shakes her head, her brow knitted. "Romy never married."

I spin and glare at Romelia. "But you said you had an ex-husband. Another lie?"

"She is marked, branded," Aurelia explains. "The curse of the werewolf is on her, too."

I step back. "She's a werewolf too?"

Aurelia shakes her head. "No, is not werewolf. But day after she spoke curse, she awoke with werewolf's paw print on her neck."

"That tattoo? What does it mean?"

"It means," Romelia says, her heels clicking on the hardwood floor as she walks closer, "that Franzl was *supposed* to disavow his love for Melani. He was *supposed* to fall in love with me. Instead, I was robbed of love. His, and any other man's."

I can't help but smirk. "What goes around comes around."

Romelia grabs my shoulders and shakes me. "How could he keep loving her? She was a monster."

I shove her hands away. "I'm beginning to understand what the curse did to you." "No one else could fall in love with you."

"That's right," she growls through clenched teeth.

"But I don't think it was the curse. You say my mother is a monster. But I think it's you. I think *you're* a monster to wish something so horrible on anyone. How could anyone love a monster like you?"

"No, Lani, she is not monster," Aurelia says. "Only misguided. She has never had skill or intuition to embrace her heritage. I am monster for teaching her Roma curse, and not Roma laws and ways."

"Then teach her now." I look from sad-eyed Aurelia to Romelia, whose eyes are as veiled as a cobra's. "Tell her she can't kill my mother."

Aurelia shakes her head slowly. "Is too late for your mother. But not for you. That is why the werewolf must be killed."

"But Dad said you could help." I rush to her and hold her hands, the way she held mine a few minutes ago. "You can revoke the curse."

She shakes her head. "Is not possible, *copil.*"

Romelia darts to her mother's side, elbowing me away. "Mother, did you bring the bullet?"

Aurelia pushes up one of her long, gauzy sleeves, revealing a silver charm bracelet. Among the hearts and stars swinging from the bracelet, one charm stands out. It's shaped like a bullet.

Aurelia unclips the bullet charm from the bracelet and hands it to Romelia.

"Finally," Romelia sighs.

"That's not a real bullet," I say. "It won't work in a real gun."

Romelia laughs, the sound cold and heartless as a night on the moon. "The little ring where it attaches to the bracelet would probably get in the way, right? Watch." She twists the bullet charm and it comes apart like a Russian nesting doll. The real bullet is inside.

Suddenly the front door slams and we all look up. Ben stands in the entryway, covered in mud and sopping wet.

"Ben!" I leap into his arms and hug him tightly around his neck. I kiss him full on the lips. "You're okay! Thank god you're okay!"

"No thanks to that friend of yours," Ben says, nuzzling my neck.

"Jace? What did he do?"

"Just tried to shove me down the bank, is all. I think he wanted to kill me."

I lead Ben to one of the chairs in the lobby. He

flops into it, exhausted.

"You're wrong, Ben. He went after you to make sure you were all right."

"Maybe he saw a chance to knock off the competition."

"Ben, all he ever did was flirt with me." I kiss him and he brings his thumb to my cheek to wipe away some mud. "It was never a competition."

"Boys can be heartless," Romelia says.

I wipe Ben's glistening black bangs out of his eyes. "There's a big difference between heartless and homicidal, Romelia."

Ben wraps his arm across my shoulder, pulling me close. "All I know is, one minute I was leaning over the river bank, being carsick. Next thing I know, Jace comes running down the bank and shoves into me. Sends me rolling toward the river. I was lucky there was a big ole tree root to grab onto, else I would've fallen in and drowned."

"Oh my god. Are you hurt?" Now I see his right eye is purple and swollen. "You are! You're hurt!"

"I'll be black and blue for a few days. Nothing a little TLC can't cure."

He has a rip in his shirt sleeve that shows a nasty scratch on his upper arm. "You're bleeding! You need more than TLC!"

"I just got scraped up a bit."

Suddenly I hear the muted strains of an old folk song. *Wish that I was on ole Rocky Top, down in the Tennessee hills.*

"Ben, that's your phone."

Ben digs his cell phone out of his back pocket and

flips it open.

"Hello? Yeah, she's right here." He hands me the phone.

"Hello?" I wonder who would be calling me on Ben's phone.

"Is this Lani?" a vaguely familiar voice asks. "It's Lisa, you know, from the art gallery?"

"Lisa! I thought you were, well, dead!"

"Not dead, girl, but we sure been through a lot. I'll tell you all about it, but first, the reason I called is to make sure you were okay."

"Me? Yeah, I'm okay. What about Stuh, Stuh –." My voice sticks on her father's name. I'm afraid to ask the question.

"Stan? He's right here. Oh, I didn't tell you where we are. We're in the hospital in Chattanooga. They have an ace amputation team here. They're taking good care of SP. But he won't be making any more art for a spell."

In the background I hear a booming voice, "Don't be so sure, LP! I still got my left hand!"

"So what happened?" I ask.

"After you and your aunt left the gallery, I called your friend, and he promised to come get you. Since he answered his phone, and you're there too, it looks like he found you, huh?"

"Yes, he found me." I smile at Ben and he smiles back.

"Thank God. Pardon me for saying, girl, but I got real bad vibes off your aunt."

"Lisa, it's sweet of you to worry about me. But what about you? What happened at the gallery? The news said you and Stan were attacked by a serial killer."

"Serial killer? No. This was no serial killer. I can see how they must have thought that, what with the way the gallery looked."

"Then who did it?"

"Some psycho wolf-hybrid."

I feel like I've just been punched in the gut.

"A wolf? You were attacked by a wolf?"

"Friggin' thing took SP's arm clean off below the elbow, but the docs here stitched him up. He'll pull through fine."

"How did it happen? I mean, can you talk about it?"

"It was later that same day that you were here. One other dude came in, a young biker guy. Really hot."

"Tall, lanky guy with jet-black hair?" I ask. "Maybe eighteen years old?"

"Yeah, you know him? Is that your friend Ben?"

"No, not Ben. Another guy. What did he want?"

"He and SP talked about his bike for a while. I thought he was real nice, but SP thought he was hiding something, maybe casing the joint for a robbery."

I stand close to Ben and tip the phone so he can listen with me. "Did he come back?" I ask.

"No, after he left, nobody else came in, so SP and I were able to catch up with the housekeeping. Let me tell you, we had the gallery sparkling by about ten p.m. That's when SP went to lock up and all hell broke loose."

"What happened?"

"I heard this ferocious growl, then SP screamed and this crazy black wolf came crashing right through the screen door. He was laying into SP, chasing him around the gallery. SP hollered at me to get out, but I was too terrified to move. Then the wolf cornered SP in the back room. He lunged again, and the force of him hitting SP knocked them both into SP's masterpiece. You know, the one you and your aunt admired so much."

"*The Bait-iful Sea.* It was on the news. All that was left of Stan was his arm, sticking right through the painting."

"That's when I knew it was up to me," Lisa continues. "I guess I got my fear muscles on. I grabbed a broom and told that wolf to sit and stay, and he did. I know it sounds bizarre, that a wild animal would know dog commands. That's why I think it wasn't pure wolf. He seemed like he'd been trained, and a pure wild wolf wouldn't respond that way."

"Wait, Lisa. Are you sure the wolf was a he?" I ask.

"Yeah, a young male, maybe two or three years old, I'd guess."

I hear Stan's voice in the background again. "Fourteen to twenty-one in dog years."

"So anyway," Lisa says, "SP and I are living proof that you can do super-human things with an adrenaline rush. I pulled SP right on out of there, loaded him into the back of the van, and high-tailed it to the hospital. They stabilized SP, put some stitches in me from where I must have stepped on some broken glass, and life-flighted us to Chattanooga."

"I'm so glad you're okay."

"I'm glad *you're* okay. Even though I hardly know you and all, I guess I just felt a connection when you came in the gallery. What with you losing your dad and me losing my mom. I wanted to make sure your friend found you and you were safe."

"Thanks, Lisa. I feel the same way about you. Listen, can I call you in a few days? To check on you and Stan?"

"Girl, we'd both like that."

I end the call and with a trembling hand give the phone back to Ben.

I turn to Romelia. "You were right about a werewolf tracking us from Tennessee," I say. "But you were wrong about it being my mother."

"Who was it, then?"

A day ago, her response would have been haughty, as if she were just feigning interest to humor me. But today, she is just as scared as I am. She and Aurelia both look at me with wide eyes like frightened owls. Ben is too exhausted to look scared, but he's waiting my response, too.

"The hobo at the rest stop. Stan and Lisa. Even the hiker on Cloud Pass. It wasn't a bear, or a freaking maniac. It was a wolf. I saw him myself at Mill Creek House. So did Romelia."

He said he wanted to help me, that he'd never hurt me.

"I can find him and bring him back."

"You're different to me."

It was all lies.

"It's Jace," I say. My chest aches in that rib-cracking way it did at Dad's funeral. "Jace is a werewolf."

CHAPTER 19

"That's a nice theory," Romelia says. "And you might be right about Jace. But it doesn't change the fact that your mother is a werewolf."

Ben and I change into dry clothes and sit next to each other on the couch in the lobby, waiting for the rain to stop.

Now that she's got the silver bullet, Romelia is determined to end the curse. I go along because I'm curious to see if she can produce my mother – alive. Ben goes because I'm going. This is one time when his bodyguard devotion might come in handy.

Romelia stops the SUV in front of an old house on a narrow, oak-lined street. The porch columns aren't as big or as grand as I remember, and the paint is dirty and chipping off. The boxwood hedges have grown into gargoyle-like guardians.

But it's the right house. My memories of it are bone-deep.

"Go on. See if she's home," Romelia orders. "We'll wait here."

Ben pats my shoulder. "It's okay, Lani. I'll be right here in the car if, um, anything happens."

He means, if my mother the werewolf leaps out of the house and attacks me.

"Just keep an eye on Romelia."

I feel like a little girl again as I run up the walkway and swing open the screen door. I almost open the front door and walk right in, but remember that this isn't my house any more. Someone else might live here now.

I take a deep breath and knock.

The minutes tick past to the beat of my heart, pounding in my chest.

The door opens an inch. I see a shadowy figure and shiver, thinking this is it. This is when I get ripped to shreds by my own mother.

Then the door opens all the way, and there she stands.

Not a werewolf. Not an old woman. My mother. Her sleeveless, knee-length shift dress is a burnt-sienna color that matches her hair.

Looking at her is almost like looking in a mirror. Her skin is smooth, except for a jagged scar on her right cheek. Her chestnut hair has more red in it than mine. Her sizzle-red lips glisten just the way I remember.

She hasn't changed at all in ten years. Just like Dad said.

"Lani?" she says in a dazed voice. "Oh, my Lani!"

"Mama!" My voice is a twin of hers.

We hug each other tightly. Tears flood from my eyes but I don't care.

She pulls away and holds me at arm's length. "You are more beautiful than –." Her voice trails off as the joyful smile fades from her sizzling red lips. "Oh, honey, I'm so sorry about your father."

"You know? How can you know?" An image flashes through my mind of the reddish-brown wolf I saw at Dad's window, and again at his gravesite. "You were there."

Instead of answering, she hugs me again. "How did you get here? How did you find me?"

"Romelia brought me."

Romelia struts up the sidewalk, her hair whipping in the wind.

"She's got a gun, Mama."

"She's tried that before," Mama says. "I think she knows now that it won't work."

"She has the silver bullet."

Mama's eyes dart from me to Romelia. "Get in the house, Lani."

"No, Mama. I'll stand beside you."

Romelia pulls the Baretta out of her purse as calmly as if it were a fold-away umbrella. "Hello, Melani."

She holds the gun at her waist so Mama and I can see it, but she is careful not to flaunt it in case a curious neighbor is watching. "I guess you know that Franzl is dead."

"I feel sorry for you, Romy," Mama says. "Your jealousy killed the man we both loved."

"Me? I didn't kill him." Romelia's voice raises, not quite to a shout. "You're the one who bit him, made him age like a dog because he wouldn't commit murder the way you do."

"I do what I have to do to stay alive," Mama

admits. "But I never bit Frank. I sent him and Lani away so that wouldn't happen."

"Somebody bit him. It wasn't grieving over you that made him old. He didn't grieve."

I feel hot blood rushing through my body, filling the veins in my neck and ears, pounding in the spaces behind my eyes till the world looks red. "You don't know what you're talking about. He grieved every day since we left Georgia."

Romelia laughs. "He didn't grieve for her because he never considered that he'd lost her. He loved her to the end, even knowing she was a monster."

"That's what you never understood, Romy," Mama says, her voice soft and filled with empathy. "Soul mates like Frank and me, we love each other for better or for worse, like we vowed. Till death do us part."

"Then death will reunite you," Romelia growls. She flicks the gun barrel at us. "Let's not do this in public, shall we? Inside, both of you."

But Mama ignores the gun. She is looking beyond Romelia.

I follow her gaze. Ben is walking up to the house.

"Ben, thank god," I yell, not caring who hears. "Get the gun from Romelia!"

"I see you've brought a pet," Mama says to Romelia.

I shake my head. "No, Mama, that's Ben. He's not with Romelia. He's my friend."

"Don't bet your life on it," Mama whispers to me, not taking her eyes off Ben.

Ben walks up next to Romelia.

"Grab the gun, Ben! Now's your chance!"

But Ben just stands there. His eyes are wide with fear, but it isn't Romelia he's afraid of, or her gun.

Can it be? He's afraid of Mama.

"Ben! Get the gun!" I shout again. "She's going to shoot Mama!"

Ben flinches and seems to come out of his stupor. He reaches a trembling hand toward the gun.

Romelia nudges him away. "No," she scolds. "Stay."

I'm dumbstruck by the way she talks to Ben, like he's some sort of dog.

But even more than that, I'm completely floored by Ben's reaction. He cowers at Romelia's command. He's such a big guy; I've never seen him so intimidated.

This is no lovesick-puppy act.

This is a pet, like Mama said, obeying the voice of authority.

"I said, get in the house," Romelia snarls at Mama and me through clenched teeth.

Mama steers me into the house, walking backward and keeping herself between me and Romelia's gun. As soon as Mama is inside too, she slams the front door and bolts it. "Run for your room, quickly!"

I dash up the stairs. Mama is right behind me. I remember which door leads to my room. I fling it open and stumble in. Mama rushes in and closes the door.

"Why'd we do that?" I ask. "We're trapped. Romelia will shoot through that door like it's nothing."

Mama smiles and I think my heart will break with happiness. It's the first time I've seen that smile in ten years. "You don't hunt pigeons when you're loaded for bear," she says.

When I give her a quizzical look, she explains, "She'd have to unload the silver bullet before she shot the door."

"Okay, so that gives us maybe three minutes instead of two."

"Darling, you have gotten so grown up. Look at you!"

"I missed you too, Mama. But we're about to get some company."

Mama just smiles some more. "I love your sense of humor."

I wonder if lycanthropy isn't the only reason she was sent to Hunt House. Maybe it was for her own protection. "Mama, don't you realize you're in mortal danger?"

I hear a voice calling from the yard. "Lani!"

I run to the window, almost losing my balance before I remember the way the floor dips.

A sudden chill races across my shoulders. "Oh my god. It's Jace."

"Another friend, sweetie?" Mama says as if we are having an afternoon chat about somebody I'd met at school. She slips silently to my side and looks out the window.

"I used to think so, Mama, but that was before I found out he's a werewolf."

"What makes you think he's a werewolf?"

Bam!

"That was the front door," I cry. "Romelia's inside!"

"Answer me, Lani. What makes you think he's a werewolf?"

"Mama, do we really have time for this?"

"This is the *only* time we have for this."

I try to ignore the fact that a woman with a handgun is about to come crashing in on us, intent on murdering my mother. "He tracked me here, all the way from Tennessee. He was staying in Knoxville, but I never met him till Romelia and I stopped at a rest station on the way down here. Then a homeless guy was killed at that very same rest station. Then I found out Jace followed me to an art gallery where I went to call Ben for help, and soon after that, the art gallery owners were attacked by a wolf."

"Seems pretty circumstantial, sweetie."

"That's not all! He turned up at the B&B where we're staying. Turns out, he's the grandson of the owners."

"Sounds like he has a valid reason for being there."

"But then he chased Ben out of Mill Creek House, and tried to push him down the bank. He almost killed Ben, and then I saw him in wolf form. He tried to attack me, but I made it to the bridge."

"Wait a minute, Lani," Mama interrupts. "Ben and Jace were *in* Mill Creek House? Actually inside the bridge structure?"

"Ben's been there twice, actually. The first time, me, Romelia and Ben passed through the bridge on our way to Hunt House. On the way back, Jace was with us. We had to stop on the bridge because it was raining so hard."

"How did Ben act?"

I hear crashing noises from downstairs. Then Romelia's voice: "They must be upstairs. Let's go."

"Ben got carsick," I tell Mama. "On the way back, he thought he was going to hurl. He ran out into the rain as soon as we parked on the bridge."

"And the other boy?"

"Jace? He ran out after Ben. He said he was going to help, but now I think he meant to kill Ben. And he almost did."

The stairs creak.

"Did you see Jace change?"

"No, but –."

"They're coming up," Mama says. She looks out the window and puts her fingers to her lips in the classic "Shh" gesture.

I look out. Jace is still there. He glances around nervously, then nods at Mama.

Mama unlatches the window and opens both panes wide.

"What are you doing? Is there some sort of werewolf pact I should know about?"

"Stay by the window. If you have to, jump."

"But there's a werewolf down there!"

Bam bam bam! Romelia knocks on the door. "Little pig, little pig, let me come in," she sings.

I reply defiantly, "Not by the hair –."

Mama shushes me with a glance.

"I don't feel too good," I hear Ben moan. From the sound of his voice, he must be standing right beside Romelia.

Blam!

The gun goes off and wood fragments scatter into the room as the door around the knob explodes. Romelia kicks the door in and steps over a piece of broken door frame. "I hope I haven't scuffed my Imeldas."

"I'm disappointed in you," I tell Romelia. "You just killed a doorknob with your precious silver bullet."

"You don't honestly think I'd be that stupid, do you?" Romelia pulls her gold necklace from her blouse's neckline, revealing the bullet-shaped charm Aurelia gave her. She deftly slips the bullet out of the charm without losing her grip on the gun.

I should tackle her, try to take away the gun before she loads it with the silver bullet. But I'm frozen.

Romelia slides open the Baretta and chambers the bullet.

Ben stands behind her in the doorway. The idiotic puppy-dog expression that he usually gets on his face when he's around Romelia has been replaced by a wide-eyed look of fear mixed with nausea.

"Ben, what's wrong with you? Get the gun from her before she shoots Mama."

"Stay where you are," Romelia orders him. She snaps the gun barrel closed.

"He's scared to come in," Mama says.

"Well, no duh," I say defensively. "She's got a gun."

"He's not scared of Romelia," Mama says. "He's scared of me. I'm the alpha."

"The alpha?"

"The alpha bitch," Romelia answers. "This is her

den."

"Why in god's name would that matter? Ben, do something!"

Ben looks like he is going to throw up. "Get … married," he chokes out.

Romelia throws him a contemptuous look. "Is that what you think? If she gets married before she turns sixteen, the curse will be broken? Valiant of you to take that chance, but no. That won't work."

"Is everything about the curse to you? Ben didn't even know Mama was alive until a few days ago."

"He knew about your father, though," Mama says calmly.

"What about Dad?"

Romelia steps further into the room, holding the gun in both hands, her arms extended and locked at the elbows, unwavering. "We don't have much time, Lani. In fact, you're so close to sixteen, I'm surprised you haven't experienced pre-lycanthropy yet."

"Pre-?"

"Not a full change. Just feelings. Dreams, maybe. Possibly stronger just before you start your period each month?"

I shake my head. "How could you know that?"

The memory flashes through my mind like a scene from a horror movie.

The car window shatters from the impact. Shards of glass rain in my lap and scratch my arms.

"Mama!" I scream.

As Mama reaches in through the shattered window, her hands morph into paws. Her face becomes a wolf's face.

Romelia points the gun at Mama's chest. "If you

won't do it, I will. It's your life."

"No!" I lunge at Romelia, knocking her off balance. She tumbles backwards into Ben, and they both fall to the floor in the hallway.

The gun flies out of Romelia's hand and I scramble for it, landing awkwardly against the door frame. I clutch the gun in both hands and aim shakily at Romelia.

Ben moans and clutches the back of his head. He must have knocked into the wall or the floor when he fell.

Using the wall for balance, I stumble to my feet. "Are you okay?"

I step toward Ben, but Mama pulls me away, back into the bedroom.

"Wait," she says. "Watch."

As Ben wobbles on his hands and knees, his moans change, deepening into something more guttural. His head hangs down as if he's too dizzy to stand up.

He looks up at me with blood-red eyes. "I wanted to save you," he whimpers. "I knew what your father was. What he did to my father. But I loved you anyway. I thought we could save ... each other."

He screams in pain and bares his teeth at me. Teeth that have become long, savage, canine fangs.

I stare in horror as Ben's face morphs into a dog-like muzzle. His jeans and plaid flannel shirt melt off him, replaced by thick black fur.

"Not you, too," Romelia cries. She stumbles away from him, into the bedroom where she cowers behind Mama and me.

The werewolf that a moment ago had been my best friend advances on us, forcing us up against the wall and the window. When all four of his paws are in the room, the wolf gags as if he is sick at his stomach, curling his long pink tongue and flexing his jaws. He shakes his head and his nausea seems to pass.

He advances again, focusing his attention on Mama.

"The gun," Romelia screams. "Shoot him!"

The wolf shifts his bloodshot gaze to me and growls.

I remember Lisa's account of the black wolf that attacked her and Stan.

"Sit!" I shout. "Ben, sit!"

For a moment the wolf settles his weight on his back haunches and sits down. The rabid fire in his eyes dims and I see the glimmer of my friend Ben begin to surface there.

I lower the gun.

In a flash, the werewolf re-takes control. The animal crouches and lunges, striking my mother full-force.

Immediately, my mother morphs into a reddish-brown wolf. She and the black wolf snarl and snap at each other, growling ferociously.

Romelia stands in the doorway, quivering.

The wolves break apart and circle, heads low and hackles raised.

Mama holds her bushy tail high. She maneuvers around to where she stands between me and Ben.

She's protecting me.

The black wolf's tail is between his legs. He is

obviously scared of Mama but too full of fight to back down.

"He's a werewolf," Romelia screams. "Shoot! Shoot!"

I raise the gun with trembling hands. I can't bring myself to fire.

"He's going to kill us all!"

"No! He's my friend!"

Saliva drools from the black wolf's jaws. He raises his muzzle and howls. In one swift motion, he crouches and leaps. But Ben isn't attacking Mama. He's going for me.

Mama tries to intercept him, but his powerful hind legs launch him over her. As he strikes me, all I can do is hold my arms out. I feel him slam into my chest with such force that he knocks my breath out and shoves me back against the window sill. With the windows wide open, we both tumble out.

I land on my back and the black wolf lands on top of me. White light floods my vision. I can't breathe.

When my vision clears, I stare at the snarling jaws of the black wolf. He growls, and a line of drool drops from his lips onto my face. Then he scrambles to his feet and lopes across the lawn, disappearing around the corner of a neighbor's house.

The reddish-brown wolf follows close behind him.

CHAPTER 20

"Lani! Lani, are you okay?" Romelia rushes to my side.

"Can you get up?" a voice close to my ear asks. I turn to see Jace lying under me.

When I'm able to catch my breath, I gasp for air. "You … you broke my fall?" I ask. With the weight of the black werewolf off of me, I'm dizzy but otherwise uninjured.

"Right place at the right time, I guess."

"Mama –"

"She ran after the other wolf," Jace says. "Was that Ben?"

I roll over and sit on the grass next to Jace, hugging my knees. "Is she … hurt?"

Jace stands up and offers me his hand. "I don't know. There's blood."

I grip Jace's arm and he pulls me to my feet.

Romelia wrings her hands together. She's white as the moon, and she can't stop trembling. "Lani, I … I … I want to apologize. I want to help … set things straight."

"We've got to find Mama. I'll drive."

The three of us race around front to the SUV and I peel out, headed for Nelson Cottage in hopes that Aurelia will still be there.

"How can you find her?" Jace asks. "And what's your plan if you *do* find her?"

"I'm going to Mill Creek House. And you –." I poke Romelia's shoulder. She's sitting stone-like in the passenger seat. Her trembling has subsided, but she stares blankly ahead. "You are going to call Aurelia and have her meet us there."

"What can she do?" Jace asks.

"She's going to think of an anti-werewolf curse to cure Mama."

"There's only one cure for a werewolf," Jace says.

"If you say a silver bullet, I will pull this car over and dump you out right here."

"Okay, I won't say it. But I don't know of any other way."

"I didn't know he was a werewolf," Romelia says. "I thought he was a redneck mountain kid, but not a werewolf."

Jace reaches up from the back and shakes her arm ferociously. "Listen, lady. You're the reason for all this. You have no business badmouthing anybody, werewolf or no."

Romelia blinks at him, too stunned to speak. Finally, she hangs her head. "I know. I'm … I'm sorry. I told Lani I want to help set things right, and I do."

She looks at me and her eyes well up with tears. "I'm sorry about your friend. I swear I had nothing to do with him being a werewolf."

"You know, I hadn't thought about that. How *did*

Ben become a werewolf?"

"Maybe Buni will know," Jace says.

"Natasha? You can't tell her! She'll think we're all nuts."

"I think she already knows," Jace says. "She gave me this."

He pulls at the gold chain around his neck, drawing the pendant out from under his shirt. Dangling from the chain is a milky-white, egg-shaped gem. A moonstone.

"Give her a call," I decide. "Ask her to bring Aurelia, and meet us at the bridge."

***

I pull off the new road and park inside the old covered bridge. Remembering what Mama said, I observe Jace for any signs of nausea.

When he steps out of the car, he clinches his side and stifles a groan. "My ribs are a little sore," he admits when he catches me watching him.

Romelia stays in the car. As we wait for the others, I gaze at the small brass plaque that marks how high the water reached in the flood, years ago. I hear the water rushing under the bridge, the river still swollen by the downpour. "Do you think the river will get much higher from all this rain?"

"Doubt it. That marker's from the only time in recorded history this bridge wasn't a safe place."

I scan the road leading back toward town, but because the new road is built higher than the old road, only a short stretch is visible. "How long till the others get here?"

Jace checks his watch. "They should be here by

now."

"I hope they're okay."

A deep furrow appears between Jace's thick eyebrows and ocean-blue eyes.

"What?"

He scratches the back of his neck. "What if the werewolves get here first?"

"They won't," Romelia says.

I jump to realize that she has once again snuck up on us. I didn't even hear the car door open or her shoes echoing on the bridge.

"The Roma are here."

Jace and I exchange a quizzical look. "Where?" I ask.

"There." Jace points to a red pickup truck that rolls off the main road from the opposite direction of where we had been looking. The truck parks on the bridge next to Romelia's SUV.

Jace helps his grandmother from the driver's seat. "Where's Nicu?"

"We drop him off at morgue," Natasha says.

"The morgue?"

"Ivan works there. Did Jace not tell you?"

I shake my head.

"He has business to take care of. Important."

"Important?" Romelia coughs in disbelief. "More important than our werewolf situation?"

Aurelia stumbles out of the passenger side of the pickup truck. Romelia rushes to her side and grabs her elbow to keep her from falling.

Aurelia looks up at her daughter. "It must stop. . . . It must stop."

Romelia nods. "I know. I know."

Natasha walks over to me. "Let me see your arms."

"I'm fine, really. Ben didn't hurt me. I just fell out of the window."

She grabs my arms and pushes my jacket sleeves up to my elbows, unconvinced.

"Jace, tell her. I'm fine."

"I'm the one you should be worried about, Buni." Jace pulls up his shirt to reveal a big, purple bruise on his lower chest. "I think I broke a rib when Lani landed on me."

Natasha chuckles softly. "*Prostie copil,* how could you think my grandson was werewolf?" She pats my cheek affectionately. "I tell you he only has one flaw."

"He snores," I say with a smile.

Jace tugs his shirt back down and crosses his arms defiantly. "I do not snore."

"This is no time for jokes," Romelia says. "Don't you all realize we now have *two* werewolves to kill? That means we need *two* silver bullets."

I search Natasha's face, silently begging her to tell Romelia we're not going to kill my mother.

But all I see in the old woman's face is sympathy.

Not the fake, pasted on sympathy-masks worn by the mourners at Dad's funeral who were only there because it's what you do when someone dies in the small community you live in.

Natasha's emotion is deep and heartfelt. I think I can see straight into her heart through her eyes.

I pull away and stiffly stumble a couple steps backward. "You . . . you've done this before, haven't you? Killed a werewolf."

"I have seen enough to know what needs to be done," Natasha says with a shrug.

"Where are we going to get another silver bullet?" Romelia demands.

Natasha sighs. "Where is gun?"

Romelia pulls the Baretta out of the back of her waistband. "I have it."

"And bullet?"

"Loaded. Lani couldn't shoot the male."

"Give gun to girl."

I look around and realize Natasha means me. I shake my head. "Oh, no. Romelia's right. I couldn't do it. He's my best friend."

"Don't be fooled by that old 'dog is man's best friend' thing," Romelia says. "A werewolf doesn't care about friendship or love. Their only emotion is hunger."

"You're wrong. My parents loved each other. Even after Mama became a werewolf."

Romelia opens her mouth to say something else, but her words are cut off in a gasp. She points at the road.

I don't know how long she's been there, watching us. A sleek, reddish-brown wolf with long, skinny legs and a scar across one side of her muzzle.

The wolf moves closer. But is it a wolf, or a werewolf? The only way I can tell a regular wolf from a werewolf is to see it change.

The wolf pauses at the edge of the bridge and sniffs the wooden floorboards.

I'm sure it's Mama. I rush to meet her, but Jace

grabs my arm. "Stay on the bridge."

Stepping onto the bridge, the animal morphs from her wolf form to her human body, barefoot, dressed in the reddish-brown shift that matches the shade of her tousled hair.

"Mama," I cry, running to her open arms.

"Are you hurt?" she asks, smoothing my hair, then squeezing my shoulders and holding me at arm's length to examine me.

I shake my head. "Jace broke my fall."

"I hope that's all he broke," Mama says, casting a sad smile at him.

"A little bruised, no broken bones," Jace answers.

"What about you, Mama? Did Ben bite you?"

"Maybe a little," Mama says. "But I'm okay. I don't have to worry about being bitten by a werewolf, after all."

Although her words are light, her voice trembles. I notice she seems to be shivering with cold.

"Are you sure you're okay?" I ask.

"Actually, I'm feeling a little queasy."

"It's the bridge," Natasha says. "It has protection rune from long ago."

"A protection rune?" I ask. "Who would do that? Who would need a protection spell?"

"The werewolf curse is around for centuries before I ever tell Romelia how to use it," Aurelia answers. "Your mother is not first victim."

"Mama and Dad both used to tell me that Mill Creek House was a safe place." I look at Jace. "You've talked about it being safe, too."

Jace nods. "Buni always tells me to come here if I

need shelter." He walks to his grandmother's side and gives her a hug. "You never explained, but I always knew you meant more than a dry place in a storm."

Mama moans and doubles over, clutching her stomach.

She half-runs, half-stumbles out onto the dirt road. As soon as she is off the bridge, she stands up straight and takes a deep breath. "Whoo! That's much better. I'll just stand out here."

I walk to Aurelia and gently grasp her cold, tiny hands. "You are the one who brought the curse on this family. Please. You have to think of a way to end it. Even Romelia has promised to help. But we don't know how."

"I told you," Romelia says, sounding as tired as Dad in his dying days. "The only cure for a werewolf is a silver bullet. I'll do whatever I can to help you end the curse, but there's only one way."

"I think you're wrong." I rush to my mother's side, brushing Jace away this time when he tries to keep me on the bridge. Mama and I wrap our arms around each other's waist.

"Do you know how many years I have spent trying to find another way?" Romelia asks.

Mama laughs, a harsh bark that echoes through the bridge. "You don't care what happens to me."

"For a long time, I didn't care what happened to anybody. But Lani's innocent. I can't stand by and watch the curse claim her as well."

I feel Mama stiffen. She takes a few steps toward Romelia, but stops before her foot touches the bridge floorboards. "What do you mean?"

Romelia stares at her. "Don't pretend you don't know what I'm talking about."

Mama opens her arms wide, palms up. "I never killed anyone. I never even bit anyone, until I had to fight Ben. And he's already a werewolf, and was in wolf form."

"What about your escapes from Hunt House? When you hunt . . . people."

"I don't hunt people, Romelia. I do what I have to do to survive."

"What about the man on the highway, just a few days ago?" Romelia accuses.

"She showed me the picture, Mama. You didn't kill him, did you? You couldn't have."

"I didn't kill him," Mama says without taking her eyes off Romelia. "He crashed his car when he swerved."

"To avoid hitting you," Romelia says, returning Mama's stare.

Mama lowers her gaze. "I didn't kill him, but I suppose in a way I was responsible for his death. And his … injuries … weren't all caused by the crash."

"Mama?" My voice quivers. "What *do* you do to survive?"

Mama lowers her head. Her long, auburn hair falls in front of her face. "Not killing, but something else, almost as horrible."

I wrap my arms around her. "I don't care what it is," I promise. "It won't make me not love you, Mama. We'll find a way to stop the curse, so you don't have to do anything horrible ever again."

She cradles my chin in her hand. "I want to tell

you the truth, Lani. Like Romelia said, I often escape from Hunt House to … satisfy my cravings. One of the guards helps me, because he knows I won't kill. Ivan lets the guard know when a traffic fatality comes into the morgue."

"Nicu?" Jace asks.

Natasha nods. "He is helping as he can."

"But Melani, if it wasn't you who attacked those people in Rock Bluff, who was it?" Romelia asks.

"I don't know," Mama answers. "I don't know."

I remember the call I got from Lisa. "They were attacked by a wolf."

"Yes, a werewolf," Romelia says. "You're looking at her."

"It was a werewolf, but it wasn't Mama. It was a werewolf who tracked us here from Tennessee. He killed that homeless guy at the rest area. He attacked Stan and Lisa at the gallery. And he attacked Mama and me at our house."

Romelia taps her finger against her chin. "You think it was all Ben? You believe Melani when she says she had nothing to do with any of it?"

A shudder wracks my body. *Are those the choices? Either my best friend is a mass murderer, or my mother is?* But there is no way around it.

"Yes, I believe Mama. It was Ben who attacked Lisa and Stan. Lisa said it was a black male wolf, not a red female." Another detail strikes me. "Ben called Lisa my Goth friend. How could he have known what she looks like if he hadn't been at the gallery? If he'd only talked to her on the phone?"

"But how did Ben become a werewolf?" Romelia

asks.

"Werewolf is not created only by Roma curses," Natasha says.

"Some are created by other werewolves," Aurelia agrees.

"I swear I didn't attack him," Mama says. "But I might know who did."

"Great," Romelia says. "That means *three* werewolves."

A voice from the road startles us all. "I can tell you a thing or two about werewolves."

CHAPTER 21

"Ben!"

He's in human form. His shirt is shredded on one side, revealing three bloody slashes across his chest.

Jace tries to push me behind him, but I shove his arm away.

Romelia blocks my path. I think she is going to try to stop me as well, but instead she presses the Baretta into my hand.

I am too focused on Ben to refuse the gun, but there's no way I will use it on a human being, much less my best friend. I couldn't even shoot him when he was attacking me in werewolf form.

"Ben, how long?"

"I was bitten long ago, the night Jolie died," he says.

"You were there? You saw what happened? You never told me."

"Would you have believed me?"

"It wasn't a bear or an insane criminal that attacked Jolie, was it?"

Ben shakes his head.

"A werewolf?"

He nods. "Our father. Our own father attacked us."

"But how did he become – ." The words trail off as I realize that I already know. "My father."

A shiver runs through Ben's body, and I wonder if he is about to turn back into a werewolf at this very moment.

I fight the urge to run back to the safety of the bridge. Instead I grip the gun more tightly.

"But I didn't change until I turned sixteen. That's how I know what will happen to you if you're not protected by the time you're sixteen."

"That's why you want to marry me? To protect me? How would that help?"

"I read up on it. If we marry before you turn sixteen, you'll be under my protection. You won't be cursed. I even marked your house after your father died, so it would be protected. Please, Lani, say you'll marry me."

"But Ben, you're a werewolf. You tried to kill me and my mother. You've killed –."

He grabs my hand – the one he can see, the one that's not hiding the gun behind my back – and rubs it against his cheek. "Does that mean you couldn't love me?"

I stroke his face, the five-o'clock shadow rough on my palm. "My own mother is a werewolf. But I love her."

I turn to look at her. "I love you, Mama."

As I smile at my mother, a look of terror comes over her face. The others are wide-eyed in alarm as well.

"Lani, be careful!"

The next seconds seem to pass in slow motion.

I turn back to Ben.

I pull my hand away from his face, which bulges grotesquely and sprouts short, black hairs like a beard. Only the hairs grow at super speed. His cheeks, neck, and chin are soon hidden by shiny, black fur. It covers his forehead, rings his eyes, and spreads across what used to be his nose but is now a canine muzzle, complete with a wicked set of teeth.

Ben drops to all fours. His clothes have disappeared, replaced by glossy black fur that shines almost blue in the sunlight. He is now a werewolf. He bares his fangs and lowers his head but keeps his eyes on me.

I don't see hate in his eyes, but I don't see Ben, either. All I see is hunger.

As he lunges for me, I raise the gun and pull the trigger.

I hear the *pop* of the gun, feel my wrist snap as the weapon recoils in my hand.

Jace runs toward me, yelling, "No!"

The wolf's body slams into me, full-force, knocking me to the ground.

I missed! He'll kill me, then the others. They'll all die, and it's my fault for not killing him. For wasting the silver bullet.

Then I realize that the wolf lies motionless on top of me. I smell the earthy scent that is so familiar, but it's tinged with a muskiness that is more raw and wild. I grab the fur at the wolf's shoulders and roll him off of me. I stare at my hands. They glisten with blood. Ben's blood.

Jace is at my side. He pulls me to my feet and enfolds me in his arms.

I struggle to get away. "Get back! Get back!"

But Jace doesn't let go. "It's okay, Lani. We're safe. You killed him."

I swipe tears that trickle down my cheeks, trying to keep them from turning into a major spill. I feel the stickiness of the blood that now smears my face.

Jace leads me to my mother.

I slump from Jace's arms into Mama's. She holds me and strokes my hair. "It's okay, sweetheart," she murmurs. "It's okay."

My mama is here to make everything okay, I tell myself. How many times did I miss that when I was growing up? It was the one thing I wanted most in the world, and now, it was real.

"We should probably move this body out of the road," Jace says. "Before somebody sees us and thinks we killed their dog.

Standing arm-in-arm with my mother, I stare at the motionless animal lying on its side in the muddy dirt road.

"You can't just dump him in the woods," Romelia says. She pushes a button on her keychain and the hatch of her SUV pops open.

Jace picks up the wolf's limp, lifeless body and lays it in the back of the SUV. "Where can we take him?"

"Werewolf must be cremated," Natasha says. "To set soul free."

I think of my father, his soul trapped in the fancy

casket, waiting to be set free.

Jace turns to his grandmother. "Buni, why *did* you give me your moonstone pendant? Did you think I would need it in Tennessee?"

Natasha shrugs. "The signs were there."

"I guess I can give it back to you now." He walks toward his grandmother, pulling the leather cord over his head.

Both Natasha and Aurelia jump toward him.

"No-no-no," Aurelia says.

"Keep it on," Natasha agrees. She glances quickly at my mother. "You may yet need its powers."

I feel like Natasha has slapped me across the face. "You mean for protection? Against Mama?"

"Protection, yes," Aurelia says. "We all need protection."

"But Mama *is* my protection. All the years I believed she was dead, she was protecting me with her moonstone ring."

And then another thought flashes through my mind like a revelation. "She protected me against Ben, and against herself."

"It seems," Aurelia says slowly, "that the moonstone might not be enough any more."

"The werewolf grows stronger with each passing moon," Natasha agrees. "The beast will gain more power, and all the while, human part of Melani will weaken, until one day, is no more Melani left. Only beast will remain."

"How can you talk that way about her?" I storm. "She's right here. She's human. She's my mother."

"Aurelia, can you get ahold of another silver

bullet?" Mama asks.

I gawk at her. "No. You can't be serious."

Aurelia shakes her head. "The one I had, it was made years ago."

"Is blacksmith in Columbus," Natasha says. "Old friend of family. Ivan will take him silver. Making of bullet might take two, three days."

"But can't you do anything to end the curse?" I look from Natasha to Aurelia and back. "Either of you?"

Natasha shakes her head sadly. "Other than moonstones and silver bullets, is nothing to be done."

Aurelia casts her eyes down. I think for a hopeful moment that she has remembered another way.

Without looking up, she says, so softly I can barely hear her, "No, is nothing else."

"What about this bridge?" I gesture to the ancient wooden structure. "What makes it safe?"

"The legend goes that the builder's daughter had a protection spell cast by the local Roma," Mama answers. "So her children would be safe from the Ku Klux Klan."

"But it works against werewolves, too?"

"Nobody has ever been attacked by a werewolf in it," Jace says. "Right, Buni?"

For a surreal moment, I forget about werewolves and curses and silver bullets. The way Jace smiles at his grandmother bears little resemblance to the "bad boy" I had romantically cast him as when I first met him. Warmth rushes through me, relief that he's not a werewolf.

I gaze up at the rafters of Mill Creek House, look

around at its lattice-work walls.

A century ago, a mother blessed this building out of love for her children.

And my own parents had made my home safe harbor. Both the house here in Lafayette and my home in Tennessee. All to protect me.

"That's it!" I run to Jace and hug him. I hug Natasha, Aurelia, Mama, and Romelia.

"What did I say?" Jace asks.

"He wants to know so he can say again and get another hug," Natasha chuckles.

"It's not so much *what* he said as the way he said it." I stand just outside the bridge and lay my hand on the framework. "Ben got an upset stomach in the bridge. Mama too."

"Ben was gagging like he was going to throw up in our house, too," Mama says.

"Right. But how did *you* feel in our house?"

Her bare feet pad softly on the muddy dirt road. She stops beside me at the very edge of the bridge and cups my face in her hands. "I was scared to death that Romelia was going to shoot you." She casts a scathing glance at Romelia. "Other than that, I felt fine."

"That's because it's your house, Mama," I say. "You're the Alpha wolf there. The house is protected against other werewolves."

"But Ben came inside your place in Tennessee," Romelia says. "He didn't seem sick to me."

"Ever since we were kids, Ben said he thought our house was haunted. I don't think he set foot inside for more than a couple minutes at a time. Until after Dad died."

"Your Dad was the Alpha there," Mama says. "When he died, the house was unprotected."

"That's how Ben was able to come inside and mark it." I walk to the back of Romelia's SUV and look at the animal lying there. Its jet-black fur is smudged with mud and blood.

Romelia scrunches her nose. "You mean the animal that peed in your house was Ben? Eww."

Jace touches my arm gently. "Your dad was a werewolf, too?"

"I never knew it." I stroke the fur on the wolf's head.

Romelia closes the hatch.

"You were right," I tell her. "I never knew my own father."

"So both your parents were werewolves," Jace says slowly. "If both your parents are werewolves –."

"Oh, no." I shake my head. "I know what you're thinking, but I'm *not* a werewolf. And I'm not going to become one when I turn sixteen."

"Are you sure?" Romelia asks. Her tone is soft, sympathetic even. But her words rankle me.

"Would it *kill* you to be a little more supportive?" I ask, exasperated.

"It might."

"Don't you see? We have a safe place here in Lafayette, until we can find a way to remove the curse."

"*If* you can find a way," Romelia says. "The silver bullet is the only sure way."

"I'm not a werewolf," I say again.

"I believe you, Lani," Jace says.

"So we've got a couple things to figure out. How to break the curse on Mama, and what to do about Ben."

"The *pricolici* can rest in freezer at our *pensiune* until Ivan can arrange for cremation," Natasha offers.

"Until he gets that silver bullet, the other problem will have to wait." Romelia taps her finger tip against her chin. "Shame one of you didn't kill the other in your dogfight."

I stare at the wolf's body through the tinted glass. "Someone has to tell Mrs. Stoat."

"I remember Sally," Mama says. "I can call her about Ben."

"But Mama, she thinks you're dead."

"I have finished living that lie. It was to protect you, and I thank God that your father had the strength not to harm you himself. I wish he would have told me."

"What good would that have done, Mama?"

"You weren't safe. I would have found someplace else for you to live. Maybe with Romelia down in Florida."

I don't even want to think what it would have been like to grow up with neither a mother nor a father. Much less having Romelia as a mother figure.

Romelia laughs, that high-pitched, slightly hysterical giggle. "You know, Ben's mother's going to think we're all crazy."

"We have to tell her anyway. I'll do it.

Romelia lends me her cell phone and I walk down the road for privacy.

Mrs. Stoat picks up on the first ring, as if she's

been waiting by the phone. "Ben?"

"No, ma'am. It's me, Lani."

"Lani, I'm worried sick about Ben. Is he with you? He said he was going to get you, to bring you home. Then he took off outta here and I haven't heard from him since."

"He found me, but I'm afraid I've got bad news."

I can almost hear Mrs. Stoat's heart pounding through the silence on the other end of the line.

"He's dead, isn't he?" Ben's mother stifles a sob. "How did it happen?"

"He, I mean, I," I stutter, not sure how to tell her. "He attacked me, and I . . . I shot him."

Silence buzzes through the phone line like listening to the ocean in a sea shell.

"Mrs. Stoat? Mrs. Stoat, are you there?" I'm afraid she might have fainted.

"Lani," Mrs. Stoat finally says. "Tell me where you are. I need to come get my son."

I tell her, then add, "But Mrs. Stoat, there's something I need to tell you."

But she's already hung up.

I rejoin the group huddled in the road around the SUV. "She hung up before I could tell her Ben is a –." I can't even say it. "She's coming for Ben."

***

We all return to the B&B. Jace unloads the wolf's body from the back of the SUV and carries it into the B&B's walk-in freezer.

"I have to work the night shift at the morgue for my grandfather," he says. He puts his hand on my neck, plays the dangling moonstone earring between his fingers. "Will you be okay?"

His touch is warm but his words leave me cold. The reason he has to take his grandfather's shift is because Ivan has taken a sack of old silver coins to the blacksmith in Columbus. So I'll be able to kill my own mother. They all think it's a done deal. That I will kill my mother to save myself.

All except Natasha. She has locked herself in the private quarters she and Ivan share at the foot of the stairs. She is searching through her ancient books from the Old Country. My hopes rest in her ability to find a cure.

"I'll drive Mother home," Romelia announces.

"Can't we stay at our house?" I suggest. It seems like a safe haven now, the house where I lived before the world went crazy.

Mama tucks a strand of hair behind my ear. "The utilities have been shut off for years. It's fine for me when I need a den, but I won't allow you to stay there until we get the power turned back on. And until we've resolved my, um, werewolf issues. Then it will be your home again."

"*Our* home."

She smiles sadly and a cold dagger of fear drills into the core of my body. *I can't kill her. I won't.*

That night, we sit in the kitchen, Buddy curled at my feet, and eat cold sandwiches for dinner. I pick at the bread and sip hot tea. Mama attacks her roast beef sandwich as if she hasn't eaten in days. I realize she might not have.

The phone rings, and a minute later, Natasha

comes to the kitchen. "Romelia is spending night with Aurelia," Natasha says. "They have much to talk over."

Later, I sit with Mama on the floor of my room. We talk and giggle like girlfriends at a slumber party. I tell her about growing up on the mountain. We laugh at how I love Boulder Man, even though my friends think he's spooky.

I tell her about taking care of Dad, how I thought he was hallucinating when he said Mama was still alive. That she was a werewolf.

"Mama, how did you know Jace wasn't a werewolf?"

"I wasn't *sure* he wasn't one. There were two possibilities. If he was a werewolf, he was trying to keep from killing."

"And the other possibility?"

"He was trying to ward off werewolves."

"The moonstone."

"I could smell it," Mama says. "It has an effect on me."

"What kind of effect, Mama?"

"It helps me not want to, well. . .." Mama's cheeks turn pink.

"You don't have to say it," I tell her.

Kill. Feed. That's what she means.

She hugs me close to her and gives me a relieved smile. "Moonstone also protects humans from werewolves," she says. "That's why I gave you my ring."

"I wear it all the time." I tilt my head and remove the moonstone earrings that I took from Romelia. "And now I have these."

"My earrings. Romelia knew what might happen to me without them."

I drop them into her hand and she puts them on. "Your father gave me these. The earrings and the ring were a set."

I jump to my feet. "I just remembered. He wrote you a note."

I grab my backpack and pull out the letter.

When I hand it to Mama, her hands tremble. She runs her fingertips over the wax seal.

"I'm sorry I opened it. I thought you were dead, and I…."

"It's okay." Mama slides the paper out of the envelope and reads quietly.

When she finishes, her eyes glisten. "It must be done, and soon."

"No way." My fingers worry the moonstone ring. "Natasha is looking through all her books. She'll find a cure."

Mama lays her hand on top of mine. "There aren't many books. Most Roma lore has been handed down by word of mouth for centuries. If Natasha and Aurelia haven't heard of a cure, there likely isn't one."

"At least we don't have to worry about it for a few days. Natasha said it would take Ivan that long for the silversmith to make a silver bullet."

An eerie howl drifts in through the window. Mama and I share a look of surprise, but Mama's expression soon changes.

"That's not a regular wolf," she says.

The next moment, we hear a crash.

Mama and I scramble to our feet and dash for the door.

Mama gets there first and blocks my way. "Don't leave this room."

"What are you going to do?"

"Hopefully, prevent some death and destruction."

As soon as she steps out into the hall and closes the door, I open it a crack and peer out.

Natasha has joined Mama on the stairs. "She's here, downstairs," Natasha whispers.

She and Mama stand close together. Although they speak softly, they don't know I'm listening, so they are only trying to keep their voices from being overheard by whoever is downstairs.

"She wants to see her son, and your daughter."

"Is she human?" Mama asks. A chill sweeps over me. Are they talking about Mrs. Stoat?

"For now."

They walk downstairs, Mama in the lead, and turn the corner toward the parlor.

As soon as they are out of sight, I tiptoe after them.

I pause at the foot of the stairs and crane my neck so I can peek around the corner without being noticed.

"Sally, I'm so sorry for your loss," Mama says, reaching for Mrs. Stoat's hand. "Especially after what happened to your husband and daughter."

Mrs. Stoat coughs onto the back of her hand, and I know she's trying to choke back tears, like at Dad's funeral. But she doesn't shake Mama's hand. Then she stiffens her back. "What would you know about that?"

"I … visited the mountain a few times over the years."

"You never let anyone know you was there. Everybody thinks you're dead."

"Frank and I thought it was best that way."

"I had my suspicions, though. I surely did."

I've never seen Mrs. Stoat so confrontational. I guess it's a reaction to finding out that her son is dead. And that my mother is alive.

I take a deep breath and step into the parlor.

"Hi, Mrs. Stoat."

Mama whirls when she hears my voice. "Lani! I told you to stay upstairs." She shifts her position so she is standing in between Mrs. Stoat and me.

I step around her. "Mama, there's something I need to say to Mrs. Stoat."

"Lani," Mrs. Stoat sobs when she sees me.

She holds out her arms, and I want to run to her and give her a hug. But for some reason I hold back. Maybe because my real mother is here, and I feel guilty that I let Mrs. Stoat fill the maternal role, however briefly, after Dad died.

Or maybe it's because I just killed her son, and the thought of running into her arms seems wrong.

"Mrs. Stoat, I feel awful about what happened."

"I do, too, child. You can't imagine what I've been through. I've been worried sick since Ben took off after you, dreading the news I might get whenever I answered the phone."

"Yes, ma'am. And then it was me on the phone, telling you what you didn't want to hear."

I clear my throat. *You have to tell her,* I tell myself.

When it is clear I'm not going to run to her, Mrs. Stoat folds her arms across her chest. Her shoulders droop. "First Jolie, now Ben," she says. "And I can't run away from it like their father did. It's a mother's duty to stand by her children."

She shoots a fiery look at Mama. "It was your duty, too."

Mama's voice is flinty and cold. "I did what I thought best to protect my daughter."

"Mrs. Stoat," I cut in. I don't know the cause of the animosity I feel flickering like electricity between Mama and Mrs. Stoat, but I can't let it detract me from *my* duty, which is to confess the truth to Ben's mother. "I haven't told you the worst part."

She glares at me, all traces of the motherly figure I've grown to know over the past ten years wiped away in a heartbeat.

"You," she spits the word like a bad taste she wants to get out of her mouth. "Where the tarnation did you find a silver bullet?"

"How. . . how did you know I used a silver bullet?" I stammer.

"It is the only way you could have killed him." Mrs. Stoat cocks her head at Mama. "Don't tell me she doesn't know."

"She knows now."

"Didn't her precious father tell her what he did to my family?"

"What do you mean?" I ball my fists stiffly at my sides, so tight I feel my fingernails digging into my palms. "What did Dad ever do to Ben?"

Mrs. Stoat's eyes flash. "Frank and my George got in a fight. George claimed he saw a wolf in the woods behind our house, and as he watched, the wolf changed from a wolf into a woman. Into Melani."

"But why would they get into a fight?"

"George was going to shoot me," Mama says. "But I ran off. I don't know what happened. I never saw a fight, and Frank never talked about it."

"Frank attacked my George, that's what happened." Mrs. Stoat's voice is like a stump grinder. "On the next full moon, George went crazy. I tried to protect the children, but George turned into a wild animal. A werewolf. He attacked us all. He mauled Jolie so badly, she bled to death in my arms. Then George jumped out the window and I never saw him again."

"My god." My head is spinning.

Mama sways as if she is about to faint. I grab her waist and we cling to each other for support. "I never bit him," Mama says. "How could he be a werewolf?"

"The letter," I remind her. "Dad said he had been cursed, too."

"Didn't you know he was a werewolf?" Mrs. Stoat asks. "I find that hard to believe, I surely do. You just said you'd been visiting him all these years."

"We never spoke. I didn't trust myself to get that close. And he never changed form in front of me."

I pull together in my head what I've learned in the past few days since Dad died. God, has it really been just a matter of days?

"Romelia said Dad was supposed to stop loving you when you became a werewolf," I tell Mama. "But he never stopped loving you."

"Love," Natasha says, "can be a curse."

"The doctor said his heart had too much stress," I

remember. "Could Dad have taken the curse on himself, out of love?"

"Does it matter?" Mrs. Stoat shakes her fist at me. "He destroyed my family. I wanted revenge. Oh, how I wanted revenge. But Ben wouldn't let me. He loved you. Can you imagine how I felt when Ben insisted I make all Frank's funeral arrangements? I could have just screamed, I surely could have."

"I'm so sorry, Mrs. Stoat. So sorry."

She points to my finger. "Between that moonstone ring, and that obnoxious statue protecting your house, I couldn't do anything about it anyway. But now, the smell of the moonstones is not as strong. It hardly bothers me at all."

I shake my head slowly. "I don't understand what you mean."

Before my eyes, a change comes over Mrs. Stoat. She stiffens and rolls her head on her shoulders. Then her shoulders beef up and hunch over, and her face elongates. Her lips snarl around long, sharp canine teeth. She drops to all fours as her dress disappears, replaced by silver fur.

I hear a low rumbling growl come from deep in Mama's throat. She pushes me behind her and begins to morph into the lanky wolf with chestnut-colored fur.

Natasha grabs me and pulls me backward into the lobby. We duck behind the registration desk, but I have to watch. I peek over the desk top.

The two wolves tear at each other. They clash on their hind legs, biting and clawing. They break away and circle, snarling. Their heads are low, the hackles raised across their muscular shoulders.

Suddenly the silver wolf charges.

The red wolf – Mama – yelps as the larger, silver wolf pins her to the floor.

The silver wolf lifts her muzzle and howls.

It's a spine-tingling sound, and I know it means she is going for the kill.

But before the echoes of the silver wolf's howl have faded, the red wolf tumbles and rolls. The silver wolf lunges but her gnashing fangs, meant for Mama's throat, sink deep in her shoulder instead. I hear the rip of flesh as the silver wolf tosses Mama into the wall with a thud.

The red wolf whimpers and lies still.

"Mama!"

The silver wolf's head snaps up when she hears my voice. Natasha slaps a hand over my mouth and pulls me down behind the counter.

We huddle on the floor, with nothing to defend ourselves.

I hear claws tapping on the hardwood floor. A canine muzzle, dripping blood, appears around the corner of the counter, on Natasha's side.

"Get back, you soulless *fiara!*" Natasha screams.

With more force than I thought possible from such a tiny woman, Natasha punches the silver wolf in the snout. Smoke sizzles from the spot where Natasha's moonstone ring connects with the werewolf's muzzle.

The wolf yelps and withdraws. She paws her muzzle, then glares at Natasha. Her lips curl back, exposing blood-streaked fangs.

"No!" I try to trade places with Natasha, but the space behind the counter is too cramped.

The silver werewolf lunges, ripping into Natasha's neck.

Natasha is motionless. Her dead body drapes against me.

The werewolf turns her attention once again to me.

I hold out my fist, trembling. My moonstone ring won't save me from the werewolf any more than Natasha's ring saved her. But it distracts the silver wolf for a split second.

And that's all it takes.

The red wolf leaps on the silver wolf's back. Biting and clawing, they writhe together against the wall, inches in front of me.

The silver wolf turns, and her throat is momentarily exposed. The skinny red wolf doesn't hesitate. She sinks her fangs into the larger wolf's jugular.

I hear a hideous *snap*, and the silver werewolf drops to the ground, her body limp.

The next noise I hear is a small "eep," like a frightened mouse. I'm startled to realize it's me.

The red werewolf looks up from her kill and spins her head in the direction of the sound. She looks right at me, lowers her head and snarls. Her muzzle and teeth drip blood as she steps over the bodies of the silver wolf and Natasha.

She is inches away. Saliva drips from her bloody muzzle as she snarls at me.

I scuttle backwards, flailing my legs. "Mama, no! It's me, Lani! Your daughter!"

Recognition flashes in the werewolf's eyes. She lifts her muzzle and howls, a long, mournful cry, then lopes out the door into the night.

CHAPTER 22

Blood is everywhere.

On the walls, the floors, the rug, the chairs, the mahogany counter.

Natasha's body looks like a broken doll.

The silver werewolf lies like a crumpled fur coat at Natasha's feet.

The front door swings open and, a moment later, shuts with a click.

A wiry old man walks in. A golden hoop dangles from one earlobe. The other lobe is mostly missing, as if gnawed off.

"Is bad?" His accent is the same as Natasha's.

"Are you Ivan?"

He nods. "Where is Natasha?"

I glance at the bodies.

He follows my gaze and a shadow of grief strikes his face.

"Natashka." He drops to his knees beside her body and cradles her head in his lap. "I brought silver bullet, but I am too late."

"You're too late for Natasha," I say, my voice cracking because I can't believe I'm saying this. "But we still need it."

***

Back in my room, I strip off all my clothes. My jacket and jeans are soaked with blood. I cram the jeans in the tiny bathroom wastebasket. I can get a new pair. But the jacket – it's the one Dad gave me. I run cold water in the sink and dunk the jacket, kneading it like bread. Tears stream down my face. "I can't save it. I can't save it," I sob. I slump to the floor in front of the sink. "I couldn't save Dad. I couldn't save Natasha. I am so useless."

When I have cried out all my tears, I run a hot shower and stand in it until the water runs cold.

Moving as if in a trance, I put on a tank top, a pair of shorts, and my dingo boots. I chamber the silver bullet Ivan gave me in the Baretta and walk down to Mama's room. I curl up in bed, pulling the sheet and quilt up to my chin. I slip the cold weapon under my pillow and grip the handle.

I know Mama will come back. She won't leave me, not after I've come all this way to find her. Not after all she's done to protect me.

And when she comes back, I will kill her.

Though weary to the bone, I can't get to sleep. I thrash restlessly, kicking the sheets off only to pull them back up a minute later. When I finally drift off to sleep, the old nightmare returns. Mama morphing into a red-furred wolf. Lunging at me through the car window. Then the red wolf melts away and in her place, a large silver wolf attacks Natasha.

Then four faces float before me: The four

werewolves in my life.

First, Dad. Transformed out of love, he refused to feed his werewolf hunger. I see his face as he lies in the casket, red lipstick on his cheek.

Second, Ben, my best friend. He loved me, wanted to protect me from his own fate. How did I reward him? I shot him. I knew the silver bullet would kill him. I shot him anyway.

Third, my mother. For ten years, I thought she was dead. Instead, she was living as a prisoner. Imprisoned at Hunt House and imprisoned in her own secret skin – the skin of a werewolf.

And fourth, Mrs. Stoat. All these years, she was a werewolf too. She knew her son was a werewolf, too. She came to Georgia to seek revenge. It was me she was after, as revenge for her family's deaths.

I open my eyes and stare at the ceiling with a hollow feeling in my stomach. It's my fault Natasha's dead.

I think of Ivan, the look on his face when he saw Natasha's mutilated body. As if his whole world had crashed around him. He had scooped her up in his arms and carried her to their room across from the kitchen. When the door shut behind him, I saw the brass plate that says, "Lovari – Personal Residence. Please knock."

I had held my fist up to knock, but stepped away when I heard his sobs. I crept up the stairs to my room, feeling more alone than ever. Even more alone than when Dad died.

Finally, my exhaustion takes over and I fall into a deep sleep.

Just before dawn, I feel Mama slip into bed beside me.

"Mama?" I ask groggily. Under the pillow, I tighten my grip on the gun. "Are you okay?"

"Yes, baby. Just very tired."

"I love you, Mama." I drift back to sleep as she strokes my hair.

***

When I wake up, Mama is gone.

I throw on some clothes and head downstairs. As I pass Romelia's door, I hear soft voices.

"It has to be done soon," Romelia says.

"I know, I know," Mama says. "Time is running out."

I don't want to hear any more. I stumble downstairs.

Jace's hound dog is standing in the kitchen doorway, tail between his legs, a low growl humming in his throat.

In the kitchen, Ivan wraps the bodies of the two dead werewolves in old quilts.

Jace lifts the larger of the two forms in his arms and carries it out the front door. I see a black tail sticking out of the quilt. Ben.

Ivan's legs wobble under the weight of the other body.

"Can I help you lift her?" My words choke off.

"I am all right," Ivan says. "Please to get door."

I hold the front door open and Ivan steps carefully down the stairs. The little red pickup truck is parked close to the front porch, out of view of the road. Ivan lays the shrouded form of the larger wolf gently on the truck bed, alongside that of her son.

Ivan and Jace handle both bodies with tenderness and respect, even the body of the murderer who robbed Ivan of his wife and Jace of his grandmother, his Buni.

"Where are you taking them?" I ask.

"Bodies of werewolves must be cremated," Ivan says. "I will be taking them to veterinarian who will send to pet crematorium."

"And Natasha?" My eyes well up with tears as I think of Natasha's last moments, how I could do nothing to protect her. "The police will want to know how she died." I can't tell him my most selfish fears: That they will hunt down the savage animal that is responsible. That they will kill my mother, or try to. I doubt the police are armed with silver bullets, but this thought does nothing to assuage my fears.

I had convinced myself I could kill her last night, but when she crawled into bed beside me, my convictions crumpled. How could I kill someone I love so much?

Ivan reads the emotion on my face. "Do not worry, *copil*. I have friends at morgue. No questions will be asked. No wolf hunt will be organized."

Before he puts the tail gate up, I lean in and unfold the quilts. I stroke Mrs. Stoat's silver fur and kiss Ben's soft muzzle. I breathe in his earthy smell of ginseng and hemlock for one last time. I cover them with the edges of the quilts and tell myself that these forms, wrapped in muted shades of green and blue and cream, are no longer my best friend and his mother.

Those two people were consumed by the werewolf side of their personalities.

My mother is doomed to the same fate.

Unless I stop it.

As Ivan and Jace drive off, Aurelia comes down the steps of the B&B, holding her flowing skirts up to knee-level. I do a double-take when I see Romelia and Mama following, arm in arm.

"I've charged the utility deposits and hook-up fees to my credit card," Romelia says.

"Thank you, Romy," Mama says.

"Melani, I hope we can set our differences aside and be friends again. For the short time we have left."

Mama smiles and wraps Romelia in a big hug as I stare. "We're sisters, aren't we?"

I stare at them. "You are?"

"Step-sisters," Mama says. "My father married Aurelia after my mother – your grandmother – died."

"Why didn't Dad ever tell me?"

"It was a deep scandal," Aurelia says, spreading her fingers wide. "A Roma marrying an outsider."

"And we weren't exactly one big, happy family," Romelia adds, casting a guilty look at Mama. "I wasn't thrilled to have a new sister, especially one as pretty as your mother."

"We were so competitive," Mama says, wiping the corner of her eye. "About grades, dancing…."

"And Franzl," Romelia says.

"Yes, especially when it came to Frank."

"Water under the bridge," Romelia says to Mama. "Come on, I'll drive us all over to your place. We have a lot of work to do to make it a home again."

Mama sits up front with Romelia, and I sit in back with Aurelia, my step-grandmother.

The scene would be perfectly natural if one member of the family wasn't a werewolf and another wasn't carrying a concealed weapon and trying to gin up the courage to use it on the afore-mentioned werewolf.

And I still can't get past the fact that Aurelia is the one who gave Romelia the curse that she used on my mother, her own step-daughter.

A question eats at me. "Romelia, why did you try to make me think Aurelia was your mother-in-law?"

Aurelia snorts through her nose, the same way I've heard Romelia do when she thinks the answer is obvious.

In the rearview, Romelia looks at me over her sunglasses. "Tell me, Cinderella. How many storybooks feature loving step-mothers and step-sisters who are ? If I had told you we were step-family, would you have trusted me enough to come with me?"

I shake my head. "I barely came with you as it was. I only agreed because you promised to take me to see my mother."

"I am the evil step-mother," Aurelia mumbles. "The fairytale come true."

"Fairytales have happy endings," I say hopefully. "Maybe our story will too."

Aurelia strokes my hand. "Happy endings are rare in real life, *nepoată*."

"Romy," Mama interrupts. "Do you mind if we make a short detour?"

While Mama and Romelia chat in the front seat, I

stare out the window.

Can I really do it?" I ask myself.

"Turn here," Mama says.

Last night, I held the gun in my fist, waiting for Mama to return. I was sure I could do it.

But when she crawled into bed beside me, and stroked my hair, I felt like a little girl again. A little girl with her mother lying right beside her to protect her while she slept.

I couldn't kill her.

Tears well up in my eyes.

I can't do it.

There's been so much death. I want it all to be over.

Somehow, my mother will survive. She'll overcome her werewolf needs. I will be here to help her. To protect her from herself.

I want the fairytale ending. I want us to live happily ever after.

I lean my head against the door and stare out the window. Gradually I recognize what road we're on.

"Where are we headed? I thought we were going to the house."

"Slight detour," Romelia says.

"Change in plans," Mama adds.

"Good idea," Aurelia says.

"What's a good idea?"

Up ahead, I see the familiar old covered bridge with the distinctive red roof. We pull off the main road and park on the bridge.

"Mill Creek House? What do you need to do at Mill Creek House?"

Aurelia pats my hand. "Something must be done about the werewolves."

"I know. We have to find a cure for Mama."

"I am afraid there is only one cure for a werewolf," Aurelia says.

"See, Mama? I knew there was a cure!" My emotions soar. I hop out of the car onto the bridge and twirl like a ballerina. After a moment of total happiness, I come back to earth, thinking of all the deaths. "I just wish you'd found it sooner."

The others get out of the car. Mama clamps her hand over her mouth and dashes to the road. As soon as she's off the bridge, she takes a deep breath and stretches, the wave of nausea gone.

Aurelia walks up to me and strokes my hair. "You're not going to like it, *mândră*."

"Don't tell me. A silver bullet."

"Oh, no," Aurelia says vehemently. "The silver bullet will not cure *pricolici*! It will only kill her."

"Then there *is* another way?"

"There is only one way." Aurelia takes my hands firmly in hers, forcing me to look her in the eyes. "You must kill werewolf that bit you, Lani. You must do it before you change for first time, or you will become werewolf yourself."

I yank my hands away. "She didn't bite me," I yell. "She didn't!"

"The night you left," Mama says, so quietly I barely hear her. "I didn't bite you, but I scratched you. It was an accident, but I did scratch you with my … my claws."

"You must kill werewolf," Aurelia says.

"It's the only way," Romelia agrees.

"You're talking as if she can't hear you or understand you any more than … than Jace's dog could."

I run to Mama. She enfolds me in her arms and I grasp her waist, holding her tightly to me.

"They're right, Lani," she whispers in my ear. "It must be done."

"But I can't. You're my mother."

Aurelia shrugs. "Who else should do it? Who else loves her enough to do it?"

"The silver bullet will kill the werewolf, whether it is done in love or hatred," Romelia says. "The point is, you are the one whose mortal life is in danger."

"Lani," Aurelia adds. "If she is still alive when you turn sixteen, you will be cursed as surely as she is. Your mother's love will not protect you once you are old enough to be on your own. You will change, and once you change, you will crave taste of human flesh."

"But Dad said he defeated the curse. He didn't kill anybody."

Mama pulls away from me and paces in the road, her head down, wringing her hands. When she looks at me, her eyes – her peridot eyes – are filled with anguish. "Frank had remarkable control, dear. But he did attack George Stoat."

A cloud covers the sun and a gust of wind whips my hair around my face. "No. You're wrong. You said you didn't see it, that you ran away."

I slump to my knees in the middle of the road and rock back on my heels as the truth dawns on me, fully, for the first time. "Oh my god. Dad *was* a werewolf.

But how could that happen if you never bit him?"

"He loved her so much," Aurelia answers for Mama. "They were true soul mates. Two halves of whole."

Romelia sits down on her knees next to me, apparently no longer worried about her linen skirt. "You know how, when you find out someone you love has cancer? You say, 'Why couldn't it have been me instead?' I think that's what happened with Franzl. You might not be able to contract cancer out of love, but he took on the werewolf curse through empathy."

"Can that happen? Can someone become a werewolf out of love?"

Aurelia paces in the road, tapping her chin with a long, purple fingernail in a gesture that Romelia often uses. "Two ways only have I ever heard. The bite of a werewolf, or a Roma curse." She looks at the clouds scudding across the sky. "But love is powerful thing. Can it not be curse? Perhaps the most powerful curse of all."

"The other werewolves. Dad must have known about Ben and Mrs. Stoat. Why didn't he just move again?"

"They could have followed you. It was better to stay in a place where you had protection."

"Then why did we have to leave Georgia? Why did Dad and I have to leave you?"

"Lani, it's not like your father *left* me. We loved each other; we didn't break up. It was a decision that we made together."

"But what about the moonstones? If they're so powerful, we could have stayed here and had a whole collection of moonstone jewelry and moonstone statues and moonstone rocks in our pockets."

"Your Dad and I talked about what we should do, how best to keep you safe," Mama says. "We thought having him take you away was the best way to ensure your safety. We didn't know that his love for me would –." She chokes up and Romelia has to finish.

"Would bring the curse on himself."

"Moonstone is quite powerful," Aurelia says. "But even protection of moonstone won't be enough once you turn sixteen."

"Oh, Lani, I should have let Ben or his mother kill me," Mama says. "It would have been better than forcing you to do it."

"Maybe easier, but not effective," Aurelia says. "If Lani doesn't kill you herself, the curse will find her."

"No, I won't do it!" I scramble to my feet and whirl to face them all – a gathering of mothers and daughters. "How can you ask me to kill you, Mama? When I just found you!"

"Frank and I gave up everything to protect you, Lani," Mama says. "If you don't end the curse before it strikes you, all that we sacrificed will have been in vain."

I stuff my hands in my shorts pockets and feel the cold, hard metal of Romelia's gun. I pull it from my pocket. "After I saw Mrs. Stoat kill Natasha, I was going to do it. To stop all the killing. But I can't."

I throw the gun to the ground.

"Lani, you have to do it. You owe it to Natasha. To all the innocent people who will wind up like her, if you don't end it now."

"I don't care if I become a werewolf. I won't kill anybody. The moonstones will protect me. They'll protect me and Mama."

"Lani, I'm very lucky that Ivan works in the morgue," Mama says. "That's how I've been able to survive without killing. It's not the life I want for you."

"And it's no guarantee," Romelia adds. "Remember, your mother has been institutionalized to prevent her from wanton killing."

The image of the photo Romelia took flashes across my mind. The one with Mama crouched over a dead man on the side of the road somewhere.

"That's why I asked for Romelia's help," Mama says.

"You mean, you wanted her to come get me? Did you know she wants me to kill you?"

"Yes, Lani. Aurelia came to visit me at Hunt House. She told me what would happen when you turned sixteen."

A car rumbles by on the main road. Mama follows it nervously with her eyes until it disappears from view. "Let's do this, before someone sees us."

Romelia nods. "It's time."

Mama grimaces and stretches her arms at her side. She points her face at the sky and groans. The groan becomes a scream, and the scream becomes a howl as Mama morphs into wolf form. She stands six feet away from me, her hackles raised and her teeth bared.

"Mama, no!" I yell.

Mama, now a lanky red werewolf with bloodlust in her eyes, pads toward me, one slow step at a time. Her ears lie flat against her head. She doesn't turn away like she did at the B&B, or when I first saw her, in the back yard in Tennessee. Instead, she draws closer, snarling with every step.

"The gun! Pick up the gun," Aurelia cries. She runs into the road, between me and the wolf.

The animal that a moment ago was the person I love most in the world advances on Aurelia.

"No, Aurelia! Get out of the way!" I run to her and grab her tiny wrist. She pulls away from me and falls backward onto the road.

"The gun!" Romelia shouts. She scoops the gun off the road and presses it into my hand.

I remove the safety, the way Romelia taught me.

The werewolf comes nearer, growling louder.

"Get Aurelia out of the way," I yell. "Go back to the bridge!"

Romelia pulls Aurelia to her feet and they stumble a few feet away.

The werewolf growls at me but shifts her attention to Aurelia and Romelia.

As long as she was concentrating on me, I wavered. But now she is focused on Romelia and Aurelia. I can't let her kill them. I know they are responsible for this curse, for the werewolf my mother has become. But if I let Mama kill them, their blood will be on my hands, just as Natasha's death is my fault.

Tears spring to my eyes and flood down my cheeks. "Mama, I love you."

The werewolf crouches and springs.

"No!" Romelia jumps at the werewolf just as I fire the gun.

Romelia looks at me and smiles in the split second before the werewolf slams into her.

They both fall to the ground, the werewolf sprawled on top of Romelia.

I drop the gun and wipe my tear-clouded eyes.

I'm not sure I'm seeing right. As I watch, the red werewolf transforms into Mama's human form.

At the same time, Romelia's body trembles and morphs into a wolf.

CHAPTER 23

"Mama! What have I done?"

Mama's body – her human body – is draped over the body of a black wolf. Romelia.

I throw myself on top of Mama's lifeless form, crying into her auburn hair.

Am I dreaming, or did Mama just draw in a breath?

I sit back and feel her neck. A faint pulse throbs beneath my fingertips.

"Mama? Mama!"

She sits up and rubs her forehead. "I'm not dead?" she asks.

"No, Mama! You're alive! But look."

I point at the wolf that lies motionless in the road. A small bloody wound behind the wolf's shoulder marks where the silver bullet entered her body.

Mama looks around. "Where's Romelia?"

Aurelia points at the dead werewolf. "There."

"Romelia? She's a werewolf too?"

"She was Romelia when she jumped in between us. I fired the gun at you, but the bullet hit her instead. Then she turned into a wolf."

"Is she alive?" Mama sounds woozy, as if she just woke up from a long sleep.

I press my fingers down through the fur on the wolf's neck to feel for a pulse. I look at Mama and shake my head. "She's gone."

Aurelia claps her hands over her mouth. She crumples to the ground and cries into the wolf's blood-streaked coat.

"I feel … different," Mama says. "Like something inside me is gone, too."

"Mama, she knew what she was doing."

"What do you mean?"

"She wasn't just trying to keep you from attacking Aurelia. She knew she would get shot."

"But why would she do that?"

"Out of love, Mama. Love for both of us." I stroke a glossy black paw, with a pang of guilt. It's the first time I've shown any affection for Romelia. "I can't believe I killed her. I can't believe I would have killed you, if not for her."

Mama wraps her arms around me and we hold each other tightly.

"What happens now?" I ask.

"I don't know," Mama says. "I don't know."

***

Two weeks later, the full moon casts enough light that we don't need flashlights as we gather around the fountain in the garden behind the B&B. The night air is fragrant with the perfume of the rose bushes that border the gurgling fountain. An owl hoots in the oak tree, and another owl answers in the distance. Dozens of fireflies trace curlicues in the air along the garden wall.

Starglow on a lake, Ben's voice echoes in my head.

I hold two tin boxes. The cremains of Ben and his mother.

Aurelia and Ivan each hold a tin box as well. The metal gleams silver in the moonlight.

Aurelia sways back and forth, clutching the can with Romelia's cremains close to her chest.

Ivan clears his throat. "Funeral is celebration of life. Here are four lives. Only one can I speak for. My Natashka." Ivan grimaces, overcome with grief that stabs me in the heart like a hot knife. Natasha would still be alive if not for me.

Jace puts his hand on his grandfather's shoulder. The touch seems to steady the old man and he takes a deep breath. "I pray for her soul to be at peace."

For a moment, the only sound in the garden is the water flowing in the fountain. Then Aurelia speaks, her voice quivering. "I am here for my daughter. Every mother wants to protect her child. But Romelia protected me. She protected Lani, too, so her death is not in vain."

"Romy protected us all," Mama says, wrapping her arm across Aurelia's bony shoulders. "Including me."

Aurelia opens the box lid and pulls out a bag of grey ash. She reaches in the bag for a handful of ash, which she sifts through her fingers over the roses. She shakes the rest of the cremains around the base of the bushes.

Jace takes the tin containing his grandmother's

ashes from his grandfather's trembling hands and opens the lid. Ivan pulls out the bag and walks, slow and stiff-legged, to the nearby bench. He releases Natasha's ashes over the ferns, then sits on the bench and folds the empty bag, smoothing it on his lap. A tear trickles down his cheek. "I can feel Natasha, my *Natashka iubita mea soția,* in wind in trees."

Ivan looks up at me, and in his eyes, I don't see sadness, or blame, or even forgiveness. Just acceptance.

In this moment, I feel a shift in my life that's hard to put into words. It's like I'm beginning my life again. I find I am loved and accepted by this new family. A family that once again includes my mother, but also includes these new friends. We are all bound by our past, all related by more than blood.

The others look at me, waiting.

"Ben and his mom need their own home. I'll wait till I can get back to Tennessee, and bury them in Ben's cathedral."

"Ben's cathedral?" Mama asks.

"A special place he created by the river. It's what he'd want."

Jace stands at his grandfather's side. "Nicu?" he asks quietly.

"I will stay here a while," Ivan says. "Take our friends inside?"

I follow the others into the formal dining room. I put the tins of Ben's and Mrs. Stoat's cremains on the sideboard. Trays of tiny sandwiches and pitchers of iced tea crowd the dinner table.

"I'm not real hungry," I say.

"Sit with me in the kitchen," Jace offers. "I'll make

us some hot tea."

As I slip into a chair at the porcelain-topped table, I feel a weight press down on my shoe.

I look under the table. Jace's hound dog Buddy is resting his head on my foot. He looks at me out of the tops of his eyes, making the whiskers that sprout from his eyebrows jerk up and down.

"You can stay here tonight if you'd like," Jace says, setting a steaming cup of tea in front of me.

I pick up the cup in both hands and blow across the surface of the tea.

"I'm not afraid to stay at my house," I say. It felt nice to call it *my house* again.

"What if she, you know, changes?"

"She hasn't changed in two weeks."

"But tonight's the full moon," Jace says.

"Mama's not a werewolf anymore."

"How do you know?"

"It's like Aurelia told me. Love is a powerful force."

He stares at me with ocean-blue eyes. "I believe that."

My cheeks burn and I want to look away, but I can't break his gaze.

He slides his chair closer to me. The dog whines and repositions himself under the table, resting his head on my feet again.

"Lani," Jace whispers. He puts his hand on my cheek and pulls me close.

I draw in my breath as his lips brush mine. This is nothing like kissing Ben, no matter what I tried to convince myself at the time. Ben was fireflies; Jace is fireworks.

The kiss is short, but I don't mind. After all, we have just said goodbye to his grandmother and my aunt. There will be more kisses in our future.

"That's what I thought," Jace says.

"What?"

"Your lips taste like chestnuts and honey, only better."

After a few minutes sipping our tea in silence, Jace asks, "How can you be sure? About your mother?"

"Romelia was responsible for Mama becoming a werewolf. By dying of the silver bullet before Mama killed any human, Romelia ended the curse. It died with her. I can feel it."

***

Summer is almost over now. I'll be starting school at Lafayette High in a week. Jace will be there, too, but since he's a senior and I'm just a sophomore, we won't have any classes together. He's promised to meet me for lunch, though. He says I can try out new dishes that he plans to add to the menu once he takes over the B&B for Nicu Ivan and turns it into a restaurant.

I live with Mama in my family's house on Mossy Creek Road. Mama hasn't changed again, or experienced any cravings for a werewolf's special diet.

We drove up to Tennessee the day after the funeral. As we passed our house – Dad's and mine – Mama and I stared at it wordlessly.

I led Mama down the pine-straw path to the bank of the Garnet River where Ben took me the day of Dad's funeral.

"It's beautiful," Mama said. "He made this for you, didn't he?"

I scattered Ben's ashes, and his mother's, following the circle of rocks Ben had placed there.

Mama and I stood arm in arm and listened to a pair of cardinals calling to each other in the hemlocks.

Afterwards, we visited Dad's grave. The hydrangea bush had lost its flowers, and the wind had scattered a few petals across the fresh mound of earth.

"Mama, I want to have Dad cremated."

"But he's already been laid to rest."

"He can't be happy there. His soul needs to be freed. Ivan said werewolves have to be cremated."

She nodded and squeezed me close.

I looked at her silhouette as she gazed at Dad's headstone. Her hair so glossy and red, without a single strand of gray. Her skin so smooth, so unwrinkled by time or the stress of raising a child.

Tears flooded my eyes. I blurted out what I'd been thinking since I found out my mother was still alive. "I hope I don't stress you into an early grave like I did Dad."

"Sweetheart, look at me." She cradled my face in her hands, wiped my tears with her thumbs. "Don't you know by now that taking care of you isn't what made your father old before his time? You and I will have many, many years together. And when I die, you can spread my ashes with your father's, in his garden on the mountain."

***

Ever since we got back to Georgia, we've been

busy cleaning the house, inside and out, sweeping and painting and installing new light fixtures. Mowing and trimming and planting a new flower garden. Moonseed bushes and hydrangea and blood-red amaryllis.

Mama and I discovered a shared love of mosaics. Every day for a week, we have been creating a mosaic frame around the front door.

The mortar is inset with hundreds of moonstones. Two large stones – Boulder Man's eyes, retrieved from the road at Mill Creek House – are placed at the very top. Under the eyes, an arc of smaller stones forms the new Boulder Man's smile.

Tonight is both my birthday and another full moon. Mama and I rock together on the front porch swing, waiting for Jace to join us with sparkling apple cider and his famous sandwiches.

My cell phone vibrates in my back pocket. I look at the caller ID and smile. "Hey, Lisa! You remembered my birthday."

"Um, well, no, but happy birthday."

My smile fades and goose bumps speckle my arms. "What's wrong? I can hear it in your voice."

"It's SP. He's wierding out."

"Wierding out how?"

"He's locked himself in the back room at the gallery. He told me to close up shop and go home."

"Maybe he's working on his next masterpiece and doesn't want to be disturbed."

"Oh, he's disturbed all right. He's talking about 'that damn dog' and I can hear him throwing things around."

I hear a commotion in the background.

"Dammit," Lisa says.

"Lisa! Are you okay?"

"Yeah. The bait bucket I was standing on just capsized."

"Bait bucket? Lisa, where are you calling from?"

"I'm on my cell. I'm out back of the gallery, trying to look in the window and see what he's doing in there."

I stand up and shout into the phone. "You have to get the hell away from there! Now!"

I hear a long, wailing howl. Lisa screams, and the connection goes dead.

ACKNOWLEDGMENTS

I could not have written this book without the patience and support of my family. Special thanks to my daughter, who not only acted as beta reader, but also created the cover and chapter illustrations.

I owe a debt of gratitude to the Founding Mothers (aka the Crit Crew), all published children's authors who provide unlimited encouragement and who annually morph with me into Cove Critters for weekends of writing awesomeness.

I acknowledge my longstanding fascination with werewolves, including a recurring nightmare shared with my twin sister when we were teenagers.

And I would like to add, rest in peace, WZ. You were a genius.